OPENING ROUND
The Tournament

By

AR ELIA

To Joe & Nicole,
Thanks for everything
Hope you enjoy this.
Love you both

Copyright © 2005, 2006 by A.R. Elia

ISBN-13: 978-1-4116-8885-8
ISBN-10: 1-4116-8885-6

Contact:
Mulebox Books
www.mulebox.com
openinground@mulebox.com

Cover Design: A.R. Elia

To
My Mother and Father

OPENING ROUND
The Tournament

"Who is the third who walks always beside you?
When I count, there are only you and I together...
-But who is that on the other side of you?"
T.S. Eliot, *"The Wasteland"*

"They are soft wisps of air that pass over your
arm, a brush of a butterfly's wing. They whisper,
the night is now the dawn."
Christopher Waits, *"Reflection Shoals"*

1

As Harry studies the morning mist, he wonders if the vapor is rising from the trees, or descending from the heavens. He watches it close in around the three men and a boy standing together on the damp grass. It is the way Harry has always liked the world to be, cool and gray.

Holding a flag that reads "18", Harry prefers to watch the trees and the mist, rather than Jack lining up his putt.

"Are you gonna' hit that some time today," Frank Danvers says. Danvers, an obese attorney, stands nervous and twitching next to a red-haired boy, a caddy called Jimbo who chews on a mouthful of gum.

"This putt's for five hundred, so I'll take all the time I need," Jack Connoll replies. "What do you think Harry?" Jack says, turning to his caddy. "I've got it going downhill, right to left, maybe straightening a bit at the hole."

Harry places the flag on the fringe of the green and carefully walks around the hole. Crouching next to his golfer, his friend Jack, he eyes the line. He has performed this task so many times in his life. He has examined the possible path of putts on greens around the world and for prizes way beyond today's game. Harry could have told Jack how to hit this putt before he ever moved from where he stood, without ever looking away from the trees and the mist. All this theatrical crouching, the arched consideration is what Jack Connoll wants. He wants Harry to draw it out, to get under the skin of his opponent. So Harry goes through the motions, giving the young caddy, "the young sherps" as he calls them, a good example.

Harry crouches behind Connoll's ball. He then stands slowly and walks, counting five paces, fifteen feet to the hole. He takes a position in front of Danvers, forcing Danvers to stare at the back of his head.

Danvers says, "Do you guys want to consult with a goddamn engineer?"

Harry and Jack continue their examination. Harry shakes his head, feigns confusion, walks up to Connoll and whispers, "This about enough, or should I stretch it out some more?"

Jack shoots him a nod and says, loud enough for Danvers to hear, "What do you think Harry?"

"Eight inches off the right edge," Harry says, "Stroke it smooth."

"Remember, this is for five dimes," Danvers remarks, elbowing Jimbo, who leans on the golf bag at his side.

Connoll stands over the ball, takes two practice strokes and, after a breathless moment, gently starts the ball down the slope. Danvers and his caddy concentrate on the ball and both gasp when it hops on a small stone. Connoll has yet to look up from the spot where his ball began its journey. Harry has turned his attention back to the dissipating mist above the trees.

The sun will burn it all off soon enough, Harry thinks. The empires will vanish into day. Harry's seen it a thousand times over the thirty years he's been carrying. Soon enough it will be hot and close, unbearable, everything will seem visible then, but he knows there is so much more, so much more. Harry does not turn back to the hole until he hears the ball drop into the cup.

"Son of a bitch!" Danvers shouts. "Screw you Connoll. Screw you and your little weasel caddy."

"Nice match Frank," Connoll replies, offering his hand to Danvers.

"Go to hell Jack," Danvers answers.

Harry places the flag back in the hole, walks up to Jimbo, shakes the boy's hand and pats his back. "You're a good caddy kid," Harry says

"Thanks, Mr. Dimmig," Jimbo replies.

"Nice match Frank." Harry turns to Danvers, his right hand extended.

"Screw you Dimmig," Danvers answers, still shaking Harry's hand.

As the group walks toward the clubhouse, Jack falls in step next to Harry, placing his arm over the caddy's shoulders.

"You're getting old Harry," Connoll says. "You better have your eyes checked. You didn't see that pebble in my line and it almost cost us the match."

"What do you mean? I saw the pebble; it was part of my read. Eight off the right edge, that's what I told you. It broke left and dropped in the hole. That was how I saw it. I just can't tell you to hit it off a god damn rock... wouldn't sound professional. Would it?"

Jack laughs. "Harry, you're still a piece of work. I'll meet you at Rose's around noon and we'll settle up there."

"Yeah, Rose's and you're buying," Harry replies, turning to walk to the caddy house with Jimbo. Walking with the boy, Harry Dimmig tries to understand how, for the first time in thirty years, he did not see the pebble in Connoll's line.

2

The creases at the corners of her blue eyes are all she sees in the mirror. How can this be, Kathryn Torrance thinks, my face is the key to everything I have and now it's going to hell. It was that letter, that horrible letter.

In other times, when the unexpected had set her on edge, she would picture herself as the black Madonna, a beautiful and evil queen of smooth marble, the avenger and protector of herself above all else. Beauty was her shield, and now in the mirror, she sees only the cracks.

She considers the options, injections, surgery, or maybe just let it go, age gracefully, give up and sit by the pool with the other failed pretenders who ascended only so far.

A knock on her door interrupts her planning and a girl says, "Miss Torrance, excuse me Miss Torrance, your car is waiting."

"Thank you Lilly, I'll be right down," Kathryn replies.

"Would you like me to have Mr. Paul come for your bags Miss?"

"Not yet Lilly," Kathryn answers, opening the door and startling the young girl. "I'm sorry dear, I didn't mean to frighten you."

"Oh no, I'm sorry," Lilly replies, smoothing her black and white maid's uniform. "May I help you with anything?"

"As a matter of fact you may. I was trying to decide what to do about the continuing deterioration of my face. You know, should I go with needles or knives? Maybe I should just pack it in and get a chair on Collins Avenue? What do you think?"

"Miss Torrance. You're a beautiful woman." Lilly blushes.

Kathryn Torrance is forty-five years old. To everyone, but herself, she looks much younger than her age; tall and blond, with pure white skin, and milky blue eyes.

"You're a sweet girl," Kathryn says. "But you're too young to understand this affliction,"

"I'll be twenty-four next week. I have seen the men, even the women, moving to you, trying to get in close."

"That's the power of money. But thanks anyway my dear. However, while you're here, I could use some help packing."

They work at filling two large black suitcases, trying to reign in the clothing, which is scattered everywhere. The girl's presence lightens Kathryn's mood. She places a hat with pink flowers on Lilly's head, taking Lilly's maid cap and placing it on her own. They laugh, looking at their reflections in the mirror, the pretty brown haired girl wearing the three thousand dollar hat and the statuesque woman in a maid's cap.

"Lilly, how long have you worked for me?" Kathryn asks.

"Almost four years Miss Torrance."

"Your Aunt Sylvia was with me for what? Twenty years?"

"Yes Miss."

"I miss that woman."

"So do I. She always said you were her friend more than her boss."

"She was my friend," Kathryn agrees, stopping to study Lilly. The girl is pretty, Kathryn thinks, full of energy, still unaffected by dark thoughts of her meager and finite life, of what it takes to survive and get to the top, still so unaware of the inevitable collapse. Kathryn is reminded of herself at that age.

"Lilly, have you ever been to New York?"

"I've never been out of Florida, Miss Torrance."

"Well, what do you think about joining me? We'll escape this heat for the cool north. I could use a traveling companion. Your Aunt Sylvia would have made this trip."

"But Miss Torrance, you mean I…"

"Pack a bag and meet me at the car in ten minutes."

"Of course Miss, it will only take a minute, please excuse me."

As the girl runs out, Kathryn recalls her former maid, Lilly's Aunt, her old friend, Sylvia. Kathryn had first met Sylvia after marrying her second husband, the horse breeder. Sylvia appeared old when they first met. Today, Kathryn thinks, she is the same age Sylvia was that day.

Another terrible thought. That damn letter. It will be nice to have this girl along in Saratoga, Kathryn tells herself.

When Kathryn finally leaves the house, she finds Lilly standing next to the limousine. The girl is wearing her tweed jacket and skirt; her hair pulled back, trying to suppress a smile.

Kathryn senses the girl's nervousness. Probably wondering if I've changed my mind, Kathryn thinks. "Everything ready Lilly?" She says.

"Yes Miss Torrance."

"Good, dear."

Kathryn turns to the house staff that has assembled on the steps. She catches them whispering, maybe about how decrepit she looks, most likely about the surprising traveling companion she has chosen.

"All right everyone," Kathryn announces. "As always, Mr. Bertram is in charge. I've instructed him to give you three extra days vacation in recognition of the fine work you did this winter. Have a good summer and I'll see you in September."

The driver helps Kathryn into the back seat of the car, while Lilly sits in the front. The staff watches the car glide down the drive to the beach road until it turns left along the ocean towards the airport.

3

It is just past noon and Harry sits in the ruddy old tavern waiting for Jack and watching the old timers, Tommy "One-Eye" Dugan and Roy "Buggy" Benton. They are in their usual spots, down at the other end of the long bar, returning his attention with a hard silent stare.

Just like the old days, Harry thinks. One-Eye and Buggy would be the only ones left from the night before, too tired for arguing, still working on a twenty-hour jag.

Rose's Bar has always been part of Harry's life. Located on Webster Street, it has not changed since the days when he was a boy, since when this was a real neighborhood, with families, kids everywhere. Back then Ronny Anson lived next door, with his brothers Mac and Carl.

Zimmy Lehrman lived across the street. Harry had his first crush on Zimmy; her big brown eyes were always on his mind. The Connoll family lived down the street, five girls and three boys. Jack was the youngest.

Jack Connoll was the leader of a group of neighborhood kids known as the "Parkies," because they spent most of their time on the baseball diamonds in the park off Webster, behind the high school. Harry, a small boy, always sick, kept to himself and watched the others play from a safe distance.

Harry recalls the summer before his first year of high school. Harry's father, thinking a horse jockey might be the appropriate career for a boy of Harry's stature, got him a job sweeping the stalls at Sportsmen's Park. Harry hated the stupid stinking animals and that job.

It was at the end of that summer, on the first day of ninth grade, when the blond kid, Jack Connoll, took a seat in front of Harry. Harry recognized Jack from the neighborhood. The difference of only two city blocks had sent them to different grade schools, but Jack was a neighborhood legend, known for swatting pitch after pitch over the heads of the other "Parkies." Then in homeroom, by the coincidence of alphabetical order, Jack sat at the desk in front of Harry.

A crowd of boys and girls gathered around Jack's desk. Jack, his blond hair tousled, his brown eyes infused with ease and humor, welcomed all that came to pay their respects.

"Hey, Jackie," Billy Pipson said, "I've got a pack of Camel's, you want to catch a smoke at lunch?"

"Sure that'd be great," Jack said. "I'll meet you out back."

"Hi Jack," Karen Bethel and Sheila Thompson said in unison, a giggle bubbling through their voices. "Looks like we'll be in homeroom all year together."

"How lucky can I be?" Jack smiled and winked at them. Harry watched as both girls' trembled.

"We got a game starting after school," Danny Gallagher said. "You in Jack?"

"Maybe. I'll let you know," Jack replied.

Harry watched from his desk. There were so many kids standing around him that he barely heard the homeroom teacher, Mrs. Mancini, when she said, "All right, everyone take your assigned seats. I'm mean now."

As Mrs. Mancini took attendance, Harry scanned the room. All eyes looked Jack's way and by default they saw Harry. Probably envying him for his chair, he thought.

"I know you," Harry heard Jack whisper, not realizing that he was the one being addressed.

"Hey kid, I'm talking to you. You sit in the park and watch us play, right? My name's Jack, Jack Connoll," He said turning to face Harry.

Harry looked up, stunned. "My, uh, my name is, Harry. Harry Dimmig,"

"Right, Connoll and Dimmig, makes sense, C then D. How come you never get in the game Harry?"

"Uh, well I have to work and, uh… I'm not that good."

"Not any good, how do you know?"

"Well... because I've never played."

"Never played?"

"No."

"You're not working today, right?"

"Right."

"We got a game starting after school, you can play on my team."

"But, I..." The shrill bell that ended homeroom cut off Harry's reply.

When the periods changed, a crowd of kids swarmed Jack. He called back to Harry, "I'll meet you out front after school and remember you're on my team."

Later on the ball diamond, the other boys scoffed when Jack told them that Harry was playing.

"Can he play?" Philly Boyd asked. "He looks too small."

"Sure he can play, besides I'm taking him on my team so what do you care?"

Now, so many years later, Harry sits at Rose's Bar, wondering how different his life would be if he did not follow Jack to the park that afternoon. He wonders if the spirits would still visit him. Harry considers this, as he watches One-Eye sip on a knuckle glass of whiskey and Buggy sleep with his head on the bar. T.J., the bartender, wipes the place where they sit with a grubby rag; he cannot see his two old costumers.

T.J., Tommy Junior is really Tommy the third, the third Tommy Flynn to run Rose's bar. No one was ever crazy enough to call his father Junior, so the name stuck to his kid. Still, Harry always found it uncomfortable to call a man who is twenty years older than him Junior, so he started calling him T.J. A moniker picked up by everyone else, to Tommy Junior's delight.

Harry watches the old ones, wishing that T.J. could see One-Eye and Buggy too. More than that, Harry wishes that he could talk with these two sad souls from his past.

"Afternoon T.J.," Jack Connoll says to the bartender, shaking Harry from his thoughts by slapping him on the back. "T.J. get us two beers.

How you doing old buddy?" Jack says to Harry, pulling up a stool. "Have your eyes checked yet?"

"No," Harry replies, glancing to the two customers at the end of the bar only he can see. "I figured I'd check them by counting my share of the winnings."

"Right, here you go, fifty-fifty, as usual, here's your two-fifty."

Harry takes the money and places it carefully into his wallet. "Fat Danvers ever calm down?" Harry asks.

"Yeah, I bought him a couple bourbons for breakfast. He'll be all right. He's already looking for a chance to win his money back and he gave me a lead on a job. He knows a guy who's been looking for help. Says we're perfect for the job. He gave me a number."

"Shit, I hope it's not another divorce," Harry says. "That's not our bread and butter, we waste too much time on these surveillance cases. We need more investigative work; you know like that Cicero Bank case. That was something. That was interesting."

"That was too much like work," Jack replies. "I like the cheaters, it's quick and easy. A couple days of sitting around, you snap a couple photos and we're back on the golf course. Besides, we've got all the bread and butter we need."

"You don't mean that."

"You know what I mean. Let's get some lunch and head over to the office so I can make this call. By the way, you're buying today."

"What about fifty-fifty?"

"My fifty is with the bourbon in Fat Frank's stomach."

"Two corn beefs on rye T.J.," Harry orders. "And another beer for Mr. fifty percent here. And don't forget my friends at the end of the bar."

"What friends Harry?" T.J. asks.

"Ah, just joking," Harry replies.

"It's the eyes Harry," Jack says. "They're going. I swear it. At least I hope that's what's going."

4

The drone of the jet's engines wash out all else, leaving Kathryn alone with her thoughts. She holds the dusk colored envelope, fingering the fold, studying the handwriting for anything familiar, anything that may provide a clue to the person she used to be.

When the envelope was placed on her desk last week, she considered throwing it unopened into the trash. Written across the top of the heavy stationary was the name: "Martin Waring," a person she once knew, a wrecked ship from her past, that has floated again to the surface.

Now, with the letter in her hands, the world moves below her and the plane is motionless. There is a buzz, a vibration that moves through her. She closes her eyes and she travels through time. She remembers herself, a girl, and Martin, an elegant German boy with an accent in his deep voice. She had listened to him and abandoned the last person in her life she had ever loved. Martin was a door she stepped through into a life in pursuit of things, of money and power, a life that has brought her here, to this jet flying north, a shadow now, her powers on the fade. His mere letter causes her to question, to remember, to regret, and she uses a poor young girl, a maid who sits back in coach, as a crutch.

"It has been so long and I have never forgotten," Martin wrote. "We were so young and now... and now all the money in the world couldn't buy back those days."

All the money in the world, Kathryn thinks, as she orders another scotch.

She has made this trip to Saratoga every year, for twenty years, since the year she married the horse breeder.

For one month every summer Saratoga is a convention of sorts, a chance to mingle with the others who have the wealth required to play the big games. It was the Kentucky horse breeder who first brought her there; with his million dollar stallions that ran last or next to last every time. She made him buy her the house. He thought it was too small, but she loved it because it reminded her of a place from her past.

Even after the divorce, after she moved from his farm and away from those foul losing horses, she kept the house and the box seat at the racetrack. Even after she married Seymour Torrance, owner of quarries and oil fields, she continued to make this August trip with her friend and maid, Sylvia.

Saratoga is the place where she checks her standing and tallies the score, to find who has married, who has divorced and who has died.

Now, she holds a letter informing her that her past waits for her there, a past before Seymour Torrance, before the horseman, before Kentucky and Saratoga, before that horrible attorney who was her first husband. Waring's letter has brought back a past that was dead, buried under the millions of dollars, under the mansions, under the jewels and the parties. Every year, this trip to Saratoga has provided proof that what she has buried remains safely hidden, and now, Martin Waring waits for her there.

5

The office of Ryan Investigations, Inc. is located on the second floor of a three-story brick building, on Belmont Street, in the heart of Chicago's North Side. Below, on the first floor, is Alkie's Greek Diner.

Margaret Cahoon, at her desk in the second floor office, awash in the stale odor of fried onions and potatoes, is Ryan Investigation's bookkeeper, secretary, receptionist and only employee.

Margaret, Maggie, is older than her bosses, Harry Dimmig and Jack Connoll. In fact, she recalls seeing them the afternoon Jerry Cahoon took her on their third date. The two high school boys sat on the curb at the corner of her block, smoking cigarettes.

She remembers that afternoon; because it was the day she knew she would spend the rest of her life with Jerry. It was a day that ranks second on her list of days when she believed herself the most beautiful. The first on this list was her wedding day; the wedding dress was perfect, her red hair resplendent against white silk, and her green eyes sparkled; there was no denying that day is number one on her list.

Now, so many years later, she works for the two boys she saw smoking cigarettes on the curb and they are tied for third on the list of people she loves. Jerry is first, all of the Chicago Cubs are second, Harry and Jack are third.

Unfortunately, ranked number one on the list of things she hates the most is the smell of fried onions and potatoes. This is the case, even though she believes it contributes to Jerry's pre-dinner affection. More effective than any expensive perfume, she has often thought.

Maggie suffers at her desk on this hot summer afternoon. She is sure she can actually see the grease rising from the exhaust fans of the restaurant below. It is just after one o'clock when she is relieved to hear Jack and Harry finally making their way up the creaky wood stairs to their office. She cannot, for all her annoyance, suppress a smile when they enter the office.

"Afternoon Maggie my dear," Jack says. "First thing, before you do anything else, make an appointment to have Harry's eyes checked. He is losing his renowned vision."

"That right Harry?" Maggie says.

"Before I answer," Harry says, "Can I say you look especially beautiful today Maggie."

"His vision is perfect," Maggie replies. "Maybe I should get someone to check you out Jack."

"That would be great, as long as, she's tall and blond," Jack smirks.

"Definitely someone who would need a vision test," Harry says.

"Can we forget about Harry's eyes for a second," Maggie says. "I am begging you two, please do something about that Greek madman down there. I can't take that smell anymore in this heat."

"Do you want us to ask him to stop cooking during your office hours?" Jack says.

"Isn't there something they could install, how about you guys springing for a window air conditioner?"

"Air conditioner?" Harry says. "Since when do you need air conditioners in Chicago? It's hot two weeks a year."

"Two weeks? Is that so? Well you're cheap fifty-two weeks a year," Maggie replies.

"You've got that right," Jack says, throwing an envelope on Maggie's desk. "Here, this will get you out of the onions for a few hours."

"Cubs tickets?" She says, holding the envelope. "The game starts in a half hour, why didn't you tell me before?"

"I just got them at Rose's, from T.J.," Jack replies. "I thought you'd be happy. You're the only one who could put up with the torture of watching them play."

"I'm happy, trust me, it's just now, I've got to rush down there and I didn't bring my ball cap."

"Call Jerry, he'll bring it," Jack says.

Maggie grabs the phone and Harry stops her. "Excuse me Mags, before you get down to your more important business, can you tell us if we've had any calls this morning."

"Uh, yeah, just one," She says, hastily searching through the pile of green spreadsheets on her desk for a pink note pad. "It was from Frank Danvers, he said it was important, about a good lead, maybe a big one. He wants you to call his friend and he wants; these are his words, not mine, he wants; 'The asshole Connoll and his weasel caddy for a rematch.' Anyway here's the number. Now, can I call Jerry?"

"Sure," Harry says, grabbing the note from her hand. "You hear that Jack, he says it's a big case."

"Yeah sure, sure Harry, hold on a second," Jack says, turning to Maggie. "Maggie is that Jerry on the phone? Good… Tell him to give me five hundred on the Pirates over the Cubs this afternoon, thanks. Now Harry, what were you saying?"

"I was saying that we may actually have something with this Danver's lead, but I forgot about the priorities around here."

"Yeah, I've noticed that about you," Jack replies. "You have to watch yourself. What if Maggie and I weren't around? Who'd take care of you? Now give me that number from Danvers and let me sort this out."

6

Lilly Rivera watches the countryside pass from the window of the limousine that takes them from the Albany Airport.

"From here it's a half-hour drive up to Saratoga," Miss Torrance tells her.

Lilly's Aunt Sylvia had told her stories about Miss Torrance's summer home in upstate New York, but her expectations are far exceeded; the trees larger, the air fresher.

On the plane, Lilly had gone up to see if Miss Torrance needed anything. She found three businessmen attending to Miss Torrance and had returned to her seat. Now in the limo, alone on a seat facing Miss Torrance, she will ask the question that had come to her that morning as she packed her small bag. "Miss Torrance?"

"Yes Lilly, what is it?"

"Do you have a staff in Saratoga?"

"A staff? Hardly, in the summer I rough it. Only old Mrs. Durgiss and her husband, I think his name is Fred. She cooks and cleans, he tends to the grounds and the house."

"What about me?" Lilly asks. "What are my responsibilities?"

"I am your responsibility."

"Yes Miss Torrance, of course."

As the car enters the town of Saratoga, moving up Broadway Avenue, Lilly notices that Kathryn Torrance is smiling. The maid turns to the window to find the reason. Outside she finds a town that appears to be at odds with time, the old holding sway over the new. This afternoon, the Victorian era business district is lazy with summer. The grand hotel, the small shops, the restaurants and bars adorned with beautiful flowers, appear to Lilly, to be only the shadows of things that approach from around a corner, their real forms yet to appear.

"This place is beautiful," Lilly says, responding to Kathryn's smile.

"I like it best now," Kathryn answers, "It is still quiet, in a few weeks, when the racetrack opens, this place will change. Now, like this, it is still dead to the world, still innocent, still dreaming."

The car turns off Broadway onto a tree-lined street of colorful, wood shingled Victorian homes; homes with wrap-around porches, odd shaped windows, lush landscaping and illogical turrets that rise into the blue summer sky. Lilly is sure she has entered into a fairy tale.

Turning right into a long drive, they stop at a house painted in soft yellow and white. A gray-haired man kneels over a flowerbed and a large woman appears at the front door. Seeing the car, the woman walks onto the porch, drying her hands on her apron.

After attending to Miss Torrance, Mrs. Durgiss shows Lilly to a room. Lilly follows the fat old women up the spiral staircase, the walls sheathed in dark wood, to the third floor, to a room in the turret on the East side of the house, a round room with a ceiling that rises to a peak.

When the woman leaves her alone, Lilly scans the room and is enchanted by its sparse and beautiful quality. This morning I woke in the basement, she thinks, and now I will sleep in a round room in the sky.

There is a painting, framed, hanging above the dresser. It is something she remembers. It depicts a ring of trees under a smoky sky. She recalls herself as a child, sitting on the couch in her Aunt Sylvia's room while her Aunt painted this very scene. As a girl, she thought the trees appeared frightened of the approaching fog.

Lilly moves closer to the painting and discovers something she does not recall. There is a shoreline painted in the distant background. On the beach there is a small, apparently incongruent, group of colors overlaid on the sand. Lilly squints, trying to determine if these colors were placed intentionally, or if they were just a missed brush stroke. As she focuses, the likeness of her aunt emerges from these colors.

"A self portrait?" Lilly says to herself, but when she looks again she sees only colors. This brief image of the woman who raised her, the woman whose death left her alone in the world, fills Lilly with sorrow. This was her Aunt's room and now Lilly has now taken her place.

Lilly pulls herself from the painting's spell and walks to the window that faces out to the street. Standing looking down to the lawn, she recalls what her Aunt had told her while painting. "Life is in the waves,"

She had said. "It will roll to the shore. If you dare wade in, there will be no fences, no end and you will dance in this world forever without regret."

Lilly shudders and pulls herself from this trance, telling herself, "It is time I saw to Miss Torrance."

7

"A strange place to meet a client," Harry says to Jack, as they walk across the gravel parking lot to the little shack.

"You think?" Jack says. "Is it stranger than the monkey house at Lincoln Park? Remember that one? We met that Pierson fellow there in the Abdul case."

"I forget about Abdul and the monkeys," Harry replies. "Still, a broken down driving range in the middle of a cow pasture isn't far from a monkey house."

"I didn't ask him why he picked this dump for a meeting. I prefer to keep my conversations short."

"Did you happen to ask him why we're meeting?" Harry asks.

"No. He said he was a friend of Danvers and he had something that would fit us perfect."

Harry and Jack stand at the door of the shack. The sun is almost dead above them and the heat is rising off the dirt brown field in waves that distort everything beyond. Through the quivering air, Harry can see the twisted flagpoles, the distance markers, and a rusted jalopy that is used as a target.

Peering in through the dirt-crusted glass, Jack laughs, "I can't believe it, there is somebody actually working here. It looks like some old guy is behind the counter. I can't tell if he's sleeping or dead."

Harry pokes his head through the rickety door. "Looks dead to me."

"I ain't dead you assholes, I'm just trying to get some rest," The man says, raising his disheveled gray head. "Now, do you want a bucket or do you want to just stand around looking like a couple of downtown jerk-offs."

"You don't actually charge people to hit balls at this rat hole?" Jack chides.

"I ain't charging you nothing cause I want you out of here." The old man's grizzled gray face is turning red. "Now get going, before I call the sheriff for disturbing my peace."

"Now wait," Harry says. "He didn't mean anything. We're here to meet someone and hit a few balls. It's just the heat; it's getting to everybody. My name's Harry, Harry Dimmig, and this is Jack Connoll. Give us a large bucket." Harry slaps down ten dollars in front of the old man. "Has anyone been asking for us?"

"No," The man says, fingering the bill. "I guess if you want to hit some in this heat, be my guest. Just be careful of all them rats you think you see."

Jack starts to say, "Now old-timer, there's no need..."

"Don't call me old timer. I'll come over there and give you a beating you'll never..."

"Listen," Harry says cutting off old man's threat. "My friend doesn't... Just give us the balls. You sure no one's been asking for us?"

"Asking for you? Like you're supposed to be somebody. What'd you say your names were? Dim Egg and..."

"Harry Dimmig and Jack Connoll," Harry answers.

"Dim Egg and Connoll. Huh... damn... I knew a Connoll once."

"That so?" Harry says.

"Some kid. Played him head up in a state amateur match, a semi-final that went twenty-one holes. Musta' been more than twenty-five years ago. Just a kid... shit, was that you? Yeah I remember, blond hair, brown eyes, this small skinny guy here was your caddy. He was always whispering. I don't believe it; the two of you are still together. My name is Irv, Irv Lavinsky. You remember me?"

Jack hesitates, but Harry answers immediately. "I remember you Lavinsky. They called you Lucky."

"You got it Dim Egg."

"Irv Lavinsky? It can't be," Jack says, giving Harry the quick wink. "I remember Irv, he looked like he was on his deathbed back when I beat him in the state amateur thirty years ago."

"That's it," Irv says standing. "I had enough of you..."

"You were a great player," Harry says, distracting Irv from his anger. "You dropped two thirty footers on us that day, gave a us a great match."

"Damn right I was," Lavinsky says. "I don't goddamn believe it. Jack Connoll, after all these years. You were something back then. Everybody said you were gonna' be somebody, somebody big. Look at you now. What happened to ya?"

"Obviously nothing good, seeing that I ended up here talking with you and about to hit balls at this broken down pigsty."

"Ain't that the truth," Lavinsky says, pushing the ten-dollar bill back at Harry. "Come on, let's go see if the kid's still got it."

Irv Lavinsky stands, grabs a metal bucket of beat up golf balls, an old driver and hobbles out through the door. Harry and Jack follow him into the blazing midday sun.

"Here try one," Irv says to Jack. "Use my club, let's see what's left of the punk's game."

Jack grabs the club from Lavinsky. He finds a white golf tee lying in the dirt and forces it into the hard earth. Reaching into the bucket for a ball, he places it on the tee, steps behind it, sights his target and absently swings the club in slow circular movements. As he takes his stance, a bead of sweat appears on his forehead, he checks his grip and then, to the astonishment of old Lavinsky, lets everything sag a bit, as if allowing the life energy to run out of his body and into the earth.

Lavinsky remembers the kid, Connoll, making these very same moves. Harry's seen them a million times.

With a twitch of his right knee Jack's body turns, corkscrewing, the elastic muscles stretching. Taking the club back, Jack visualizes the image of his ball already in flight; for him the swing is already complete.

For Irv and Harry the visions have just begun. For them, as Jack's club moves back, away from the target, time appears to slow and reverse.

Harry knows the affects of Jack swing; the breeze waning, the birdsongs quieting and the memories from their past emerge.

*   *   *

Harry recalls following Jack to the baseball diamond after their first day of high school. He remembers how Jack took him, the very next Saturday, out to Oak Grove Country Club, north of Chicago.

"I've been carrying bags here all summer," Jack told him. "There'll still be seven or eight good weekends left in the season."

"You mean caddying?" Harry asked.

"Yeah looping. Great job, good money, people are nice. You'll see some good action and you play the course for free on Mondays. If you happen to wander by the pool, you can happen to meet some cute rich girls."

"You make decent money?" Harry asked, as they sat on the train heading out to Oak Grove.

"Sure, they give you five dollars a bag. If your man has a good day you can make double or triple that in tips. On busy days you can go around twice. Hell, you get the right kind of guy; he'll even buy you a Coke and hot dog at the turn. It's a sweet job. You'll see."

"Sounds better than walking those big dumb animals and shoveling horse shit."

"About the same, except the scenery is better and the big dumb animals don't smell as bad."

From that morning on, Harry has been a caddy. It was not long before Harry's services were in demand at the club. Caddying, the quiet observations and calculations on behalf of his player, was as natural to him, as hitting a golf ball was to Jack.

On Mondays, the boys were allowed to play the course; that is Jack played and Harry carried his bag. They would have worked as caddies for free, just to have those Mondays. They would meet before dawn at the "L" and ride it north to the Dempster stop. From there they would walk the three miles to the club, stopping at Herb's Diner for hot donuts and coffee. They were always the first on the course, going around three times some days, finishing in dusk, always playing the eighteenth in after the sun had set, the fireflies flashed around them and the lights of the clubhouse were their only target.

On those Mondays, their friendship, and partnership, was resolved into a plan; Jack would become a golf pro and Harry would be his caddy.

Jack, the fearless boy, with his long fluid swing, began playing and beating the best in the region. He trusted Harry, when he was told to lay back or go for green; he never questioned the club he was handed.

Harry knew he could never hit a ball like Jack and, for all his ability, Jack knew he would never know as much about the intricacies, the unseen aspects, of the game, as Harry. As time passed, their reputation grew on the courses around Chicago.

Then Harry remembers, a night, they are on the road, years after leaving high school behind, driving the old black and white Checker Cab they had purchased for two hundred dollars from Freedy Palka's West Chicago Taxi Company. It was the perfect road vehicle, huge back seat for sleeping, big trunk for their equipment and indestructible. The odometer had frozen at 314,488.

Jack was driving the cab, somewhere just over the Iowa state line, when he asked, "Are you awake?"

Harry, curled up in the corner, grunted a reply.

"Good, I'm kinda' losing it. Nothing to look at but half grown corn."

"You told me you'd get us to Ames," Harry said, sitting up straight. "Don't start trying to weasel out of driving now."

"Relax, I said I'd get us there and I will. I just need to talk or you might wake up in corn patch or whatever the hell they call them around here. You know what I mean?"

"What's on your mind?"

"Well I was wondering what the schedule is, you know, what's the plan?"

"The plan is for you get us to Ames and we'll call the friend of that banker we met at the Brookton Club, who might be looking for a game. Then, maybe we get a couple more games from that one, make a few bucks before the matches start at the Ames Club on Thursday."

"Yeah I know that, I mean what's the big plan?"

"You really must be bored," Harry said. "Since when do you give a damn about the long range?"

"Don't know, I was just wondering… What about that shot I hit on fourteen this afternoon? That could have been the best shot ever hit at old Brookton."

"It was a beauty. That boy you beat will be having nightmares for years."

"Yeah a beauty… So Harry…"

"Yeah Jack."

"What about the plan?"

"From Ames to Boulder, from Boulder to Topeka and then we start making are way to Arizona. We need to be there at the end of November."

"The end of November, that's it, huh?"

"That's it, the tour qualifying tournament. Next year, we'll be flying instead of driving this old piece of shit."

"That's if we get the card."

"We'll get it, we're the best there is out here. Shit, you know that, we've beat them all and a few of their fathers."

"This is different Harry. This will be all the college boys, the players from Europe and who knows where else. There'll be tour players trying to make it back. All hungry. These guys won't be the same as the yahoos I just whacked at Brookton Country Club."

"Yeah, sure, there'll be some good players, but Jack, I've seen them all. We've won state amateurs and who knows how many of how many other titles. We've beat the best out there. I haven't seen a course yet that can stop us."

"Maybe we should take a run at the U.S. Amateur before we try to qualify for the tour?"

"No, you got the game to be a pro. We can do it. How long have we been on the road?" Harry asked.

"Since we were seventeen, over five years."

"Five years of playing every amateur event we could find and any money game that came along. I've watched you; I've seen the tour players, we're as good, we can do it. There is no doubt we've got the game."

"Five years…" Jack said. "Shit, five years of driving this junk around the country. How did it go by so fast? I trust you Harry. You know that. I get the glory; you clean my clubs. I sleep in the member's house; you sleep in the back seat. I dance at parties, you sit at the local dive and plan our next move."

"We're partners Jack. We'll both be celebrating soon."

"Right Harry. Flying next year, instead of driving a broke down cab. That's the plan."

Harry remembers the morning they drove the Checker into The Ames Country Club. He distinctly remembers the sound of a hound dog barking and how only he saw the vision of the bootless cowboy spirit sitting on the top rail of the horse fence. There was a smile on the phantom's indistinct face and Harry wondered whom he was here to haunt.

That week everything went to plan. They had won a few hundred from the friend of the banker from Brookton. Jack registered for the club's tournament and was assigned to stay with one of the club's least prominent members, Jonathon Cantwell. The word was that Cantwell owned a failing shoe store chain and lived in a suburban home that was in desperate need of a renovation.

Harry recalls that moment in his life, for them, all signs were promising a golden road to paradise.

*   *   *

As Jack takes the club back to the farthest point and everything comes to a pause, Irv Lavinsky watches in awe, he feels the forgotten twinge of envy. How easy he makes it look, Lavinsky thinks.

Harry dreads this moment. The moment when Jack's swing approaches a perfect rest and then changes direction. A moment in which he knows their future will never be what they had planned. It is in this pause that he recalls their time in Ames.

*　　*　　*

The first time Jack saw her, K.C. Cantwell, the eighteen year-old daughter of the failing shoe salesman, he was convinced that this was not the only life he had lived.

The first thing he said to her was, "I know you."

K.C. laughed, saying, "That's impossible," although she understood exactly what he had meant.

Harry remembers the matches in Ames; it was the best Jack had ever played; none were close, the girl seemed to inspire him. Although K.C. was beautiful, she was not any different from the other affairs Jack had as they moved from town to town. She would be another fling, another small town girl falling for Jack's easy way.

Soon, Harry knew she was different.

At the club's Saturday night reception, Harry parked cars, picking up some extra money. K.C. and Jack arrived in Jonathon Cantwell's old Buick. When they stepped from the car, Harry was struck by how perfect they were together, two reflections connected by a radiance that appeared to him as basic and eternal.

K.C. laughed when she saw Harry wearing the short red valet's jacket. Harry recalls how she self-consciously tried to cover the hand-sewn repair in her dress and how Jack looked to her for clues on when to move and when to stop.

The party went on inside, while Harry, alone on the club's front steps, saw the spirit of his grandmother standing on the lawn. There were other ghosts milling about behind her. When he approached her, she faded from sight, a tear dropping from her cheek.

At dawn on Monday, the championship trophy in hand and dreams still fresh in the minds of the young lovers, the three of them left Ames together.

*　　*　　*

Irv smiles, as Jack starts the club forward from the moment of rest. Like Hogan, he thinks, so simple, like any child could do this.

Harry, during his world travels, had met musicians who would sell their souls for the natural timing displayed in this scrap of Jack's swing; everything pure, innate synchronicity.

Connoll's body begins to unwind. It is the onset of the release, the first move toward an unknowable end and the moment when Harry's thoughts return to the road to Arizona.

*   *   *

Jack, K.C. and Harry, drove from Ames to Boulder. There was the diner outside Redstone where Harry sat in a booth with K.C., sipping coffee, as Jack replaced the fan belt on the cab.

"So this is what you do?" K.C. asked Harry.

"You mean diners, golf? I guess this is it," Harry replied.

"No, I mean carrying a golf bag. That's all you do. Jack plays, wins money, repairs the car, makes the contacts and you carry the bag. Right?"

"I do more."

"Jack tells me you're partners. Fifty-fifty. That right?"

"He told you that?"

"Doesn't seem fair to me."

"It doesn't matter how it seems to you."

"Don't be too sure about that Harry. Jack and I have had some discussions about this."

A chill snaked through Harry and his attention was drawn to a couple sitting at the booth two down. They were small, maybe dwarves, their heads and hands out of proportion to their bodies.

Without looking back to K.C., Harry asked, "Jack and you have talked about this?"

"Yes. Let me ask you Harry, have you ever had a girlfriend? I mean, Jack says he can never remember any."

Harry did not answer. He turned back, stared into her eyes and saw only black where he had remembered blue. He pulled his attention back to the dwarves and they now wore the costumes of a king and a queen.

Harry knew they were only spirits, that only he could see them, but for that moment he believed they ruled the world.

"What's the matter Harry? Cat got your tongue. All I want to know is have you ever had a girl?"

"No," Harry replied.

"Just like I've told Jack," She smirked.

*   *   *

As Jack brings the club down to the ball, it moves in towards his turning body, his arms uncocking, his wrists now forming the final axis, the moment of impact is approaching. Irv Lavinsky experiences a surge of energy, a rage from his youth that he believed was lost with the years.

Harry feels it too and it brings him to that parking lot outside of Topeka, two weeks before the tour-qualifying tournament.

*   *   *

Harry was sitting on the bumper of the Checker, polishing Jack's spikes, as K.C. made her way across the asphalt lot. Harry had been avoiding K.C., but she was always angling to get him alone and now she had him.

"The qualifying starts in a couple weeks," K.C. said. "I'm getting nervous already."

"Yeah, we can do it."

"We? You mean, Jack," She said.

"No, I mean Jack and me," Harry replied.

"Do you really believe Jack needs you?"

"We've been partners since ninth grade, he'll tell you, always fifty-fifty, a team. Just leave it alone."

"Fifty-fifty now, but once he's on the tour, you get what the other caddies get, no more than ten percent."

"We're different…" Harry said, stopping his reply.

"Different? Listen, you're nothing without him. Jack loves me and I won't let you take advantage of him."

"Take advantage of him? We have a plan."

"I know how this works," K.C. said. "I saw it happen to my father. People like you took advantage of him, of his talents; I won't let this happen to Jack. I won't let that happen to me again."

"To you, what do you have to do with our lives?"

"Wrong Harry, this is my life now. If you try to get between us, you're done. Maybe I'll do it for fun. I'm out of Ames now and I won't let the likes of you stop me."

"I thought you cared about him. I thought you loved him."

She hesitated before she answered him. The cold veil around her faded for only an instant. "I do care..." She started to say before stopping herself, the ice returning to her eyes. "I care for myself and I'll take care of Jack. He doesn't want a faggot for his caddy anyway. I've told him all about you."

"What? What are you talking about? I..." Harry could not continue a reply. There was dead silence between them. With K.C.'s eyes on him, Harry did not have the strength to lift his gaze from the black tar under his feet. He was burned inside and out, crippled beyond movement and yet she still did not turn away to release him.

Harry summoned strength to reply. "You hate everything, me, Jack, yourself, everything. You want to steal our dream, the thing we worked and sacrificed everything for. I won't let you do this to us."

"You're not strong enough to fight me. You are a stupid little Dimmig and your time is almost up."

Harry did not understand what this meant. He could not know that from that moment on, nothing again would be sacred.

*   *   *

As the heat rises in waves from the dust of the desolate driving range, the two men watch Jack bringing the club's head to meet the ball. The energy Jack has created is about to be released into the world of action. Irv Lavinsky stands, as if girding for a stomach punch, and Harry turns away, back to Phoenix.

*   *   *

Jack had been sullen since Topeka. Harry had tried to talk with him over the last week, but off the golf course Jack was never separated from K.C. and on the course he began to falter. In their last match before they left Kansas for Arizona, against a club pro, a match that Jack would have normally closed out in short order, they lost a thousand dollars. It would be their last tune up before the qualifying tournament. Jack played a game that Harry had never seen before; hooking tee shots, pushing wedges, missing three-foot putts and reacting with anger at his mistakes. Harry's suggestions fell on deaf ears and he eventually decided to follow his player in silence. This silence lasted until they arrived in Phoenix.

The morning they arrived at the site of the qualifying matches, Harry saw K.C. slide down in her seat, ashamed to be seen riding in the beat up old cab. As soon as the car stopped, she bolted with the excuse of needing to use the bathroom.

The St. Martins Club was hushed with activity; with men pulled there by the slim thread of their hopes and dreams. Jack and Harry made their way to the registration tent through the funereal atmosphere that shrouded the course and suggested that bodies were about to be buried. Even in the biggest championships in which they had played, they had never experienced this type of atmosphere. This was about life and death.

As other golfers waited to be set off on the course in those muted surroundings, they occupied themselves by swinging at phantom golf balls. Those others, their opposition, looked stronger then ever before; neatly trimmed hair, new spikes, caddies carrying bags emblazoned with sponsor's names that held the newest clubs. As they passed, strange languages and intonations drifted in and out of Harry's perception.

Into the middle of all this walked the ragged Harry and Jack from Webster Street, an old taxicab their home, equipment that had seen many seasons and fresh off a thrashing by club pro in Topeka. They could not bear to look at each other.

"Your tee time for the practice round is 3:15," The tournament official said to Jack.

They were paired with two other competitors and their caddies. There were the Spaniards, who only nodded when introduced and a

British golfer, Glyn Parker, a tall thin man whose tweed cap could not contain his wild straw blond hair. When Parker introduced himself, his smile caused his face to crinkle in around two blue eyes.

"Nice to meet you men," Glyn said in his casual British accent. "I've played these Spanish boys before, in a tournament outside Surrey, a few years back. Very fierce, as you might expect, they don't talk much, except to swear. I guess it's just you two and me today for company. I don't hold much hope for my caddy. Some kid I just picked up out front. He seems more interested in the football results than my golf game."

Jack laughed when he shook Parker's hand and Harry felt at ease for the first time in weeks. During that round, Jack struck the ball beautifully. Harry thought it was that last laugh before teeing off. Jack returned to taking his cues from Harry. As they played, Harry mapped the course in his notebook, running scenarios over in his mind, noting how the other golfers played the holes.

When Jack reached the island green at the 540-yard par five fourteenth in two shots, Harry caught the Spaniards staring at Jack and making signs with their fingers in his direction. Harry assumed it was a Spanish curse.

There were others on the course that day too, but only Harry saw them. There were the spirits who followed their group. There was a tall balding man, elderly, who walked with a limp and wore a blue blazer; he followed silently behind Parker. There were two men dressed in rags that hobbled around after the Spaniards, huddling close by wherever the golfers stopped. A woman Harry knew as Jack's mother stayed far back, just at the edge of the tree line.

There was more to see on the course that day. Harry watched, as Parker struggled with his caddy, Taylor. Parker was constantly waiting for his clubs to catch up with him and needed to instruct the boy at every turn.

"Taylor you've got to do better..." Parker would say. "Did you write the yardage from the trap down in my book? You must remember to do this."

The boy shifted the heavy golf bag and just shook his head.

"Damn it Taylor, you have to concentrate. This is serious business," Parker would say, stomping away.

Jack and Harry were having no such problems. They played a round built from the summer Mondays at Oak Grove. The balls dropped feathery on every green and they tallied a round in 63 shots.

"That's some very good golf my friend," Parker said to Jack. "Some of the best I've ever had the pleasure to witness. You put a couple together like that and you will certainly get yourself a ticket."

Word spread quickly around the course. Jack Connoll's name was on everyone's lips. The best round of the day by five shots. A reporter from a golf magazine asked Jack questions on strategy and two Japanese golfers bowed to Harry when he passed.

When K.C. found them she was excited with the news, grabbing Jack and kissing him hard on the lips.

$*$ $*$ $*$

And then, Jack's club connects with the ball. It is an instant that is impossible to observe, unknowable, always a mystery, even to Jack. The explosion of energy into action, shattering the visions into reality and the world is changed forever.

$*$ $*$ $*$

At dusk, on the evening of the practice round, Harry walked the course alone; one last check on his notes. Earlier, Jack and K.C. had left the course together to find a place for dinner. As he walked in the desert night, Harry thought he heard a rhyme on the wind, something from his childhood repeated on the breeze, *"They all went to heaven in a little row boat..."*

As he sat on a bench by the practice green, eating a sandwich given to him by a cook from the club's kitchen, the rhyme stayed with him. He felt confident, everything was almost normal again, the last few weeks an aberration, he thought, as he watched the black and white Checker pull into the parking lot.

Jack and K.C. walked slowly up the path toward Harry; K.C.'s left arm around Jack's waist.

"How was dinner?" Harry asked, when they approached.

"Good. You eat?" Jack said.

"Yeah, I got a sandwich after I walked the course," Harry replied.

K.C. picked up the notebook that sat on the bench next to Harry and thumbed absently through it.

"Kase, can you leave me and Harry alone?" Jack asked. "We need to talk."

"Sure Jack. I'll be in the cab listening to music." With a quick glance to Harry, K.C. walked away, leaving the two men alone.

"Harry," Jack started, "I've been meaning to talk with you for a while now, but..."

"I know it's been a rough couple months," Harry said. "But today's round was great."

"Yeah, it was. It was. Harry there's something I've been meaning to talk to you about."

"Yeah Jack, what's up?"

"It's me and you Harry, well I'm just not that comfortable with us anymore."

"Not comfortable? I don't understand."

"Well I've been thinking, this partnership, maybe it wasn't a good idea."

"Good idea? You've been thinking? Christ Jack, after how we played today, what are you talking about?"

"Harry, I played today, you just carried my bag."

"I... I... don't understand, why are you telling me this?"

"I'm telling you this because I'm done. I don't need you anymore and to tell you the truth, you're starting to embarrass me."

"What? Jack... I embarrass you? How? What are you talking about?"

"Harry it's nothing personal, but I'm about to be on the pro tour, and, well, your type, you know it isn't accepted out here."

"What type? What does that mean?"

"You know, how you've never had a girlfriend."

"Jack, listen to me, listen to what you're saying, you need me and what does it matter if I've never had a girlfriend, what does it matter to anyone?"

"Just don't make this harder, K... I mean I, already found a replacement."

"No... Jack... Please, what are you doing? After all the years it took us to get here, what are you doing? It's her, I know, she's doing this to us. Please don't let her. Remember our plans, how this is our chance. She told me she would do this. Please Jack."

"It's too late Harry, I'm sorry. I'll leave your bags by the club entrance. Here, take this; it's seven hundred and fifty dollars. It's half of everything we have and it's the end of our partnership." Jack held the money in front of Harry.

Harry could not move. He was gripping the bench seat with both hands. He was trying to suppress vomit. "How can you do this Jack?"

Harry looked up into Jack's eyes, they were red and he saw him struggling with a tear. Harry realized then how pathetic he must appear to Jack; always the small weak man, a caddy, on a bench with a half eaten sandwich, his only possessions about to left at the curb. Jack must pity him, giving him this money to diminish his guilt, working on directions from the one they picked up in Ames. It was all too much.

Harry leapt from the bench striking Jack in the face with his fist.

"You asshole," Harry screamed, as Jack fell back with Harry on top of him. "You're throwing it away for that bitch. She could care less for you."

Harry flailed at Jack and Jack did not fight back. Harry sensed that Jack had hoped he would respond this way. It was useless anyway. Harry could never hurt Jack. He rolled off of him onto the grass. Lying on his back, Harry stared up into the desert sky. He stayed there as Jack said, "I'm sorry Harry," and walked away.

*   *   *

The ball rockets off the clubface. It starts low then rises, cutting through the waves of heat, through the lost years of these three men's lives. Jack,

Harry and Irv stand and watch it rise, flying out over the hardscrabble field marked by the impotent flags, out over the rusted jalopy and the broken down fence. It soars high and arches toward the blazing sun.

"I'll be damned," Irv Lavinsky says, watching the ball's flight. "I will be damned."

*   *   *

Harry slept in the caddy shack the night Jack left him on the grass. He had collected the scattered money, found his belongings at the club entrance and then laid awake on the floor of the shack until he fell into a dream.

In the dream he was a boy again, on Webster Street in front of Rose's Bar. He was sitting on the curb across from Zimmy Lehrman's house. He was in love with Zimmy; her big brown eyes. When he turned to his right, she was there, next to him. She took his hand in hers and kissed his face softly.

"You're a special boy," Zimmy said to him. "Remember Harry, your past is the key that waits."

Harry turned away from her and looked down Webster into the sun. The blinding light caused him to open his eyes, to awake on the caddy shack floor, it was dawn; the first sherps were arriving at the course for the morning rounds. Harry gathered his belongings and made his way to the clubhouse, intent on calling a taxi.

"Morning Harry," The Englishman said.

Harry turned to see Glyn Parker, tweed cap, fresh scrubbed face, red and smiling. "You're looking a little worse for the wear. Rough night?"

"You can say that," Harry replied.

"What time you boys going off?"

"Jack's teeing of at 11:09."

"Damn, that's a bad break. It'll be hot as hell out there by then."

"Yeah, I guess. What time you going off Glyn?"

"In fifty minutes: 7:53. That is if I can find that blasted caddy of mine. You haven't seen him have you? You remember him, Taylor's his name."

"No I haven't seen him, but I'm available if he doesn't show."

"What? How's that possible?"

"I'm not sure myself Glyn, but it is."

"Well I'll be damned. A man shoots a 63 and fires his caddy that night. That's a new one. But his loss is my gain. My only regret is that Taylor isn't here so I can tell him to his bungling face."

"Let's go to the range Harry. You still got your book right?"

The notebook. Harry frantically searched his pockets and his bags, but the book was nowhere to be found.

"Glyn, can I meet you up at the range?"

"That would be fine Harry, just don't leave me waiting. We've got a big day ahead of us."

"I'll be there Glyn. Thanks."

Harry ran toward the bench by the practice green, but halfway there he remembered seeing the book in K.C.'s hands just before Jack gave him the news. She had stolen it, he was sure. All his work, ideas, strategies, club choices, she had it all now. Her job was complete. She had stolen everything.

The next five days were grueling. The new team, Parker and Dimmig, struggled with each other in the first round. Harry's club selections were often ignored, and once, when Glyn did accept his suggestion, it was obviously the wrong choice. Still, after the second round Glyn had played well enough to make the cut and by the third round they were within three shots of earning a tour card. They had also developed a routine. After each round they would first go to the range, then to a local gin mill to drink beer and talk strategy.

At the start of the final round, Glyn was within two strokes of making the tour. On the seventeenth hole, he was within one stroke when a five-foot birdie putt lipped out and hung on the edge of the cup. On eighteen, his approach stopped ten feet from the hole. The pressure had built to a tremendous level. As they lined up a final putt that would earn Glyn his tour card, Harry could hardly move his legs.

Harry said to Glyn, "Start it inside the left edge."

"I see it just outside," Glyn replied.

"Inside all the way," Harry said.

"I've got to go with what I see Harry."

They both watched as the putt rolled by the left edge.

Glyn's shoulders slumped. He immediately turned to Harry and said, "I'm sorry. I should have listened to you."

"No, I'm sorry Glyn. I could have done better for you this week. You played great."

As they walked off the course up to the clubhouse, Harry stopped and put out his hand. "Well this is where we part ways," Harry said. "It was great working for you. It meant more to me than you can ever know. Thank you."

"You're welcome Harry, but why does it have to end. I think we've got the makings of a great team. I've got a sponsor who wants to back me on the Asian tour, I still have exemptions left in Europe and my finish here should get me into a few tournaments in the states next summer. What do say? Work for me and we'll see what's out in the world. Maybe even make enough to eat."

Harry looked into Glyn's kind eyes knowing that he had nowhere else to go. The old cab and his old friend Jack were long gone, days ago, after missing the cut. Jack had left alone. During the final round Harry had seen K.C. following a tall German player who finished high on the leader board and would win his tour card.

"I'd like that," Harry told Glyn. "I've never thought about going to Asia and I promise we'll make that putt next time."

"I believe you Harry. I most certainly do. Now come on, let's go have a beer, forget about today and start preparing for tomorrow."

*   *   *

Harry, Jack and Irv stand silent watching a ball that is now far in the distance and falling to the earth. Harry is holding back tears. "It could have been so different," He says to himself.

"So what do you think Irv, do I still got it?" Jack asks.

"If anyone asked that's what I'd tell them," Lavinsky replies.

The three men on the tee are silent, contemplating everything they had just experienced. The silence is broken by the sound of someone clapping. They all turn to see a short pudgy bald man standing by the open door of a blue sedan. He wears silver rimmed glasses, a business suit, with sweat soaking through his white shirt under his loosened necktie.

"That's what I'm looking for Mr. Connoll," The man says, still applauding and approaching the threesome on the tee. "That's what I'm looking for. My name is Manley, Kevin Manley. That was quite a drive. Certainly everything I've heard about you is true."

"Mr. Manley, nice to meet you," Jack says. "This is my partner, Harry Dimmig and this is our associate Lucky Lavinsky, we call him Irv. Please step into our office."

"Nice to meet you," Manley says, shaking hands with all the three men and following Jack.

They make their way back into the shack where Irv brings out four cans of Old Style beer from a small cooler behind the counter.

"So Mr. Manley, what can we do for you?" Jack asks.

"It's Kevin. May I ask about Mr. Lavinsky here, does he work with you?"

"Certainly," Jack says. "Irv's a part of the team. What you have to say to us, you can say in front of Irv. It goes no farther than this putrid shack. Right Irv?"

"Right, I tell no one," Irv replies.

"Well all right, I guess," Manley offers.

"So what is it?" Harry asks.

"Well, let me start by saying everything I've heard about you appears to be true."

"What would it be that you heard Kevin," Jack says.

"I heard that you were a very, very good golfer, Jack. I heard you may be the best to ever play in the state," Manley says.

Irv snorts, spits up his beer and turns away.

"You heard right Kevin," Harry replies, giving Irv a threatening glance. "The best ever, so what about it?"

"Well Harry," Manley says. "I have also heard that your partner, Jack, threw it all away, his chance to be a pro, years of his life, though I never heard why."

"And you're not likely to hear the reason unless you get to the point," Jack says.

"Right," Manley continues. "Well I'm looking for a player, someone who can compete with the best and doesn't have a prominent tour background."

"A ringer," Irv smirks. "You're looking for a ringer."

"You might say Mr. Lavinsky, Irv, that I'm looking for a ringer to play other ringers, but there's more to this job than golf," Manley says.

"Get to the point Kevin," Harry says.

"Please give me some time, it is a very complicated matter," Manley replies.

"You'll have all the time you need when we're on the clock, right now get to the point," Harry answers.

"Let me help," Jack says. "Who will we be working for? You or someone else?"

"Very good Jack, that's a good starting point. I represent a man in this matter. I cannot name him at this moment. I am his lawyer and you will work for me."

"A goddamn lawyer," Irv smirks. "I smell trouble already."

"Relax Irv," Harry says. "Lawyers are ninety percent of our business. It's the unnamed one that always gets me worried."

"Let Kevin explain," Jack says.

"Thanks. Yes I am a lawyer and I happen to know your friend and weekly pigeon Frank Danvers. He is the one who alerted me to your existence. As for the unnamed one Mr. Dimmig, he will be no concern of yours. Is that understood gentlemen?"

"Get to the fucking point," Irv sneers.

Harry and Jack look at each other and laugh.

"Now easy Irv, let the man speak," Jack says. "I'm sorry you will have to forgive our elderly friend. At his age he can't afford to waste any time."

"What's that supposed to mean Connoll?" Irv glares at Jack.

"You know what," Manley says. "Maybe I made a mistake here."

"Now Kevin," Jack says. "We're just having a little fun."

Irv Lavinsky continues to stare at Jack. Manley sits red faced, sweat rolling down both sides of his face; he grips his beer can with both hands.

"I… I don't know gentlemen…" Manley starts.

"Please Kevin, just tell us what you want," Harry offers.

"All right. Where was I?"

"You were telling us we work for you and you work for someone else," Jack says.

"Right, well, uh, right, my client is, uh, he's a very special client, uh…"

"Relax Kevin," Jack says. "Irv, you got any more beers in that cooler? Get another one for our friend Kevin."

"All right Kevin, let's hear it," Harry says, as Irv returns with four more beers.

"Right. Well, as I was saying," Manley starts. "I am looking for golfers and more. I am looking for golfers, who can win a special competition and who can observe their surroundings with the eye of a detective."

"You want us to golf and spy," Jack says.

"Not quite Jack," Manley says. "I want you to golf, spy and win."

"Spying," Irv smirks. "So that's what you sunk to Connoll?"

"Okay." Harry looks to Irv. "This is where I think you should take a walk."

"What? This is my office. I'm not gonna' be kicked out into the afternoon sun like some mangy dog."

"Here's a hundred dollars," Harry says. "We'll rent the place for the afternoon. Think you can find a cool spot for a hundred?"

"I'll be down at the Oak Inn if you need to consult with me." Irv winks at Manley, grabs the money and shuffles out of the shack, the flimsy door bouncing twice on the frame before closing.

"So he wasn't an associate?" Manley asks.

"He was, only we just associated with him this afternoon," Jack replies. "Sorry Kevin, just having a little fun."

"I won't have this." Manley stands up. "This is bullshit. I'm offering you a professional opportunity and you assholes screw me around. How can I trust you two to represent my client's interests when the first time we meet you're bullshitting me? This is serious business."

"Relax Kevin. Please sit," Jack says. "He was just an old man. If it's so serious than get to the fucking point. As for trust, you'll never find two more honest guys. Seeing that you're a lawyer, maybe the only two honest men you've met in many years. So get on with it. What's the job?"

"Honest guys? Sure... huh, all right," Manley says, returning to his seat. "If I didn't think you were perfect for what we need, I'd be out of here this second. But all right. First off, there is a man," Manley says. "Very wealthy, the guy lives in something like a castle. Anyway, word is, has been for a long time, that he's half crazy, maybe because he's into that island religion. For the last ten years there's been rumors of his strange behavior and now there's this golf competition."

"What golf competition?" Harry asks.

"Invitation only," Manley says. "As far as we know, they were sent to eight of the world's most wealthy and powerful men. It's being held at his private course. A place no one's ever seen. A ten million-entry fee... The prize is the pot and more. The invitees can play the match themselves or hire someone to play on their behalf as long as who they hire has not played on any pro tour in the last ten years."

"So your boss wants us to win the pot for him?" Jack says.

"Yes, he wants the money," Manley replies. "He also wants someone in this tournament who can him tell more than just the conditions of the course. He wants players who can dig a little deeper into the man's personal life while they are inside the gates of that mansion."

Harry's eyes are wide. "Sounds interesting. What are you willing to pay?"

"Well Harry, Jack, we'll pay the normal rate for your investigative work. I believe that would be, for both of you working on the same case, four hundred a day, plus all expenses. Is that correct?"

"Yeah, maybe," Jack replies.

"If you win," Manley continues, "If you win the tournament, my client will pay you 2.5 million."

Jack turns, choking on his beer. Harry feels the blood drain from his head.

"A one in eight chance to win two and half million?" Harry asks.

"That's it. It won't be easy. But that's the opportunity we're offering. What do you say?"

"Hell yeah, is what I say," Jack replies. "I..."

"Now Jack, hold on," Harry says, cutting off his partner. "Can you excuse us Kevin? I need to talk with Jack for a moment."

"Certainly," Manley says, walking to the cooler. He grabs another beer and walks out of the shack.

Harry and Jack sit silent staring at the floor.

Finally, Harry says, "Can we believe this guy?"

"I don't know, but what do we have to lose."

Both men begin to laugh.

"What do we have to lose?" Harry repeats to himself.

"Should we try for more than 2.5, or how about a higher daily?" Jack asks.

"Let me handle it," Harry says.

Harry opens the door. "Uh, Mr. Manley, Kevin, could you please step inside, we have a few more questions?"

Manley lumbers back into the shack, mopping the sweat from his forehead with a white handkerchief. "What is it gentlemen?"

"When is this tournament?" Jack asks.

"In four weeks," Manley replies.

"Where?" Harry asks.

"At a mansion, on our host's course in northern New York State."

"What's the name of the man who is holding the tournament, the man whose life we'll be looking into?" Jack asks.

"His name is Waits. Christopher Waits," Manley replies. "So do we have a deal?"

"We'll need a two thousand dollar advance. You know, good faith," Harry says.

"Done," Manley replies.

"Tell your boss he's got his men," Jack says.

"I will and I'll be in touch soon. Remember this game is for more than money. You should prepare yourselves for the best competition."

"We'll be ready," Harry says. "Before you go, I have one more question."

"What is it Harry?"

"Why did we have to meet out here? Out at this dump."

"Oh, well, I wanted to see the swing for myself. You did not disappoint, it was everything I had heard. Guess you didn't know it, but I watched you on the course with Danvers yesterday morning. You didn't hit one tee shot like that all round. You let Danvers lose by one stroke. I know how it works," Manley says, standing up and walking to the door. "I know how it works and I will be in touch... Harry and Jack, two honest men, that's a good one, that's a good one." Manley is laughing, as the rickety door slams behind him.

8

During her free time from Miss Torrance, Lilly Rivera watches Saratoga awaken. The racetrack's opening day is Saturday and the once subtle buzz now vibrates through everything.

Over the last few weeks, Lilly's time off was spent wandering the streets, window-shopping on Broadway, exploring the narrow lanes and observing the intimate society of the tiny bistros.

Once, she visited the old racetrack, walking in through an open gate, watching the beautiful animals as they galloped for morning exercise on the historic circuit.

In her travels, Lilly found the little park where she sits today. A park surrounded with a trellis of flowers, a fountain at the center and the atmosphere a symphony of birds.

Miss Torrance is occupied with the spa this afternoon and Lilly feels thankfully alone here. She sits on a bench underneath a large oak that grows just west of the fountain.

She senses something change in her surroundings. She closes her eyes and listens. It has become silent. No birds, just an occasional soft rustling of leaves. She thinks, how strange, I heard birds when I arrived.

When Lilly opens her eyes she sees him. It is not the first time she had seen him in Saratoga. She recalls glimpsing him the first time two weeks ago. She was with Miss Torrance on some errands around town and they had stopped for tea at a sidewalk cafe. He was standing on the corner across from where they sat; an olive skinned man, probably Hispanic like her, with long black hair pulled behind his ears. His coal black eyes were focused on their table.

Then once, a week later, she looked down from her turret window and found him walking slowly by Miss Torrance's house.

Now, he is standing across the park, beyond the flowers and the fountain, at the bottom of the path that leads to the street. For the first time she is alone in the same space with him. Although she has no reason to fear him, she is frozen, she cannot run or move. He watches her, motionless, just staring across the park to her.

Lilly observes the air around him ripple and move upward. The air has weight, it can be seen, it carries what it has captured and it moves toward her. She can smell the flowers in it; the fragrance of this man must be there too. The air is distorting, causing a tangle in the colors of the park scene. Her eyes close again and she fights to keep them open. Later, when she regains her focus, the man is nowhere in sight.

For a time she scans the park for him, but her attention is drawn to the silver froth of the fountain.

"Life is in the waves," Lilly recalls her Aunt saying. "It rolls to the shore to claim you." Lilly gazes into the refracting streams that shoot skyward and fall back to the pool. "If you wade in there will be no fences, no end and you will dance in this world forever without regret."

Forever without regret, Lilly thinks.

The water streams skyward, hanging for an instant, before it falls back down, bringing the memory to her of that horrific moment from her past.

*   *   *

A child of seven, she felt the heat pour into the small apartment on the fifth floor. Her family's building was located in the scabby, chaotic, neighborhood known as Little Havana. Out on the street below, gangs of children screamed and ran wildly on the hot pavement. The music of ten radios mixed to create a shamble of noise. Her parents were so young then. They paced the floor. They argued in the small kitchen, sweat coating their faces. Lilly's mother was crying as she pushed her young child into the bathroom.

"No, no, Lilly, stay here. I must talk to your father alone," She said.

Lilly stood with her ear pressed against the bathroom door. Their words cut into her heart. They shouted of money, of a job, of names and places that the girl could not know.

The girl heard the door from the hall crash open and the voice of a man, pure English, demanding, "The name Rivera... The boss wants the name of his new competitor. The name of the man you work for..."

Lilly cracked the door and peered out. There was a fat man speaking; black frame glasses, wearing a tie, sweat glistening from his neck. The small dark man next to him was flashing a knife.

"Give us his name or you both die," The fat man demanded.

"No. No, please," Lilly's father begged. "Tell Señor that I do not know this man's name. I only work for him one time. I need money. That's all. Please leave us alone, I cannot help Señor."

"Tell us his name Rivera. Tell us how you met him."

Lilly's mother dropped to her knees, begging, saying, "We have nothing, please no, leave us."

"He came one night," Lilly's father said. "I was working, 1st and Biscayne, sweeping the sidewalk in front of the fruit stand for Contrares. Contrares gives me a dollar an hour. The man just comes to me, face of the rat, not from here. He ask if I want to make some extra. I did it, I need the money, that's all."

"That's all," The fat man said. "Well maybe he'll remember your name then."

Lilly sees the fat man pull a gun from his jacket. He signals to the man with the knife. The knife is put to her father's throat. Her mother screamed, "No," but the short man dragged the knife across Sixto Rivera's neck; blood spilled down his white shirt. One of the two he owned. Lilly's father slumped to the floor and her mother, terrified, glanced back to the bathroom door; turning back, suddenly, she leapt toward the fat man, clawing at his eyes, screaming, "You bastard, I kill you."

The fat man fell back his gun discharging; a loud blast, and Lilly watched the red stain appear on the back of her mother's blouse as she fell to the floor.

"Shit," The fat man said. "The crazy bitch tried to take out my eyes. Let's move before the police come."

Lilly watched it all through the small opening in the bathroom door. From that day she has seen the ghosts. The counselors, the doctors, and her Aunt have never been able to keep them away.

*   *   *

The sun has passed its high point. The birds perch on the black iron fence and a white dog brushes against Lilly's leg. It is time to meet Miss Torrance, Lilly thinks, it is time to leave this beautiful park and go to work.

9

The aroma of fried potatoes and onions engulfs Maggie. She is stranded on her own island of disgust. She hangs up the phone, looking across the office to her bosses who sit at the scratched dining room table they use for conferences.

"I can't take it," She says to them from across the room. "The Greek has won, I'm done. Find yourself a new prisoner for this torture chamber."

"How many times is that Jack?" Harry says, without looking up from the maps laid out in front of him.

"This week or today?" Jack asks, dropping the sports page.

"Today."

"My count is four," Jack replies.

"Mags you're falling behind schedule. You've only quit four times today."

Maggie stands and walks over to Harry, looming above him about to pounce. "You know what?" She says. "This time I mean it."

"You can't quit unless we let you," Jack tells her. "You know too much?"

"Oh yeah, I know all your high-powered secrets," Maggie smirks. "Jack, I know that you're dating three woman now, two who think they're the only one. One even thinks you love her. The third one thinks that if she leaves her husband you'll marry her. Oh yeah, I know that. I also know that Harry owes the phone company three hundred dollars and that he hasn't called his mom in Florida in over two weeks. How can you let me quit? All this critical information will be out on the streets. The empire may crumble."

"Who thinks I love them?" Jack asks.

"The girl, the twenty-five year old, Shelly," Maggie replies.

"Not Judge Reinhardt's daughter?" Harry asks.

"Of course," Maggie replies.

"Jesus Jack, don't tell me your screwing around with the judge's daughter," Harry says. "Who is the other one?"

"Kerry Lamb," Maggie replies. "The trendy restaurant owner."

"Jack, what are you doing? She's a snake."

"I can't help it," Jack replies. "They're both beautiful and I'm weak."

"I'm afraid to ask," Harry says. "Maggie how bad is it? Who is the married one?"

"Just think the guy my husband bought the car from," Maggie says.

"Jesus Jack, not Fat Benny the car dealer? Not his wife. He's connected and certified stupid."

"No big deal," Jack replies. "I've got it all under control. We've all got our secrets. Maggie you got Jerry, your bookmaking husband. Harry's got the unpaid phone bills and his mom in Florida."

"There it is," Maggie says. "The famous Jack Connoll wit with his smiling brown eyes. Thinks he can say anything, even stupid things like that, if he brushes back his hair and puts on a crooked smile. Everything will be all right, huh Jack? As long as the dashing Jack throws you a smile. Well I telling you both right now, I'm done. I'm done with the Greek, I'm done juggling your women and your creditors."

"Ah, Maggie," Jack says. "It's been a rough morning, but come on, we're on a big case. If everything works out, we'll be out of this place in a few months. I'll get you a fancy office, air-conditioned. I'll even hire you assistants whose only job is to make sure the place meets your olfactory sensitivities."

"Jack," Harry starts. "Please tell me it isn't true. Tell me you're not messing around with Fat Benny's old lady."

"Now you see that Maggie," Jack says. "You've gone and got Harry all worked up. Exactly why I can never let you quit. You just don't know how to handle all the privileged information you have access to."

"What else is going on around here I should know?" Harry asks.

"Enough," Jack says. "Let's just get back to work, everything will work out, it always does. Maggie, in between all your juggling, did you happen to find out anything about our new client, Mr. Kevin Manley?"

"Manley?" Maggie begins. "I mean it, if this case doesn't pan out, I'm gone. Last chance."

"Yeah, I promise Mag," Jack replies. "Now what about Manley?"

"Manley..." Maggie looks to her notebook. "Manley's an interesting character; you guys know how to pick them. I talked with my friend Joan over at the bar association. He's not listed as having an office in Chicago, but she found him on a national list of attorney's. His office is in Miami. So I called my Uncle Ray who lives in Dania. He has a friend that works part time as a court stenographer at the Broward County Courthouse. He knows Manley. Says he's very rich, has a house on Biscayne Bay, a yacht; always with the young models at the fancy restaurants."

"Fat, short, bald Manley with young models?" Jack asks.

"Money goes a lot farther than good looks and charm," Maggie replies. "I wish you'd learn that someday. You may need that knowledge in your more golden years."

"You think?" Jack says.

"Maggie, please get on with Manley," Harry says.

"Right," Maggie continues, "Jack's always turning the subject to himself, anyway, this Manley, according to my Uncle Ray's friend, has got it all."

"How?" Harry asks. "He didn't seem that smart."

"Oh Harry," Maggie says. "You are so naïve. Since when do you have to be smart to be a rich lawyer? You just have to have no heart and no soul. Apparently this guy, Kevin Manley, is as vacant as they get. Uncle Ray's friend says that wealthy drug dealers are his favorite clients. Cleans up their messes, you know the murder raps and such."

"Great. That's just great," Harry says. "We're working for a drug dealer and Jack is banging a Judge's only daughter, how much worse can this get?"

"Relax Harry..." Jack starts to reply when the phone rings and Maggie leaves them. "We've worked for bad guys before. You never had a problem cashing their checks."

"I know, it's just that I'm getting a very bad feeling," Harry replies.

"Not your ghosts again? I thought you were cured after you saw that last head doctor."

"It's not the ghosts Jack. It's Manley; offering us everything we wanted, no negotiating, throwing two and half million on the table without blinking. It's too easy, nobody would give us that deal if something wasn't very wrong."

"The deal makes sense to me. He needs us to win a golf match for him. He knows we can do that. He wants us to spy. He knows we're detectives. Sounds perfectly reasonable to me."

"It doesn't sound two and half million reasonable," Harry replies.

"All right, I got something else," Maggie says, returning to the dining room conference table. "Some stuff on your Mr. Christopher Waits. That was Carla Vaccaro at the Federal Building on the phone. She's been digging the dirt on this guy for the last week or so. You know calling some of her friends in the state department. By the way, I have to buy her a couple opera tickets. One-fifty a shot."

"We'll be getting that check from Manley any day, so tell her the tickets are in the mail," Harry says. "Now, what'd she say about Waits."

"So far, this is what she has come up." Maggie checks her notes. "Waits is one of the wealthiest men in the world and he's practically a recluse."

"And why are very wealthy people always recluses?" Jack asks.

"Let her talk Jack," Harry says.

"I'm just saying, if I was that rich you'd see me everywhere," Jack continues.

"Maybe the richer you get the less you can trust people," Maggie answers.

"I'd like to test that theory," Jack says.

"Maggie please, what about Waits? What did you find out?" Harry asks.

"Right Harry. Carla told me everything is sketchy; she's not even sure how old he is, thinks he may be near his seventies. Most of what's known of him comes out of his early days as a reggae musician. I'm talking the sixties and early seventies."

"He was a reggae musician?" Jack says. "What the..."

"Yeah, played guitar, sang, wrote songs, born and raised in Jamaica, worshiped the ganja, the whole Rasta deal," Maggie says.

"Are we talking about a black man?" Harry asks

"We are. A very rich, reclusive and weird black man," Maggie replies.

"How'd he get so rich?" Harry asks.

"Haven't been able to crack that one yet. Carla's working on it, says she got a couple friends in the FBI who may know something. All she could tell me was that he came out of the islands one day and thirty years later he owns a piece of everything there is to own."

"What's his connection to Manley, to golf? What about this place in New York State?" Jack says.

"Don't know, but she's working..." Maggie is cut off when the phone rings again. "Let me get this."

When Maggie leaves them alone, Harry says, "Jack, what the fuck is going on here?"

"Don't know Harry, but this is what you wanted, right? Didn't want the cheaters and divorce cases. You wanted something interesting, well you got it now. You want out?"

"No. You're right. This case fits us perfect. I'm afraid to say, too perfect. I've called everyone I can think of regarding this golf tournament. Nobody's saying anything. Then I talked with my old friend Kim Hanaki in Japan. He got very quiet and told me to be careful. You know me Jack. I don't care, whatever they throw at us we can take. But..."

"Maybe this is the break we've been looking for Harry. Maybe this is our second chance."

"Have you been sticking to the schedule?"

"Well, I'm hitting the ball great. I've cut back on my drinking and, as Maggie informed you, I'm down to three women. So things are coming together."

"Did you have a chance to talk with Danvers?"

"No. The less that ambulance chaser knows, the less he'll want from us after we get paid," Jack says with a wink.

Maggie is again standing near the table, appearing dazed; the color has drained from her face.

"That Greek must be really getting to you," Jack remarks. "You're looking kinda' sick."

"It's not the Greek," Maggie replies. "It was the phone call."

"The phone call?" Harry asks.

"There was a voice. Christ, it sounded like it was coming over a pipe from a million miles away. It said, 'Inquire no more of Waits or you will die.' That's it, 'No more of Waits or you will die.'"

"What?" Harry bolts up.

"Did you trace it?" Jack says.

"Tried," Maggie replies. "No caller ID. Jerry's brother, Billy, down at the phone company, said he'll check it out, but right now he can't find anything. And... and I..."

"I what?" Harry asks.

"I called Carla at the Fed building. She didn't answer. I called her floor and no one knows anything. She's not at her desk and she should be."

"All right," Jack says. "Looks like we got a live one here. Mag, we've had these calls before and Carla's probably just having coffee or sneaked out to a shoe sale."

"This call was different," Maggie says. "And I'm worried about Carla. She's a tough woman but..."

"Enough," Jack says. "This is part of the business. We'll check on Carla." Jack turns to Harry. "Looks like we were right. We might have to earn our money. You want out Harry?"

"No," Harry says. "But I think we should be a little more careful. Maggie, unlock the guns. You keep one in your purse. I'm going over to check on your friend Carla. Call your uncle in Florida and get me a number for Manley."

Maggie runs to the safe to retrieve the pistols, but stops when the phone starts ringing. Everyone freezes; this ring has a shattering sound, shaking the tiny office. Maggie has to gather all her strength just to walk to her desk and pick up the handset.

"Yes..." she says, as Harry and Jack listen. "I can't tell you that... I don't know. I will when he comes in. Is that a threat? Don't you threaten me..." Maggie slams down the receiver into its cradle and stands with her head down staring at her desk.

"Maggie," Jack says. "Was that about Waits again? What'd they say?"

"Shit. I can't take this anymore. It was the phone company. They want Harry to pay the phone bill or they're going to cut off our god damn lines."

"Shit," Harry says.

Jack brushes back his hair and smiles. "At least it wasn't fat Benny looking for his wife. I'm meeting her for a drink in an hour."

10

The steam rises from the bath and hangs over the room. Nothing is clear now; everything is obscured by water mist and Kathryn sinks deeper into the warmth.

It had not always been like this. Once the world moved one step behind her. Then, she watched with amusement as everyone tried to keep pace. Then, she was a goddess, devouring or discarding all without concern.

Once again Kathryn Torrance does the calculation, I'm in Saratoga, it must be summer, almost August, there was the month in Paris during the spring, the winter in Palm Beach, Southampton beach last summer and the Travers Benefit, here in Saratoga, almost one year ago. Before that, there was the time in Europe wearing muted tones and drinking wine, alone. It was six months before that Carson passed away, and that would make it eighteen months I have been alone.

"A year and half, nearly two years" Kathryn whispers into the steam. "It's never taken this long before."

Her first marriage to Samuel Barlow, the corporate attorney, was over when she met her second husband John Rouse. Rouse, the horse breeder, was a richer and older version of Barlow's bluster and cigars. Her marriage to Rouse was over when they tired of each other. He left her for a counter girl at Saks and she left him for billionaire Carson Torrance. When she married Torrance, she was already a wealthy woman as a result of her divorces. She was not nearly as rich as she would become when Torrance died.

Now it has been eighteen months since they buried Torrance and she is still alone.

They used to fall right into my lap, she thinks, now I can see it in their eyes, now, it's only the money they want. It has been eighteen months, and now, it's only the money. Kathryn knows well how that works.

In her present state of mind and cloaked by the veil of steam, the thoughts of her past, her failed marriages and Carson's death represent her better memories. She concentrates on these former conquests, but a shadow crosses her mind and she recognizes the form. This shadow has followed her for many years, always just a passing hint of a form, never before threatening.

Since Waring's letter appeared on her desk in Florida, the shadow has not left her. Last Tuesday, when Waring's card arrived inviting her for dinner on Saturday, tonight, the shadow had reached out and touched her. It promised retribution for the pain she has inflicted on those who have loved her.

"Enough," Kathryn says to herself. "I have always been stronger. I am Kathryn Torrance. I came from nowhere. I made up this world from nothing and it will always be mine."

She turns a silver handle and cold water washes over her. Martin Waring, she recalls the man, that fool, I used him and now he wants to return to haunt me, the audacity of this man. I have always been stronger and I can still swat away this flea, this Waring.

Kathryn recalls her mother, drunk, as she was most of the day, saying to her, "If you walk with Jesus he will save your soul."

My soul, Kathryn thinks now, I have never walked with Jesus and no one has ever touched my soul. I have battled and beat the best of them and I am not finished yet.

*　　*　　*

The car arrives precisely at eight. It carries her to the restaurant in the candlelit basement. Only four tables set in white and gold. Martin Waring stands when she enters and, as Kathryn approaches, she catches him suppressing an urge to bow.

"Kathryn," Martin says. "My memory is perfect. You are the most beautiful woman I have ever met."

Kathryn does not reply. He bends and kisses her lips. She is surprised at how much he has changed; no longer the young blond German boy, his hair now thin, gray more than gold, his tall stature rounding, appearing bent and broader around the middle. A wave of sadness passes through her followed by a surge of strength.

"Please," Martin says, holding a chair for her.

"Thank you Martin. It's so strange after all these years to be here with you now."

"I'm sorry, if I intrude on your time…" Martin says. He stops, desperate to recall the reason he had asked her to join him tonight.

"No Martin," Kathryn says, believing that she has stunned him into this pause. "I was very intrigued when I received you invitation and now, to be sitting her with you, well, I could think of nowhere I'd rather be. So, what brings you to Saratoga? Don't tell me you have fallen under the spell of the horses?"

"No. I'm… I'm here for the next month on business."

"Business? What type of business? When I left you there was only golf."

"Ah right, when you left me…" The waiter interrupts, filling their glasses with champagne. "Here's to the old days," Martin says raising his glass to hers.

"I never drink to the past," Kathryn answers. "It is dead. I drink to the future, to the next moment when the wonders of the world shall be revealed."

"Of course. Very well Kathryn, to the future," Martin says.

They raise their glasses, the fine crystal capturing the candlelight. They drink it in, the wine, the light and the wonders of the world.

Martin studies the blue infinity that is Kathryn's eyes. He is bewildered by his weakness. After all these years, after everything he has accomplished, he is still a child in her presence. He cannot recall why he is here with her. He has stopped trying to recall. Summoning the strength to speak, Martin says, "I don't agree with you. You know, about the past being dead. It is with us every moment. It is always more real than our future. You can imagine the future, but you can't imagine the past."

"Imagine our future. How sad Martin, you still don't realize that you can imagine your past as easily as you can recall your future. So many people are concerned with what is gone."

"What is gone is what we are."

"It is just clatter, an annoyance, a diversion. But, for your sake, let's begin with the chitchat. Please tell me about your past. Tell me about this business that brings us together."

"Fine Kathryn, if that's how you want to do this? Let me start. How about if I start the day you left me after the tournament in Atlanta. I believe it was for that attorney, what was his name? Barstow?"

"Barlow. Sam Barlow."

"Sorry. Yes Barlow. Well, you might say that put me a little out of sorts."

"Marty, you're the one who taught me that you always have to take the best option. You're the one that talked me out of Phoenix. Remember?"

"No one ever talked you into doing anything. However, you are correct. That was my rule back then, no allegiances, no permanent connections, no partners. That's what I believed when you left me cold for a better deal. I am not ashamed to say that I was devastated. I couldn't play..."

"I recall you weren't playing well before I left you. If you were, maybe I would have stayed around."

"True. My game hit a low point with you. Still, after you left, it fell off further and I fell off with it. Ended up borrowing money to get to Australia, found a spot on their tour."

"How sad."

"Yeah. That ended quickly enough too. There I was, I went from playing on the U.S tour to tending bar at a public course outside Perth."

"Oh Martin."

"Don't trouble yourself, actually it was the best thing that ever happened to me. Eventually my game came back and I started giving lessons. I met some people and found I had other talents."

"Other talents?"

"I even began to believe in love again."

"I am so happy for you Martin; playing golf, meeting people and in love again, what a wonderful story. Shall we order dinner?"

"Of course Kathryn. Let's leave it for a while."

While the food is brought and cleared, their conversation is occupied with matching up names of people they have in common. The main course and a bottle of wine are consumed before the conversation turns back to their more personal stories.

"You were saying, you were teaching golf in Australia and just about to fall in love. So go on tell me the rest."

"Ah, I see the past does hold some interest."

"Merely entertainment."

"I'll make a deal with you Kathryn, I will tell the rest of my story if you do two things for me."

"Anything for you Martin."

"I'll entertain you with my story, if you join me in two glasses of port. One for my story and one for yours."

"Only one for your story? Certainly Martin. Whatever you want."

"Good then, where was I?"

"In love and tending bar, I think."

"Right. My game came back. I was teaching golf and I fell in love with a girl, a schoolteacher. Her name was Meryl. We married..."

"Meryl, that's sweet."

"She was beautiful. We lived in a small house by the beach. I can honestly say that in all the places I've been in my life, there has been no place as wonderful as that home."

"I am so happy for you. What an inspirational story."

"I knew you would never understand, but it was..."

"Don't ever assume that I cannot understand Martin. I just recall the man I knew. The one who would have laughed in the face of anyone who told him a story about the perfect little family and the cottage by the sea."

"I haven't changed that much Kathryn. I'm telling you this because it is my story."

"Then please Martin, go on."

"Well it so happens that I was giving golf lessons to an Aussie businessman. He was about my age, he kept telling me about this new industry. He kept saying, 'telecommunications.' I'm thinking, yeah telephones, you know everyone has one, but still how much room is there in that game with the big players, but he just kept talking. He said that someday everyone will carry around their own phone, and that someday, you would have access to all the information you require over a phone, and that computers would be connected to your television set and that there would be nothing that you could think of that you couldn't get over a wire, antenna or satellite. I laughed, but I took him up on his job offer. He was right. It wasn't long before my little house near the beach became a fifteen-acre mansion on the beach. It wasn't long, or at least it didn't seem that long, that I found myself president of the largest telecommunications in Australia and, by default, one of the largest in the world. It wasn't long until my net worth was estimated at near two billion dollars and it wasn't long after that I lost my wife, Meryl, to cancer."

"I'm sorry... about your wife."

Martin notices the purple tones beginning to vibrate in Kathryn's eyes.

"But I am so happy for you. Really," Kathryn says. "So I guess your business brought you to Saratoga and you decided to look me up, how wonderful. It is amazing to be here with you. Just like the old days. Remember how in love we were? Just kids."

"Just kids. Only I tripped and fell, while you kept on skipping."

"Oh Martin, please, the past is over. Tell me, what is this business that brings you here? How long will you be here? Where are you staying?"

For an instant Martin recalls why he had invited Kathryn to dinner, but the thought is fleeting and passes before he can capture it. "Well, I'm in town because of a golf tournament and I'm staying in a house I've rented up on Lake George."

"Oh, it's so good to hear you're playing again. I would love the chance to see you out there."

"Except for that short time, after you, I have never stopped playing. Anyway that's my story. The first glass is empty, so I believe it's your turn."

"Yes, of course Marty. I'll be quick. You know how I don't like to linger in the past. Well, I met that foul attorney Barlow, with his cigars and loud mouth. The night we left Atlanta, I knew it was a mistake to leave you, but it was too late. Anyway, we were divorced when I met Rouse, the horseman; a decent fellow, with a wandering eye. He bought me the house in Saratoga. Rouse did give me that, though of course it was inevitable that our marriage would fail. That's when I met Carson Torrance."

"He was a very rich man, but older, right?"

"Yes a wonderful man, who like your wife died unexpectedly, at the age of eighty-six."

"Unexpectedly at the age of eighty-six?"

"He was a very healthy and active man. Anyway, that was almost two years ago. Since then I've been trying to put my life back in order. My time in Saratoga is a critical part of this recovery. That's it."

"That's it?"

"That's it. Now Martin, what about the future?"

"You tell me. You're the expert on recalling the future."

"Well if it doesn't interfere with your business, I would like you to come with me to the Jockey Club Benefit next Saturday. It's held every year, one of the top parties of the season. It marks the opening of racing."

"I will take you," Martin replies.

"Wonderful. I am so happy you took the time to find me and invite me to dinner."

"As you know Kathryn, it was my pleasure. You are one of a kind. Seamless, beautiful, able to change direction at the drop of a name."

"I don't know what you mean Martin."

"I don't mean anything. When I look into your eyes, I remember the time when I was a young man, when I would have laughed in the face of someone who said that his schoolteacher wife and his little cottage near the ocean was the most wonderful time of his life. When I look into your eyes, I see what I will need to compete."

"I still don't understand."

"I'm sorry Kathryn. I'll have the driver bring your car around. I look forward to the party next Saturday."

"So do I."

They stand and kiss gently on the lips, hesitating long enough to let the energy pass between their bodies.

"I had forgotten how wonderful that feels," Kathryn says.

"I did not," Martin answers.

Kathryn turns to walk out and Martin follows her to her car. Before she slips through the door, she turns and looks up to Martin. He sees the violet now saturating her creamy blue eyes. Wealth undeniable, the color of those that rule the world, he thinks, remembering the real reason for this dinner.

"Kathryn," He says, before closing the car door.

"Yes Martin," She replies.

"May ask you one question? About my business here?"

"Certainly Martin, but I thought it was the golf that brought you here."

"It is both I guess. Have you ever heard of a man by the name of Christopher Waits? He has a mansion north of here, supposedly very wealthy."

"I've never have heard of a Mr. Waits. Hard to believe if he is that wealthy and lives in this area. I could ask around for you, if you would like?"

"I would appreciate that Kathryn. Thank you."

"Well then, I'll see you next Saturday. Please come to my house at six. I can't wait."

"I'll be there. Good night Kathryn."

"Good night Marty."

Martin watches the black car drive away. He knows he is entering dangerous lands, but he has known this since he decided to take up Mr. Wait's strange offer.

Kathryn sits in the back of limousine and she checks her face in a mirror. They continue to fall into my lap, she thinks, and my game is not over yet.

11

Harry waits for a southbound bound train at the Belmont Street "L" station. As he waits on the old wood framed platform, Harry knows he is out of place among the young men and women who stand around him. Still, he likes these platforms; they are relics of a time that belongs to him. It is in the old places of Chicago, the places that survive from Harry's youth, that he is touched by recollections of his road. It is here, where his memories are as real as any of his ghosts.

I've got to find Carla, Harry thinks, trying to turn his attention back to his job.

Maggie had tried to reach Carla many times in the hours since she received the threatening phone call. It became apparent Carla would not return to her desk in the Federal Building and she did not answer at home.

Harry is taking the "L" to check out the Sandburg Apartments, where Carla lives, a conglomeration of government subsidized middle-income high rises constructed on the edge of the Gold Coast. They were built at a time when the City hovered on the brink, when everyone considered the northern suburbs to be their best option to escape the city. Now in Chicago, these apartment buildings, still rent controlled, stand in the middle of some the most desired neighborhoods in the City.

Harry recalls little of the Chicago in those times of the threatened breakdown. Those years coincided with the years he spent traveling the world with Glyn. There was little news of the City's urban crisis in Asia, Europe, the South Pacific and Australia. In moments of conceit for his connection to this city and its people, Harry links the City's flirtation with failure to his absence. He also links the downfall of Jack to the day they parted in Phoenix.

Harry had heard this story only once, but he never forgot a word.

*   *   *

Before Jack drove the Checker out of the St. Martins Club, K.C. had concealed a laugh when he asked her if she was coming with him.

"Sorry Jack," K.C. said, "I've met someone else."

"I just had a bad week. I'll take a shot at the U.S. Amateur and next year..." Jack replied.

"Amateur? Next year? I'm sorry that's not my dream."

"So you didn't love me, it was a sham, a con?"

"I didn't leave Ames for love. I left for a life, a better one. I thought you were the one Jack. I wish you were, because I do love you, but you failed. I'm sorry, but you failed.

"So you found someone who can give you what you want?"

"I found someone who is on the right track."

"And you love him?"

"No. I love you Jack, but you failed."

"So Harry was right, you care more for yourself than me."

"Of course Harry was right," K.C. said. "Still, it was in your hands and you failed. I guess you failed us both."

As Jack drove the Checker out of the club, he glanced to the driving range. He saw Harry working late with his new partner, the Englishman, Parker. Jack considered stopping to speak with his old friend, to beg for forgiveness, to ask him to get back in the car, to ride with him and help develop a new plan. Jack just kept driving. He had crossed a line, and now their lives, connected since childhood summers, would be separate.

As Jack drove numbly back to Chicago, the stark night sky left him open to the memories of the past week. He thought of his two rounds, about the shots that fell short, about tee shots that were lost and the putts that rolled by the hole never threatening to go in. He thought he could do it all himself, but, somewhere along the line, he had connected his fate to Harry. Thoughts of K.C. were also with him as he drove; her perfect American face and the eyes that promised him the world became a mocking vision of his foolishness.

The road took Jack back to Chicago, to the neighborhood. He drove non-stop. He arrived on a Tuesday morning, driving directly into Freedy Palka's taxi garage, working his first hack shift that night.

After work, he would sit at Rose's bar, drinking and listening to the old-timers, joining their efforts to drink their lives away. There was "One-Eye" Dugan dancing a jig and old "Buggy" Benton arguing about politics with Big Tommy the bartender. When there was no money left, he would stumble to his parent's house falling unconscious onto their couch. He would wake with his father staring down at him, gray-haired head shaking in disgust.

During these years, he would search the morning newspapers for the results of the international golf tournaments. He would run his finger down the list of strange names in search of a score. When his finger stopped next to the name: "Parker, Glyn" a chill would shake him and his eyes would lose focus. Often, this name was on the top of the list. Sometimes there would be a small headline: "Parker wins in Malaysia", "Another Top Ten For Parker in Singapore," "Parker Wins Playoff Battle in Madrid."

Jack would imagine Harry in the heat of competition. He would imagine it was his name instead of Parker's. Still, the years passed and his clubs never left the trunk of the Checker. He could not bear to touch them.

It was Big Tommy the bartender who suggested to Jack that he could pick up some extra money working for Jerry Cahoon. Jerry had some connections and he was in line to inherit the role of neighborhood bookmaker from Old Jimmy Rhoney. Jerry was happy to have a kid from the neighborhood work collections and payoffs for him.

With the extra money, Jack rented an apartment and cut back on his hack shifts. He even found time to take the Checker over to Lincoln Park where he would practice hitting wedge shots back and forth on an open field.

His life was caught here, no plans, just the same straight dark road, deeper into the old neighborhood. The same road he had been on since Phoenix. A road of endless nights spent in the driver's seat of a retched cab or taking the last dollar from the losers who were Jerry's customers. His only escape became the wedge after wedge he would hit in the park, each swing an attempt to wipe away regret.

It was a Sunday afternoon in October when the shack of a life he built finally collapsed in a storm on top of him.

The storm began with the red flashing light in his rearview mirror, the police officer roughly cuffing his hands behind him, the money and bookmaking receipts he carried in an envelope taken as evidence. The easy smile, the way he could brush back his hair and turn on the charm, did not help him. When Jack was brought to the jail, Jerry Cahoon was already in custody.

Jerry winked and said, "Don't worry kid. This is Chicago and I know people, leave it to me."

*   *   *

Harry catches the first brown line train that pulls into the Belmont Station. A red line train would have left him closer to Carla's building, but the brown was here and he was in no mood to wait any longer. He had to find Carla and the memories were coming at him too fast to just stand around waiting for the red.

The train trembles, rattling, it moves south towards downtown. Harry scans the passing view east, a crane, a construction site, a new building, the signs of transformation everywhere. The City is always changing, he thinks, moving forward, reinventing itself as the past is wiped away. History is being buried along with the only ones who can remember what once stood. This is survival, and Chicago, like Harry Dimmig, is a survivor.

*   *   *

The airplane landed in Tokyo. Harry and Glyn had been in the air for most of the twenty-four hours since they had departed Phoenix. They had stopped in Hawaii for two hours, but that was a small relief from Glyn, who needed to smoke a cigarette every twenty minutes. To escape the plane's smoking section, Harry would walk to an empty row of seats. Here he would look out the window, down to where the clouds hid the ocean.

The memory of that view had always defined those days with Glyn. Harry aloft in the clouds, obscured from the dark deep ocean below. His world was filled with beauty and mystery, a world he could never have imagined as boy carrying bags at Oak Grove.

67

The ghosts he encountered in those days were ancient, too ancient to give him notice. They moved less connected to the living, more rooted in eternity.

Harry never told Glyn what he saw. He never told of the visions of the dead, of the thousands of years of civilization that existed undetected in the cities they visited. Harry was sure that Glyn would not have cared that he saw ghosts. He may have even believed Harry. Still, Glyn was Harry's business, his method of survival, and Harry knew, has always known, where to draw the line when it came to what he saw. So between Glyn and Harry it was only golf and drink. There was a friendship; it just could not include all the wonders of Harry's unseen world.

So, Harry carried the weight of his visions alone. In India, at the home of a wealthy Brahman businessman, Harry watched a dark prince wandering the gardens beyond the courtyard. The prince carried a gold sword, and appeared alone in thought, as eighty-eight concubines dressed in green silk followed him. Of all those gathered at the party, only Harry stopped as the prince and his entourage passed.

On a golf course in New Zealand, Harry discovered a young girl following them as they walked along the ocean. She had large brown eyes, the wind in her long brown hair; appearing lost or alone, she signaled for Harry to look out toward the ocean, back to America and then she began to cry. Harry nodded in her direction and continued on.

In Spain, in a match with the same two Spaniards that he had first met in Phoenix, Harry saw the two men in rags hunched near the swarthy golfer and his caddy. As the match progressed, the Spaniards used their fingers to place curses on Glyn, unaware of the ragged men who were their constant companions.

At a tournament in Wales Harry saw a woman. She was tall, out of place on the green tract. Pretty, her blue eyes and smile familiar, she waved to Harry and Glyn as they passed her on the way to the first tee. When Glyn waved back, Harry almost fell over. Glyn can see them too, Harry thought.

"Harry," Glyn said. "Meet my sis, the magnificent Page. Page this is my friend and caddy Harry Dimmig."

"Pleasure to meet you Harry," Page said. "Are you all right?"

"Christ Harry," Glyn said. "You look like you've seen a ghost."

"Sorry, I thought it was you who saw the ghost," Harry replied. "It is nice to meet you Page."

That night, as Glyn sat with his brothers around the public house fireplace telling stories of his travels, Harry sat at table with Page.

"Harry, do you ever get tired of traveling?" Page asked.

"Never think about," Harry replied. "What about you? You ever get tired of staying in this small town?"

"Never think about it," Page replied. "Do you ever wish you had a home, with a wife and children,"

"No, I never do. I only think about golf and... well... just golf."

"And well, what?"

"Nothing really. I'm sorry."

"Come on Harry, what?"

"Nothing. I just think about golf. In fact, to be truthful, not only don't I ever think about having a family, I've never had a girlfriend."

"You do like girls? Don't you Harry?"

"I just guess I've been too busy or too shy."

"Shy of what, you seem comfortable enough right now."

"Yeah, it's not that, it's, that, I can't say Page, lets just keep it at shy..."

"What are you talking about?"

"Ah, let's just say it's all the moving around I do. We travel so much and most places I can't even speak the language..."

"What makes you shy Harry?"

"Page, please forget it, time has gone by so fast and it just never happened and..."

"Sounds like a lot of excuses and strange ones at that."

"Yeah, I guess it does. I'm old enough now to not care what people think, but trust me I'm just shy."

"All right Harry, all right, I think I understand. Still, you're not bad looking fellow, in fact I find you attractive."

"Attractive, I'm short, skinny, losing my hair..."

"Harry, you don't get it, I think you're handsome. You have quick intelligent eyes. I can see desire. Someone who holds a great secret, but someone who is trapped by something, larger, outside of their control."

"It seems that?"

"And you have a wonderful smile. Don't know if Glyn's told you this, but us Parker's always fall for a smile first. Thin as a rail? Maybe, but you are appealing."

"I am?"

"Yes. Now this is the moment you should tell me how attractive I appear to you."

"Oh sorry. You're beautiful, your eyes sparkle and when you smile I feel like standing up and bowing to you. I like your blond hair that flies off in every direction and how when you brushed against me earlier I felt a spark."

"What about my body. Not classically beautiful, right?"

"I think you are beautiful, long legs and a good shape…"

"Small breasts and awkward…"

"You are beautiful and I wish I could hold you."

"Harry you can. Come back to my apartment with me tonight?"

"What about your family, your brother?"

"Aren't we a little old for that?"

"I feel it wouldn't be right."

"Then tell them you're going back to your hotel room and I'll meet you out front at eleven."

"I would like that Page. I would like to meet you at eleven."

At eleven that night, Page waited in front of Harry's hotel, as Harry sat watching the ghost of a fat chambermaid wandering about his small room. Page waited until twelve thirty and then walked home alone.

$$*\qquad*\qquad*$$

Harry exits the train at the Sedgwick Station. His anxiety about Carla is peaking. Although he has never met her, Carla has helped them on many cases, one of Maggie Cahoon's friends, one of the many around Chicago who report to their office secretary and Ryan's most valuable asset. According to Maggie, Carla is the niece of Jimmy Vaccaro, who is a business associate of her husband Jerry Cahoon in the marketplace of point spreads and odds.

"God forbid anything happens to her," Maggie had said to Harry. "She's a sweet woman, just a couple years younger than you and Jack. She knows everybody. I know she can take care of herself, but still, I'm worried. You've got to go check on her. Please Harry."

Harry walks quickly, half running, down Wells Street on his way to the Sandburg Apartments. Wells Street was once a center of Chicago's counter culture, a wild street of artists and activists who fought to change the world. Harry recalls how, as a boy, he held his mother's hand as they wandered through the snake charmers and street musicians that performed on Wells in those days.

Wells Street has changed. It is now tamed, matured, lined with condominiums, boutiques and bistros. Where they once sold incense and pipes, they now offer imported wines and French cuisine. Harry knows that beyond the superficial changes, below the surface of the street, there is sadness for the failure, sadness for exchanging the dream of paradise for the reality of the necessary present.

*   *   *

After posting bail, Jack Connoll's father waited for his son in the stark jail lobby.

"So this is what it has come to," Terrence Connoll said, as they walked home. "You're another cheap hood. You embarrass your mother and me. You have brothers who are doctors and businessmen. Your sisters have beautiful families, so it's up to you to drag the Connoll name down. Is that it?"

"I'm sorry," Jack replied. "I was just trying to survive."

"Trying to survive, bullshit. You never think. Do you? You leave school to play golf, wasted all those years as a cheap hustler in that game for the rich and now look at you, in a stinking jail. A bookie."

Jack had no reply. He was occupied with the thought of the beautiful perfect face of the woman who had cost him everything.

"I'm sorry dad. I don't have anything. I'm just trying to find something. I know I've embarrassed you. I'll leave. When all this is cleared up, I'll leave town. Maybe that's what I need to do. Maybe that will help."

"Listen Jack. This is hard for me to understand. Of all my children I thought you would be the most successful. Never saw a kid that people took too as easy as you, good looks, smart, and a good heart. You could do anything and that's why I don't understand this. Something happened to you out there, I don't know what, I don't want to know. But son you've got to let it go. You're almost in your thirties and it won't get any easier from here. You don't have to leave town. I can help you. I've already made some calls, you know, called in some favors, they'll drop this charge, but you've got to stay clean."

"Listen dad, you don't have to..."

"Jack, listen to me. I have a friend, you know him, Howard Ryan. I spoke with him and he needs some help with his business. It's not anything big, but it's a start. It'll get you out of driving the cab and the bookmaking."

"Ryan? The private detective?"

"Yeah, calls himself a private investigator. He's getting to the end of his road and he's got no kids. I talked to him and he agreed to take you on, teach you the ropes. Says he'll do me the favor, but he needs the help anyway. It could work for both of you. What do you think?"

Jack stared into his father's eyes. He could see the desperation and the sadness. "I'll go see Ryan. Maybe it could work for both of us."

Ryan Investigations was operated out of a dusty second floor office on Belmont Street. The first time Jack went up to office he was overwhelmed by the smell from the Greek diner located on the first floor. Over the years, as he worked with Ryan, as that office became his home, Jack came to associate that smell with his redemption.

Howard Ryan was a retired Chicago policeman. Thirty years on the force and twenty-five years a private detective. His life had been lived on the borderline between good and evil. In fact, in Howard's eyes, everyone lived their lives there, and if they didn't think so, they were just stupid or fooling themselves.

Ryan's connections ran all through Chicago, into its darkest corners and all the way to the top of City Hall, which had its own very dark corners. The boss, the Mayor, would call Ryan out for a drink every so often, for a "personal favor," one for the "old days."

"This is the meat business," Howard would tell Jack.

"The meat business?"

"Yeah, like being butcher. You'll be wallowing in the guts and bones of this world, slopping around in the gore that is people's lives. It ain't pretty."

"Sounds like fun, when do I get a gun?" Jack replied.

"Soon enough, my boy, soon enough."

The first few months Jack followed Howard everywhere. Howard taught Jack how to stake out a motel, how to tail a car, how to bribe a desk clerk, and how to tap a phone. He told Jack whom to call at police headquarters for a lead, who would run a license plate number at the DMV and who you paid every month for such services. He would run over and over with Jack a list of names of people you always did favors for, no matter what. Howard showed Jack that the business was twenty-four hours, your life, contacts were made everywhere and information was something you bought and then sold for a higher price.

There were no rules about when you worked. If you felt like spending three hours in a strip club for lunch, that was fine, because some cases you would have to spend seventy-hours in your car.

The schedule suited Jack. Howard didn't mind if Jack took an afternoon to play golf, as long as Jack was meeting people and making connections.

"Connections are the core of this shit business," Howard told Terrance Connoll one night at Rose's. "And your kid's a natural."

Mr. Connoll smiled and bought Howard another beer.

Howard and Jack had their share of good cases. There was the case of the Evanston disappearing twins and the case of the Bucktown payphone swindler. There was the time they staked out the third baseman for the White Sox and found he was carrying on affairs with three of his teammate's wives.

"Now that what I call a triple play," Ryan had said to Jack.

There was the time they worked on the Gold Coast insurance scam; the case when Howard took a bullet in his leg and Jack returned fire. With one-shot he put the jewel fence face down in the reddening snow.

There were other jobs too; the times they would make their rounds at various downtown restaurants and bars, filling a bag with cash. Afterward, they would sit at Demos, the all night diner, sipping coffee until Big Carl Perlstein from Streets and Sanitation, would slide into their booth, chat for a few minutes and leave with the bag.

As the years passed, Howard's days in the office grew fewer. Jack became the head investigator, the man the mayor called, the man who walked the line between good and evil.

Eight years before, Jack had walked into the smell of the Greek cooking, and he had changed, he had matured, he had been saved. Still, if you observe him closely, you will see, just below the surface, sadness for the paradise that was abandoned for the necessary present.

*   *   *

The doorman at the Sandburg Apartments tells Harry he has not seen Miss Vaccaro, "Since this morning... since she left for work."

Harry stands in the lobby, confused about his next move. He hears a frail voice ask, "Why would you be looking for Carla?"

Harry turns to find an elderly woman sitting in a chair by the tall lobby window. Sparse gray hair and frail, she is wearing a tube that snakes up her arm. It supplies her with oxygen; her body requires what her lungs can no longer offer. Harry follows the clear tube down to the green tank and recalls the weight of these oxygen canisters. Changing them was one of his last duties in Glyn's employ.

*   *   *

74

The cancer was diagnosed on a hot day in Berlin. Glyn had been promising to see a doctor for months about the cough and the blood. As one tournament always led to the next, and the time was never right, Glyn just let it pass.

Then, after the Saturday round of a tournament in Stuttgart, Glyn lit up a cigarette at the bar, ordered a beer, turned completely white and fell to the floor.

It was in the stark German hospital room, on a hot August day, that he received his diagnosis. Harry was sitting with him. For a moment, for the first time since Harry had met him, the smile went out of Glyn's eyes. It would return in short order, but for only two months. During these last days, Harry pushed Glyn's wheelchair and changed his oxygen. In the end, Harry helped carry Glyn's body, in a beautiful box made of rare wood, to the family plot outside of Berkshire.

Page clung to Harry, as they walked away from the grave. "Thank you for everything you did for my brother," She said. "You were truly his friend."

"He gave me more than I could ever give to him," Harry replied. "Even in the end, in his last days, he was laughing, drinking, enjoying himself, no different from the first time I saw him on that course in Phoenix. He went through life without questions, just took it all into his heart and laughed. He rescued me, gave me my life. I'll miss him and I don't know what I'll do now."

"Harry, do you remember the time I was to meet you outside the hotel?"

"Yes. I'll never forget it. I just couldn't escape something that night, I never can..."

"It's not that Harry. I know you had your reasons. It's just... afterwards, I asked Glyn what was wrong with you.

"He told me, 'Page. Harry lives in many worlds at once. Trying to bring him into your world is a fool's job.' He said, 'Harry senses the slightest change in the wind, or a missed beat in the vibration of the world and it sets him off. Harry's a good man and I know he cares about people, but I'm afraid that he is too aware of everything to have anything to do with chaotic things such as love or sex.'

"Harry come home with me right now," Page said squeezing Harry's hand. "Have a place for the rest of your life. Let everything else go. We'll get by all the other stuff."

"Thank you Page. I loved your brother. I will miss him. As for your offer, I could think of nothing better. If I was to settle down with anyone it would be you, but I've been away too long. It's time I went back home. Back to Chicago."

"Stay with me Harry, this could be your home."

"I truly wish it could be. I'm sorry Page, some things I just can't escape. I'll stay in touch. Goodbye dear." Harry kissed Page on the lips, leaving her behind for one last walk by his friend's open grave. He dropped to his knees on the wet grass. Alone with Glyn that last time, tears ran from his eyes and he smoothed the dirt around the open hole.

"Glyn, I can never thank you," He cried. "I only wish I could repay you for what you gave me."

*   *   *

The woman attached to the oxygen tanks, sits by the large glass window of the Sandberg Apartment lobby. The dust rises up through the sunlight that streams in on her.

"Excuse me," Harry says. "You say you know Carla Vaccaro?"

"Can't you hear too well? I've already asked you, why would you be looking for her?"

"I'm a friend and I'm concerned she may need my help," Harry replies.

"I've never seen you before. What's your name?"

"Harry, Harry Dimmig. I'm a friend of her friend, Maggie Cahoon. Maggie asked me to look in on Carla."

"Maggie, yeah, that sounds familiar. Tall... loud... redhead, right?"

"You've met Maggie?"

"Hard to miss. What kind of trouble you think Carla's got?"

"I don't know that she has trouble. Maggie and I just want to speak with her."

"You try at Charlie's?"

"No, what's Charlie's?"

"A bar her brother owns. If she's got trouble that's where she'd be."

"Where's this bar at?"

"It's in a basement, on Madison near State."

"Thanks," Harry says, moving quickly to the door. "I'm sorry, what is your name?"

"Lucy."

"Thanks Lucy. Do me a favor, if you see Carla, have her give Maggie a call."

"Sure thing Dimmig. Sure thing."

Harry hails a cab on LaSalle and five minutes later he is standing in front of Charlie's Bar on Madison. Above the red door, which is six stairs down from the street, a green neon sign flashes: "Welcome, C'mon In." Harry recalls that Rose's once had the same neon sign hanging over the entrance.

*   *   *

On a blustery October evening Harry had stood across the street from Rose's, staring at the neon sign, trying to find the courage to walk back through the door.

After a deep breath, he found himself standing just inside the door, amazed at how little had changed in the years he had been on the road. Big Tommy was behind the bar and T.J., then still known as Tommy Junior, swept the floor around the jukebox. There was One-Eye and Buggy, alive then, sipping coffee from stained mugs and watching the fuzzy reception of a television that hung above the bar.

It was One-Eye who recognized him first. "I'll be damned," One-Eye said. "If it ain't the long lost caddy."

The others turned to see what the old drunk was talking about.

"Harry, is that you?" Tommy Junior said. "Shit, come on over and let's have a look at you."

Big Tommy growled, "You haven't aged a day, still the same skinny runt I remember sittin' on the curb out front. What're ya' drinking?"

"I'll have a beer Tommy, thanks. Set everyone up, on me."

"Fine, fine, finally," Buggy said. "Our boy has returned from seeing the world. What you find out there Dimmig?"

"Nothing as strange as seeing you and One-Eye with coffee cups, watching the evening news."

"You got a point," One-Eye replied. "Give me a double B.V. straight up."

Harry, the world traveler, sat and listened as the regulars told him the stories of the neighborhood; the roll call, who had died, who was working in city hall, and how much they had all drank the night before. No one mentioned Jack Connoll and, although they inquired once or twice, no one really wanted to hear what he had seen out in the world.

This was fine with Harry. He was happy just to sit. The evening before he had spent with his parents and their questions had sent him to bed with a headache. So Harry just sat back and listened to the stories, to the music from the jukebox. He drank the beer and the whiskey that was placed in front of him and swam in the stale smell of Rose's that announced to his soul that he was home.

Through the night Harry sat as the crowd ebbed and flowed, faces from his past, hands that patted him on the back.

One-Eye, drunk, the red lights of the bar shining on his round old face, finally said, "It's good to see you kid. It's always good to have one of our own come home. What about Jack? You seen Jack yet?"

"No, Eye," Harry replied. "I haven't had a chance. How's he doing?"

"He's doing okay. Had a rough time, but he's better now. He usually stops in late, so you might see him yet."

"That would be good Eye, that would be good."

It was not long after, Harry looked up to see his old friend walking through the door, the same easy manner, the same smile. Everyone turned to greet him. Jack stopped cold when he saw the ghost from his past now seated at the bar.

Harry stood and walked over to his old partner. "Jack, it's been a long time… It's…"

"Harry. Jesus Christ I don't believe it." Jack embraced Harry. "You're home. Let's get a table."

Jack and Harry made their way to a table at the back of the bar. For a time all eyes stayed on them and then the jukebox played "O'Reilly's March," causing One-Eye to stand, drunk, teetering, to announce, in his booming voice, that, "On this special night, as special as any other, magic surely has been proven to exist, and Rose's can now certainly be called the center of the universe, I will dance a jig that I have saved for such an auspicious occasion as this."

One-Eye twirled in a wild reel drawing all eyes to him. With the bar's attention now diverted, Jack and Harry sat at the small table with a bottle of whiskey and two glasses.

"Jack…" Harry started to say.

"No Harry, let me start," Jack said. "I'm sorry for the way I treated you. You didn't deserve it and I was wrong. I've paid for it every day of my life. I am proud that you made it out to the big time… that you played in the big matches. Still, I have always hoped that you would be back for a visit."

"What happened was a long time ago. I never had the time to blame. Just that once, in the heat of the moment, did I hate you… I never doubted that you would always be my friend."

"What brings you back? You just taking a break?"

"No Glyn, Glyn Parker… He just passed."

"Parker's dead. So young… Ah Harry, I'm sorry. I only met him that once, but I knew you had hooked up with a good guy."

"Yeah, he was a good man and I'll miss him."

"So what are you gonna do?" Jack asked.

"Don't know. I've had a few offers to carry bags back in Europe. Other offers as well. I just wanted to come home for a while, I guess."

"Offers, huh. Listen, I've got to run, do you have any plans for tomorrow morning?"

"No, what's up?"

"I'm thinking of playing a round at Oak Grove. You feel like carrying for a washed up amateur?"

"Sure Jack, I could think of nothing better."

"You staying with your parents?"

"Yeah."

"I'll pick you up at six-thirty. All right?"

"Six-thirty. That would be great."

"Good, I'm glad that's set. I wish I could have another drink, but I've got to get back to work."

"What kind of work?" Harry asked.

"I work with Ryan. You remember the detective, Howard Ryan?"

"You're a detective? That's what you're doing tonight?"

"Yeah, I've got to get back and relieve Ryan. He's holding my place at a motel stake out, a bus driver cheating on his wife with a meter maid. Ryan came in to give me a break. I'll pick you up in the morning."

"So you just sit in your car all night?"

"Yeah, sit, watch, take notes and photos, listen to music and think. That's the job."

"Would you mind if I came along?"

"Mind? I'd like the company. Just like the old days. Come on lets go."

As Harry and Jack sat in the car watching for any sign of the bus driver and the meter maid, they never mentioned the St. Martins Club, K.C., or the plans they once shared. After the bus driver and the meter maid went home, Harry and Jack drank coffee at Michael's Diner until the sun came up. From Michael's they drove directly to Oak Grove Country Club.

To Harry, the course appeared frail and small on this cold fall morning, a feeble reflection of his memory. Still, for the first time in decades, Jack and Harry were once again the only two on the course.

Harry marveled at Jack's swing. Although it had not changed, the effect it had on Harry was now different. The swing, the perfection, the smooth take away, the flawless moment of rest, the downswing starting in perfect tempo, the explosion of the club head meeting the ball and the sight of the ball cutting through the cold morning caused a sadness in Harry; a sadness that would rise every time Jack would swing the club and the ball tracked perfectly to the green. For Harry it was still worth it. It was the price of lost opportunity, of time passing, of friendship, of brotherhood, of being home, of life.

Two months later, Harry wrote Howard Ryan a check for a half interest in Ryan Investigations, its offices and all its accounts. Ryan signed over the other half to Jack in return for his years of service. At the age of seventy-eight Howard Ryan finally retired.

Jack and Harry were partners again, fifty-fifty, just like before. Maggie Cahoon, Ryan Investigation's most valuable asset, was hired in return for Jerry Cahoon letting Jack slide on a two hundred dollar gambling debt. It was the best move they made in the ten years they had operated the business.

The three of them have done it all. They have had good cases, and bad cases, making enough to live and doing it all as the Greek, undeterred below, sends his pungent odors skyward without consideration.

During those ten years, the old ones passed, Harry's father, Jack's dad, Howard Ryan, Big Tommy, One-Eye and Buggy. They passed out of sight of all, but Harry Dimmig. He still sees them here, as they watch over the beloved neighborhood they left behind and the two boys who once almost made it out to the pro tour.

*   *   *

Harry walks again under the neon sign that reads: "Welcome C'mon In," through the door into Charlie's bar. There is a thick man behind the bar. He is dark complected; black hair combed back, framing a round goateed face. The man appears too huge for the space he occupies and he is reaching for something under the counter.

"Can I help you pal?" The man asks.

"Yeah, my name is Harry Dimmig, I'm a friend of Maggie Cahoon. We're looking for Charlie's sister, Carla. I'm looking for her. She might be in trouble. You Charlie?"

"Worried about Carla, why's that?"

"Carla's been helping Maggie. Before I tell you any more, why don't you tell me who I'm talking to?"

"Never mind who I am. Keep talking."

Two men Harry had not seen have slipped behind him, taking a position blocking the door to the street.

"I don't say anything until I'm talking to Charlie or Carla."

"You don't appear to be in any position to be making that demand."

For an instant, Harry's attention is drawn to three dark men wearing old style suits and neat trimmed hair who sit around a table at the back of the bar. These ghosts return Harry's attention, their eyes squinting as cigar smoke twists up to the low stained ceiling. When the big man behind the bar had said, "You don't appear to be in any position..." they shook their heads and nodded to each other.

"Hey asshole, what are you looking at back there?" The big man says to Harry. "Look at me or I'm gonna get your attention and you don't want to find out how."

"Sorry pal," Harry replies, slipping his hand inside his coat, his fingertips touching the cool gun barrel. "I only talk to Charlie or Carla."

"Okay if that's how you want it," The big man says, looking past Harry. "Okay boys show the little man who is in charge here."

The two men move toward Harry. Harry reaches for the pistol in his coat and the heavy man pulls a shotgun from below the bar.

"Stop it now," Screams the woman storming out of the back room. "Everyone freeze. Jesus, you are all such assholes. I'm Carla Vaccaro. The big idiot behind the bar is my brother Charlie. These two monkeys behind you are his brain dead friends. He thinks he's looking out for me. But, you know what smart guy?" She says walking up to Harry. "I'll let him if you can't tell me what Maggie Cahoon has tattooed on her ankle."

"She has a... a... 'C.' A red 'C,' for the Cubs," Harry says. "She loves the Cubs."

"Yes she does," Carla says. "All right boys, sorry to ruin your fun. This guy is who he says he is. Relax and get him a drink. Follow me Harry."

Harry follows Carla to the back of the bar; to the very table where Harry had seen the three well dressed apparitions, just moments before. Charlie lumbers over to the table with three glasses of whiskey and pulls up a chair.

"This guy's a friend," Carla says to her brother, brushing the dark curled hair from her eyes.

"Got it Carla," Charlie says. "So tell me, my new friend Dimmig, who is this asshole threatening my sister?"

"I don't know yet," Harry replies. "Did they call you?" Harry asks Carla.

"Call me? I wish that was all. The shit started about a week ago, after I made my first call for Maggie to my friends at the FBI about this Waits character. An hour later I get a call from my bank saying someone has accessed my account without permission and maybe I should change my credit card numbers. I think nothing of it. I keep digging and a few days ago, I see this black Mercedes with this guy sitting outside my building. The same car is there when I wake up the next day."

Harry is watching Carla. She is slight built, with large brown eyes, pretty, but nervous and trying to hide her fear. She sips from her glass of whiskey, as her dark brown eyes dart from Harry to her brother. Charlie sits at her side; his eyes are riveted on her. He listens again to the story he has heard many times for any new insinuation.

"I still didn't make the connection until this morning," Carla says. "Five minutes after I hang up with Maggie, I go outside to have a cigarette and this man, looked like he was one of them stoned Rasta guys, you know the Jamaicans, long knotted up hair, only he's as big as a linebacker, wearing a business suit, and dark glasses. Anyway, he comes up to me, grabs my arm and pushes me against the wall." Charlie's face reddens and his hands tighten around his whiskey glass as his sister continues her story. "This guy pushes me against the wall and says, 'Why are you checking on Waits?' I say, I never heard of anybody named Waits, that's when he squeezes my arm harder and opens his coat to show me the automatic. 'Now,' he says, 'Give me some answers. Who has you collecting info on Waits?' Now I, I..." Carla stops her story to sip from her glass of whiskey. Charlie's eyes are fixed on her.

"So what happened?" Harry asks.

"Relax Dimmig. Don't push her," Charlie says.

"That's all right Charlie," Carla continues. "He took his gun, puts it to my head and says, 'Tell me now or you die right here…' I told him everything. I told him I had no idea why and could care less about this Waits. I said I was helping a friend, Maggie Cahoon, and her bosses, Dimmig and Connoll, that I was doing a favor and that was it."

"What did he do?" Harry asks.

"The fucking asshole threw her down on the ground," Charlie answers.

"That's right," Carla continues. "He pushed me down, leans in close and puts the gun back to my head. He says, 'If I have to come back to visit you again, this gun will be the last thing you see. You understand?' That was it. He walked away."

"Now Dimmig it's your turn," Charlie says. "Who is this guy and where do I find him?"

"I don't know," Harry replies. "Carla knows more than any of us right now."

"Listen Harry," Carla says. "I've only talked with top people about this Waits guy, FBI, the CIA. And whoever these people are, they were all over me within hours. Waits must be as connected as you get."

"Let Harry talk," Charlie says. "How did it happen you brought this name to my sister."

"All I know is that Jack and I are playing in a golf tournament at Wait's mansion, north of Saratoga, next week. We were just trying to get some background on our host."

"A golf tournament?" Charlie says. "You've got to be kidding me, all this for a fucking golf match? There's got to be more."

"That's apparent," Harry replies.

"Well then," Charlie says. "It must also be fucking apparent that I will be accompanying you and your asshole partner to Saratoga."

12

Lilly sits on the bed in the round room, studying her Aunt Sylvia's painting. She finds another patch of color and watches it coalesce to resemble the dark man from the park. He is in the circle of trees now; he is moving toward the beach, to her Aunt. Lilly watches as the man meets Sylvia. They stand while the waves wash over their feet and the heat waves rise from the sand around them.

In this moment of reflection, Lilly realizes that she is the required element, a connection, the witness, as important as the creator. Aunt Sylvia and the dark man are meeting for her benefit, she thinks. She lies back on the gold duvet, her eyes now closed. Recalling the breeze that washed over her in the park, she recognizes him in this room. She can feel him next to her on the bed, his heat. She can feel his hand as it smoothes her hair.

"Who are you?" Lilly whispers.

The man does not reply.

"Who has sent you?" She can feel his breath on her neck. "My Aunt Sylvia made that painting. You were there in the trees, you were with her on the beach." A tear falls, streaking her face and she feels the man brush it with the back of his hand.

"Since I was a child…" Lilly says, opening her eyes and focusing on the inverse point of the turret ceiling above her bed. "They have told me that the ghosts did not exist; that I was imagining; that the trauma of my parent's murder had unbalanced me. As I grew older, they gave me medicine for it and yet I still saw them. I see my aunt. I feel you here. They have always been silent and I no longer speak of what I see to anyone."

A rap on door causes Lilly to sit straight up in bed.

"Lilly," Mrs. Durgiss says. "Lilly, may I come in?"

"Uh, yes, come in."

"I'm sorry to disturb you dear. I heard your voice. You must have been talking in your sleep."

"Yes, Mrs. Durgiss, I guess I was. Can I help you with anything?"

"Lilly, Mrs. Torrance would like you to come down to her room. She is preparing for that party tonight. She's got a big date with her new man, that German fellow. She's waiting for you dear."

"Thanks Mrs. Durgiss. Please tell her I'll be right down. Thank you."

Lilly looks to the painting. The dark man now walks alone, away from the ocean, to the mountains in the distance.

*   *   *

Maggie Cahoon sits staring across her desk at the frail gray haired man in the blue raincoat. "So, you say you're name is Irwin Lavinsky?" Maggie says.

"That's right Red, but you can call me Irv," Lavinsky replies.

"Call me Red one more time, you're gonna' need a doctor. You got that?"

"Sure Honey. I like'em fiery."

"Now tell me again," Maggie says. "Why are you here?"

"Don't know sweetie. Your boss Dim Egg called and told me to be here this morning. I had to get someone to take my shift at the driving range."

The rattling panes of glass from the street door tell Maggie someone is about to head up the stairway. She hears two walking up the stairs. From the footsteps, she knows it is not Jack and Harry. She feels woozy from it all; the sound of strange footsteps approaching, this smart-ass old guy sitting across from her and the Greek is cooking at full force.

The office door opens and the frame is immediately filled with a man who appears too large to fit through. He stands there staring into the office. Maggie reaches for the gun in her purse.

"Christ," Lavinsky says, "Who let the gorilla out of his cage."

"Never mind ya' old goat," Charlie Vaccaro replies. "Where's those two assholes who run this joint."

"By assholes," Carla says, pushing in from behind Charlie. "My brother means your bosses."

"Carla," Maggie shouts, jumping from behind her desk to embrace her old friend. "It's so good to see you. After what's been going on... I wish I knew where my assholes bosses were too. Come in, come in."

"Now Maggie, aren't you gonna' introduce me to your lovely friend?" Irv says pulling himself to stand.

"You've got to be kidding me, right?" Carla says looking sideways at the grinning old man.

"I wish," Maggie replies. "Carla, this is Irv. He's the new torture that Jack and Harry have inflicted upon me." Turning to Carla's borther, Maggie says, "Charlie, my name's Maggie and you've met Irv."

"Great," Charlie says. "Now where are those two assholes? We've got a long drive ahead of us."

"Where you driving to?" Irv asks.

"None of your business," Charlie replies.

"They're all driving to New York, to a golf tournament," Maggie says. "I guess Charlie's going along."

"That's right," Charlie says.

"Going along as what?" Irv asks. "No gorillas allowed at golf tournaments."

"All right, I had enough of this shriveled..." Charlie moves across the room towards Irv.

"Let's go Coco," Irv says, struggling to stand. "What ya' gonna do?"

"Enough," Carla screams. "Stop right there."

Everyone in the room freezes when they hear the laughing. It is Harry and Jack standing in the hall watching the scene and enjoying it.

"What a team," Jack says. "So this must be the famous Charlie Vaccaro? I hear you'll be joining us."

"That's right Connoll, you, me and your asshole partner," Charlie replies.

"Call me Harry," Dimmig suggests.

"Right, sorry. I mean your asshole partner, Harry."

"You're right," Jack says to Harry, "He may be good to have along. And this must be the beautiful Carla Vaccaro," Jack says extending his hand.

"That's me," Carla says. "Nice to meet you Jack." Carla offers her hand to Jack in a way that reminds Harry of the high school girls back in Mrs. Mancini's homeroom.

"I hate to interrupt this lovely party," Irv says. "But why'd you drag me down to this shit hole of an office for anyway?"

"Now Irv, don't get jealous," Jack says.

"Jealous? I'll show you jealous," Irv says moving toward Jack. His path is abruptly blocked by Charlie's thick arm.

"Hold it right there," Charlie says, "You and me got some unfinished business."

"Stop it now," Maggie orders. "I can't take this anymore. What is going on here? Why is Irv here?"

"We're hiring him," Harry tells her.

"You're what?" Maggie, Irv, Charlie and Carla say together.

"Yeah, since we'll be away for a while," Harry answers, "We thought Irv might help out, you know, keep Maggie company."

"What?" Maggie says.

"I've got a job," Irv says. "I've got responsibilities."

"How much they pay you out there?" Jack says.

"Six an hour."

"We'll double it," Jack says.

"Now wait a minute," Maggie says. "If you think for one second, this guy can do anything but annoy me, you lost what's left of your brains."

"Yeah," Charlie says. "This piece of driftwood ain't protecting nobody."

"That right Coco," Irv says. "How's about I protect you right..."

"Stop it now!" Harry says. "We're all working together here. Remember? Irv will do just fine Maggie, he'll keep you company and at least there'll be someone around, especially after what happened to Carla last week."

"I'd prefer a blind dog," Maggie says.

"Charlie," Carla says. "Maybe you can help?"

"Huh, yeah sure, I'll have Marky and Jimmy stop by and check up on your girl," Charlie says to Harry.

"I'll stop by too," Carla says.

"I'll be looking forward to your visits," Irv says winking.

"I can't take this," Maggie says.

"Good," Jack says. "Now that's settled we can hit the road. Everything's in the car except us."

"I know I haven't worked here long, but can I ask a question?" Irv says.

"No," Harry replies.

"Why are you driving?" Irv asks anyway. "You could be there in two hours if you took a plane."

First Harry, than Jack and finally Charlie open their jackets to reveal the weapons they are carrying.

"Anymore questions?" Harry asks.

"Yeah," Charlie says, "Whose car we taking?"

"Jack's Honda," Harry replies.

"No fucking way am I driving into Saratoga in a shit box Honda," Charlie says.

"You got a better suggestion?" Jack asks.

"Fucking right. I got my Lincoln down on the street. A real car, no Jap matchbox, four doors and a full leather back seat."

"It's no Checker Cab," Jack says. "But it sounds like the deal. The Lincoln to Saratoga it is."

*   *   *

Kathryn Torrance sits at a chair in front of a mirror, quickly wiping a tear from her eye when Lilly walks in. She greets the girl saying, "I was waiting for you dear."

"I'm sorry I'm late, Miss Torrance," Lilly replies. "I was caught up in something. Thankfully Mrs. Durgiss came for me."

"Yes, she said you were sleeping."

"Not really, just thinking."

"Huh, well I'm thinking too. I'm thinking that maybe I should forget about this party tonight, this date."

"Why?"

"I'm not up to it. I'm old and I look it. There was a time when the Jockey Club Dinner was the start of a great month and now I dread the thought of it, the thought of being one of the old ones who stands and watches."

"You are far from old and you will be with your friend, Mr. Waring."

"I know Lilly. It's hard to explain, one day you feel young, at the center of everything and the next you feel left behind and alone. When you're young you don't know what life is and by the time you do, you're too far down the river for it to matter."

"You still matter."

Lilly helps Kathryn with her jewelry. As she does, she sees her own reflection in the mirror. There is no escaping it, no matter how much younger she looks, Lilly knows she can never match the beauty in the perfect face, or the rare promise in those blue eyes. Kathryn Torrance is a special creature; she makes the jewels sparkle. Lilly feels eternally smaller in this reflective comparison.

"Lilly," Miss Torrance says, looking back into the girl's reflection. "Your Aunt... Sylvia... always called me Kathryn, would you please do the same."

"Yes Miss Torrance."

"Please Lilly," Kathryn says smiling. "This whole thing, with Martin coming out of nowhere, has thrown me off. I've never been this nervous before any party in my life."

"You must really care for him."

"I think I did once, but that's not it. I'm upset by knowing where he comes from."

"You're upset because he's from Germany?"

"No, he's from my past."

"I don't understand Miss… Kathryn.'

"He's like a ghost, like in the fairy tales. I feel he has come to haunt me, to punish me for something I did once and that's what has me upset, thrown me off balance."

Lilly looks at her boss and considers telling of her own ghosts. "My Aunt Sylvia once told me that life is like the waves of an ocean, that you just have to walk in, let them take you. If you do you will never know regret."

Kathryn's face turns up to Lilly's. She smiles and the blue of her eyes are streaked with rivulets of cream.

"Thank you dear. I'm ready now."

*   *   *

Charlie drives the big Lincoln on the highway headed east. Jack, a map spread on his lap, is next to him. Harry sits in the back seat, sinking into the soft leather. Moments ago, Maggie, Irv and Carla had waved them off and now the city, their home, diminishes behind them.

Harry is thinking this will be the first time since Phoenix he will be outside of Chicago with Jack. Jack is fumbling with the radio and Charlie lights another cigarette.

"Nice car you got here Chaz," Jack says.

"Yeah, it rides good," Charlie replies. "And that's Charlie to you. How far you think we got?"

"I figure fourteen hours, maybe sixteen with stops," Jack says. "It should put us in Saratoga sometime Sunday morning."

"Where we staying?" Charlie asks.

"Manley booked us rooms at a hotel in town," Harry says. "We'll stay there for a couple days prior to the matches and then we move up to the mansion. I told him that you're working with us."

"This Manley, he's got nothing to do with Waits?" Charlie asks.

"Not that I know of," Harry says. "Listen Charlie, we know why you're along, you got your reasons, but you've got to let us do our job. You'll get your chance."

"Huh… You don't want me to screw you guys up?" Charlie replies. "Don't worry about that, I just want a shot at that freak in a suit that messed with my sister."

"You'll have to wait for the right time. Let it go for now," Jack says.

"Right time? Right time. I checked up on you Connoll, that's the story of your life, let it go, gamble, drink, and screw it all. Right?"

"You figure that out while spending your life in that basement you call a bar? Fuck you Vaccaro," Jack replies.

"You know about life?" Charlie says. "I'll tell you about life, number one, everyone takes care of themselves. After that, you decide who you gotta' protect and that what's you do until you die. That's all there is in life."

"That's your philosophy?" Jack says. "Brilliant."

"What do you know Connoll, small time bookie, easy buck hustler that you are. Now you follow the pathetic dredge of the world to make a living."

"I followed more than a few dredges into that bar of yours."

"Enough," Harry says. "We got a long drive. We can't start fighting each other. We're working together and we have to look out for each other. Like Charlie says. Charlie, how long you owned the bar?"

"It was my father's and I took it over when he died. I was twenty-four, just finished college, just a kid," Charlie replies.

"You went to college?" Jack asks.

"Yeah, Columbia College, downtown," Charlie says.

"What'd you take?" Jack asks.

"I got a degree in English," Charlie says.

"English? It don't sound like you learned too much," Jack says.

"Yeah. Hey, what are you gonna' do? I spent the last twenty years in a basement on Madison. I had to; I had to take care of my mom and sister. This is the way you got to talk down there. This is the way you got to talk to survive."

"Why English? Did you want to be a writer?" Harry asks.

"No. I thought I wanted be a teacher."

"A teacher?" Jack says turning to Harry. "Could you imagine this guy walking into a classroom? Would have scared the shit of those poor kids."

"Screw off, Connoll," Charlie says.

"So you spend your life working the bar. How long that bar been there?" Harry asks.

"Since the war," Charlie says. "My dad opened it when he got back from the Pacific."

"Must have seen its share of mob action I bet," Jack says.

"The mob, what's that?" Charlie says. "All I seen is guys taking care of themselves, protecting the one's they love and surviving."

"You're saying there's no mob?" Jack asks. "Come on, when I was booking bets I met more than a few of the boys."

"Sure you would, knowing the two-bit runner that you were," Charlie says. "All I know is, you got bad guys and sometimes they make some alliances, which aren't worth a damn, but they're still just criminals, single solitary, working for themselves, every color, religion and nationality. It's fucking Hollywood and the newspapers who want you to think there's some vast underworld, it's their creation. People stick together for a moment... maybe... that's all. The bluebloods in the newspaper boardrooms, the assholes in Hollywood, they are the mob. Me, down there in the basement, all I see is people living their useless lives, trying to take care of the few people they have decided to protect and then dieing; some sooner than others. That's it."

The big Lincoln is plowing through Indiana, past the gold dome, past the farms and the rest stops filled with small foreign cars and giant American trucks.

The underworld is only a creation, Harry thinks, as Jack and Charlie continue their conversation, you die and that's all, I only wish that was the truth.

*   *   *

"Does it seem like a illusion to you now?" Kathryn asks Martin Waring.

Martin sits across from her in the old pavilion, uncomfortable in his tuxedo and with all the attention that swirls around Kathryn. "I do not know to what you refer," he replies.

"I mean our time together, that year when we were young."

"No it seems like it was yesterday to me, very real. Does it seem an illusion for you?"

"Yes, like some trick that was being played on us."

"A trick? No," Martin says sipping champagne from a crystal glass. "I see it much differently. It is what I cherish the most, the memories."

"The little cottage by the sea... I know."

"Yes that, but also our time together. We were young, strong, ready to conquer the world. It is a feeling that I often search for now."

"Funny, you search for lost feelings," Kathryn says. "I search for lost beauty."

"You have lost nothing of your beauty. Maybe that is your weakness? Much like you think my pining for the past is mine. My last memory of you was the day you left me in Atlanta and when I look at you now, I realize that you were only a shadow of what you would become. You are infinitely more beautiful today."

"My appearance and your memories."

"They hold us... I search my memories; retrace my steps in search of the courage of my youth. You search your mirror for the beauty you think has faded. A pitiable pair, maybe the price of our good fortune," Martin says, caressing Kathryn's hand.

"So where do we go from here?" Kathryn asks, nodding at a gray haired couple as they pass the table.

"You mean us?"

"Yes."

"Maybe, whatever brought us together here has given us the opportunity to see that we need each other now," Martin replies. "In your reflection I find the strength I thought I had lost. I hope I can do the same for you."

"For what end Martin? So you can take me to the cottage by the sea."

"No. That time is gone. There is a challenge I face. The golf tournament I mentioned is much more than a golf tournament. The man Waits that I…"

"Yes Waits, I've asked about him, very mysterious fellow. He's not part of any society or charity, but the word is that he is wealthy beyond words."

"Wealthy and powerful," Martin agrees, leaning in close to Kathryn. "He is offering it all as a prize in this golf tournament."

"What do you mean, it all?"

"Everything, the rumor is that he's insane. The prize is his fortune and he's offering it to one of eight challengers. I'm not sure who the others are, but I've seen a few familiar faces around town lately, some of them are infamous and all are wealthy."

"Why would he do this?"

"Don't know. The entry fee is stiff, ten million, but the prize is billions."

"I've been told he came from nowhere," Kathryn says. "A black man."

"Yes that's all I have heard. I was hoping you would know more."

"So that is what this was all about, you were using me to get information."

"It may have been my reason for contacting you, but that all changed when I saw you. I realized then that you are the source of strength."

"Martin, it appears you did just fine without me."

"No that was different, that was luck, I met the right man, with the right idea, at the right time. With you, I am the one who changes the world. I realize that now. With you I can find the strength I need to win this prize."

"So what are you saying?"

"I'm saying, work with me on this, be with me at these matches. I'm saying, give me the edge I need, the path back to my courage through the darkness of the years. Stand with me and we will inherit Wait's kingdom."

Kathryn and Martin sit across from each other, the music of the orchestra rises around them in an ancient medieval melody. The energy between them is infused with the dream that the world will again be only theirs.

"I will help you. I will help recapture what we cherish, what you say we have never lost, the strength and beauty of our youth. I will help you take Wait's kingdom."

*   *   *

For eight hours the Lincoln has barreled east. Jack is now driving, Harry sits next to him and Charlie sleeps in the back. It is now evening and they have just passed over the border into New York. A baseball announcer's deep intonation can be heard under the static on the car's radio.

"This takes me back," Jack says. "Driving on a star filled summer night through the countryside. You sitting next to me."

"Yeah, the good old days," Harry replies.

Somewhere a baseball announcer speaks with measured words into a microphone, "Strike... two..."

Harry is not sure if the crowd is cheering the pitch or if it is just more static in the reception. "So what do you think of Charlie?" Harry asks.

"I think he's a good man," Jack says. "A little sensitive, but good to have along in case something goes funny."

"The chances of something going funny are pretty good," Harry says.

"Sure seems that way. Tell me again what Manley said when you talked to him yesterday."

"We're meeting tomorrow night at the bar in the Adelphi Hotel. That's all I know."

"What about his boss, the mystery man?"

"He didn't mention him," Harry replies.

"And you told him about Carla, the phone calls?"

"Yes. He only answered with silence."

"Silence. What is that? Wait until I see that short lawyer?"

"I'm worried about Maggie, Carla and Irv," Harry says. "I'm not worried about us. Whatever it is we're walking into, we'll handle. We always have."

"I know Harry. I just wish we were more in control here… That we had more of a plan."

"A plan. I remember the last time we had a plan. That didn't work out so well."

"Yeah, huh. Can I ask you something?" Jack says almost in a whisper.

"If I say no, will it matter?"

"Do you still see them? You know, the ghosts?"

"Jack are we back on that? You know the shrink cured me of that. Said the visions were a result of the bad fevers I had as a kid; only a creation of a sick, lonely boy's, imagination."

"So you don't see them anymore? Come on Harry, tell me the truth."

"What if I did still see them?"

"No, no, it's no problem. It's just that if you did, I would wonder what they would be showing you about this whole deal we're on."

"Well Jack, if I still saw them, I would probably be seeing them more frequently, maybe my grandmother, Eye and Buggy, even Howard Ryan would appear. They would probably have concerned looks on their faces; maybe indicating that where we're going could be dangerous, but they would not be warning me off this adventure. It would be more like they want us to do this, like they would help us if they could."

"They would say that?"

"Well they wouldn't say it, because they don't speak… but I would be able to tell."

"The shrink said you used to make all this stuff up?"

"That's what he said. Jack, are you worried about me?"

"No, we can handle it. Right? We always have."

"And what you putz's can't handle, I will," Charlie answers from the back seat. "I'll show you how sensitive I am."

"Damn it Vaccaro," Jack says. "Can't you take a five minute break?"

"I guess I can't. Now turn off your ghost stories, I'm trying to follow the game."

*   *   *

The Lincoln passing under the stars carries the three men east to Saratoga. Inside the big black Ford, Harry is now driving, as the others sleep. He sits quiet behind the wheel and listens in the static for the announcer's occasional commentary. On the edge of the highway, caught in a flash of the car's passing headlights, Harry glimpses the face of a tall man who stands watching as they pass. It is someone Harry once knew. Harry does not wake the others. He only whispers, "Thank you," into the night and drives on.

*   *   *

East, under the same clear night sky, the girl, Lilly, lies in the turret bedroom on the gold duvet. She scans the painting that hangs on the wall. She watches for the two on the beach, but the waves find only sand. The past collides with the future in Saratoga, she thinks, and there is no one alive I can tell.

*   *   *

North of town, on a bed, in a rented house on a lake, Kathryn and Martin consider the consequences of the deal they have struck. They have made themselves vulnerable to each other. This is the price they must pay as they draw strength for the undertaking. Reflected in Kathryn's eyes, Martin sees his glorious youth, his victories of strength and pure will. In Martin's eyes, Kathryn finds the image of the beautiful woman who can bend the world.

*   *   *

In a mansion, surrounded by miles of uninhabited land that rolls softly up to the mountains, a frail black man wanders through long hallways; his matted and twisted gray hair is pulled back, his face more skeleton than flesh. He is considering all he has made. Slowly, his long thin legs unfold to each step in a shudder of measured movement, a spider readying, he wanders and waits for his guests to arrive.

13

The ocean crashed against the shore; each wave in rhythm with the beat of the boy's heart. It was all he knew, the waves against the shore, the tide that comes and recedes, leaving a meager contribution. He waited in the night for the first light, for dawn, hungry; he waited for the tide to move out, for his chance. He had only the waves and those who wander the beach and disappear; the shadow people he called them. When he was younger he had tried to speak with them, but there was no response. So he waited for the ocean to leave the shells, the cast-offs that would allow him to survive.

He sold them outside the resorts, on the streets of Kingston, or along the beaches, to those brave enough to venture outside the tourist compounds. The others, the older boys, sold the green. More money in the green, but the boy liked the shells; they were beautiful, unique creations and he owed no one for them; not the farmer, not his mother, not his six brothers, or the father whom he barely knew. The shells were his alone, a gift of the waves, of the night and the shadow people.

He cleaned them at the service station on the busy street corner. Old Man Rooker, the boss pumper, let him use the water hose. After, he took his sack and made his rounds. There was no school for the boy. Fifty cents for the small ones, two dollars for the big and for his best, the largest, the most colorful and rare, five dollars.

The boy, Christopher Waits, grew up on the streets of Jamaica and the ocean beat in rhythm with his heart. Tall for his age, "a handsome boy," the tourists said, with a quick smile, ocean green eyes and a sharp mind.

Chasey Minker had watched him carry his sack for many years. He watched Waits make the hard sell on the trinkets and shells to the sunbirds. "Diligent boy, a true bargainer, smarter then my older boys," Minker said. "Hey you," Chasey would say to Christopher. "You sell for me, you make double you make on 'dem shells."

"No 'tanks Minker, I work for no man," Waits replied.

"A stupid boy, we all work for someone. You work for me, you eat better. You be smart enough, you be the boss yourself someday."

Waits knew Minker was right. The shells would feed him only so long. One afternoon he followed Minker into the hills, away from the ocean. On a dirt road they passed through the thick jungle, down a path to a house that leaned to the right. Children played in the yard and a woman worked laundry on a line. Minker and Waits walked by them all to a large shed out back. On a bench next to the door sat Looby Mills; all three hundred pounds of him, his dread hair hanging from his huge fat head. A shotgun rested on his belly and he nodded to Waits.

"Ah, Chase," Looby said. "I see you finally got the young Christopher. A born seller 'dis one. He's got the gift."

Minker winked and motioned for Waits to follow. In the shed, the green hung drying from the ceiling. Below, men with dreadlocks stood at wood tables pulling it apart. They passed a pipe and the smoke twirled up around them. A turntable spun a record and the music from the speaker seemed to stir the haze. The aroma of this factory overwhelmed the boy. It was the pungent odor of the lush swamp, the scent of birth and decay; it grabbed him and made him light headed. The smoke snaked through the music; it made everything spin and Waits closed his eyes.

"'Tis the place Chris," Minker said. "'Tis where you come get your shells from here on boy."

Minker grabbed the pipe, took a long drag and gave it to the boy. "Here."

Waits drew on the pipe, the smoke rushed in, exploded in his lungs, Christopher Waits coughed, uncontrollably, his eyes watered and the others, including Minker, laughed.

"Easy boy," Minker said. "This is strong. Gonna' show you a new world. Will show you who ya' boss really is boy."

Waits took another drag and wandered to a chair. His heart beat now in tempo with the music. The slow halting rhythm now made sense to him. He had heard it before, in the waves, in the night; it is the music of the shadow people who only he can see.

*　　　*　　　*

It was fat Looby who first gave Waits a guitar. Looby spent all day guarding the shack and all night he spent smoking and strumming an old arch-top; a yellow guitar that had been glued together in numerous places. The fat man would struggle to strum in time with the music that came out of the speaker. Rhythm and blues, Ray Charles, Calypso and now more often Ska.

After a long day on the streets, Waits would return to the house to sit and watch Looby struggle with the pine box. Waits would laugh at the sight. "Ah, Loob man, maybe if ya' lost a few 'tousand pounds, those fat fingers would make music," Waits said.

"That so boy. You 'tink you can do better," Looby replied. "Here." Looby handed the boy the old guitar. "You put 'dose fingers here," Looby told the boy. "And ya' use the fingers on the right to pull up, always up, like you be sending the note to heaven."

Two weeks later, Waits paid Looby twenty-five dollars for the guitar. Looby would have given it to him, "…but 'tis good he sacrifices for the music," Looby told Minker.

The guitar never left Waits. He played it to the records of Jimmy Cliff, to Prince Buster, to the new sound Rocksteady, to the Gaylords and Toots, to the beat of his heart, to the shadow people. He played the music of the islands, the music that bent the sultry air and tangled the humid breeze, the music born of Africa and the metal drum, of calypso, of slavery, of reverence for the return of the King of Kings. It was stirred by the ganja, it was the sound of the one heart, of a people's freedom, and their mournful lament. It was the soul of the Rastafari.

Soon, they came from all over the island to hear Waits play on the Kingston street corner. He entertained them now with an old electric Fender Squire and small amplifier; a ragged extension cord was plugged into the service station power holes. It was a fine arrangement. Waits brought the crowd in, Minker's boys sold the green, and Old Man Rooker peddled bottles of beer from a rusted cooler. At the end of the day the cash that accumulated in Wait's hat was more than Chasey ever paid. That September, word of a big show spread quickly across the island.

"A big concert… Down at the West End Cricket stadium, a touring show… Bob Marley and the Wailers, Toots Hibbert, and the Skatalites,"

Minker said, while calculating the sales potential of this event. "The promoter's an old friend of mine, that half Jamaican, half Chinaman who makes 'da records. I'll talk wit' him about getting you a spot," He told Waits.

*   *   *

Waits was given thirty minutes on that hot Jamaican Saturday. He was to perform alone while equipment was being changed for the big acts.

The sun beat down, the pipe smoke hung thick above the crowd and no one noticed the tall young man standing at the microphone. Alone on stage, Waits held tight to his fifty-dollar pawnshop black Fender Squire. He had only heard the guitar through the small amp and had never heard his voice through a microphone. He stood on stage staring out across the field at the thousands who were gathered. In the afternoon heat, he was frozen with fear. He summoned enough strength to turn to his right. There, just off stage, stood Looby and Minker.

"C'mon on boy, show 'dem what you can do," Looby urged.

"Yeah boy, go ahead, make some music," Minker said nodding. "They'll be yours. You can do it."

When Waits turned back to the crowd, he was surprised to see it had increased in size. The new arrivals were his shadow people. They had come from the beach, from the night, to hear the child they had raised.

"I... uh..." Waits started, "I would like to 'tank you all for being here," Waits said. "This is a song I wrote. I call it, *Reflection Shoals*." He laid his left had on the neck and brought his right hand up, across the strings, striking a chilling 'A' chord that echoed over and across the thousands. He could see the chord sweep the stadium, a wave of heads turning to look up to him, those of the shadows and those of the living. He began to beat out the bass line with his thumb, "bauhn... bauhn... ba-ba-ba-ba, bauhn... bauhn... ba-ba-ba-ba, bauhn..." adding the melody with his middle finger the cheap Squire started vibrating, energy arching from it, the wave he made rolled in and out from the stage. Waits had become the origin.

At the end of his thirty minutes the crowd stood and screamed his name. They shouted, "Christopher, Jah... Jah."

103

Waits turned to his right. Looby and Minker had their arms raised over their heads in victory. Next to his two friends stood Marley and Toots.

"'Tank you," Waits said into the microphone, before walking off the stage.

"You got some'ting, boy," Marley said to him. "You got family?"

"Just Looby and Minker here," Waits replied.

"'Den pack your bags, you be coming wit' us t'night."

14

There is no sun on Sunday, as the black Lincoln pulls into Saratoga. Black clouds float under a gray sky; a steady rain falls on empty streets.

"Where's everybody?" Harry asks the desk clerk at the Adelphi Hotel.

"Some are at the races," The clerk replies. "Most just called it an early weekend and returned to the city when the rains came in this morning. Funny how fast the rain came. Last night was clear as a bell."

Harry checks them in while Jack and Charlie hover nervously in the lobby of the old Victorian hotel. Everywhere are ornate antiques, stuff piled on top of stuff, dissimilar, out of place, out of time; an old bicycle with fat tires leans against a velvet chair, an old wooden tennis racquet lies on a table next to a crystal lamp.

"What kind of freaking place is this?" Charlie asks Jack.

"Never seen anything like it," Jack replies.

"There are no apparent divisions here," Harry says, returning with the keys to their rooms.

The men make their way up the wide stairway to the third floor. Harry is forcing himself to concentrate. Unknown to his partners, he has been surrounded by spirits since he walked through the doors of the Adelphi. They move about him, engaged in work, or lounging on chairs and couches. Harry recognizes the ghost of a woman in layered lush dress he had seen once at a Dimmig family wedding. By the bar are stout men, smoking thick cigars, who resemble the Connoll family. The ghosts of bellhops scurry about and long dead chambermaids move by with heads bowed. Today the Adelphi, in the center of this rain drenched town, appears inhabited more by those who have passed, than by those who live.

"My bed's got a fucking canopy," Charlie says standing at his open door.

"They all do," Jack remarks. "What is with this joint?"

Harry does not reply. He just walks straight to his green-canopied bed, falls on it and closes his eyes. There is too much time here, he thinks, I have never visited a place that held so much time.

On his bed in this transparent world, Harry drifts to sleep toward the memory that has been with him since he was a boy.

*   *   *

Harry Dimmig's fever was close to 104. The boy shivered and his mother wiped the sweat from his forehead with a cool cloth. His bedroom ceiling, once pale white, was now a black night sky of uncountable stars that closed in around him.

The legends say that the dead move in the dark spaces, in between the things that make up what we know. They have no dimension, no beauty, no present and no future. They are comprised of what is left of what they were.

Harry observed the old woman standing behind his mother. The woman's lips moved, but Harry could not hear her and his mother was not aware of her presence.

The night sky that filled his room began in this old woman's eyes and when the black night took his mother, his screams echoed hollow into a cavernous void. His room became an infinite space, a billion stars; there was no gravity, love, hate, or pain.

The old woman remained; she was familiar. Harry looked to her fleshy face, the sharp blue eyes, gray hair, but her words died before they reached his ears.

Harry understood there were others with her. They moved in the dark spaces. The old woman, wearing plain clothes, placed her hand on Harry's shoulder. With this gesture her words vibrated through him.

"You have heard my voice before," She said to Harry.

Harry nodded his head.

"I am part of you, your dreams. I am in the things that made you," She said.

"Who are you?" Harry asked the woman.

"I gave my life for you," The woman replied.

"Am I dead?" Harry asked.

"No boy, you have found the door that separates us. A special boy."

"What is this place?"

"It is where we are, always here, moving among you, between your life and our eternity."

Harry turned from her. In the distance, he recognized the red brick of his apartment building, his home on Webster Street, where outside of his bedroom window, a mob of black rats milled about.

Harry, frightened, looked to the old woman. Her face was now among the stars and he could see then, that what he thought were stars, were others who were with the woman.

"They are not real," He told himself.

"Between our worlds," She was saying, "The one who hears us speak will know the fate of all. The one who hears will move on the spiral stairway, they will have the wisdom of dead kings and they will use what they learn to lead their world." The woman hesitated, a tear falling from her face. Turning to the rodents, she asked, "At what cost? At what cost to the boy?"

"Are you my mother's mother?" Harry asked the woman, drawing her attention back to him.

"I may have been," She replied.

"Then you are dead."

"I may be."

"Is this a dream?"

"No."

"Why are we here?"

"I am always here. I want nothing from you Harry. You have found our world and now you know that we can speak. This you can never forget. You must go, but I will tell you something. Yes," She said. "I must tell you something. There is one person who speaks to us. One day you will meet him. When you do, know that I am here, that I will protect you, assist you if I can. I have others that will work for you. More arrive every day. I can offer only meager assistance, many are stronger and the living one, waits, possessing the key will soon go mad. For you to come willingly to this door again will be at great risk. Still you are a special boy."

The mass of milling rats became aware of Harry and the old woman. Harry wants to run but someone was holding him. He screams, turning to where the old woman was, to the others, to the stars, but they had already gone. A rat with the face of a man laughed, hideous, he was close, close enough that Harry smelled its horrible wet stench. Harry struggled to move, but her hands gripped his arms. She was holding him.

She was speaking his name. "Harry, please wake up," She said, "It's just the fever, a bad dream, please wake up, everything is all right."

Harry recognized her voice and his mother's face emerged out of the blackness, tears fell from her eyes; the same eyes as the old woman in the stars. "It's all right Harry," She said, smiling, relieved when he looked up to her.

"I saw her," Harry had said to his mother. "She was with me, the old woman, she was here, grandmother, but the rats…"

"It's all right now Harry, it was just a dream, I'm here with you now. I love you."

"She said she would always be with me, that there is a man who can hear them…"

"That's good Harry, just rest now. Everything will be all right, it was just a dream and you are very sick."

*   *   *

The bar in the Adelphi is off the lobby. It is part of a series of small rooms connected by hallways that ultimately lead to an open courtyard. Large thick leafed plants intrude in spaces around old wicker chairs near low tables, on which tiny white candles flicker. Other than the man behind the counter, the bar is empty this Sunday evening.

Harry, Jack and Charlie stand looking at the solitary barman. Harry, although rested and showered, cannot shake a feeling that he is still lying under the green canopy in the dream.

"Smirnoff on the rocks with an olive," Jack tells the bartender.

"Canadian Club," Charlie counters.

The bartender waits, but Harry is distracted by a small man he sees sitting at a table in a dark corner.

"What can I get for you sir?" The bartender asks.

Harry does not reply.

"Harry, wake up," Jack says, grabbing Harry's arm. "What do you want?"

"Uh, sorry," Harry says breaking free of his vision and turning to the bartender. "A gin and tonic please."

Harry turns back to the dark corner, but the small man has vanished. He had recognized this spirit and it had shaken him. It was a man that had never visited him since he had left this world. It was his father.

"Strange joint," Jack says.

"You can say that again," Charlie says, sipping his whiskey. "What do you think Dimmig?"

"I've never seen anything like it, the whole town," Harry says. "I started getting feelings last night when I was driving. The closer I got, the worse it got. Now this place, this place tops it all."

Jack studies Harry. He has never seen him this distracted and he assumes the cause. "Harry everything all right?" Jack asks. "You look a little off. Remember what the doctor said, it was the fevers."

"What fevers?" Charlie asks.

"No I'm fine," Harry says.

"What fevers?" Charlie asks.

"Nothing, just fevers I had as a boy, sometimes they still make me weak, but don't worry, I'm fine," Harry replies.

"Not the goddamn ghosts you assholes were talking about last night?" Charlie says. "Jesus Christ, you weren't serious were you?"

"No," Harry replies. "No we weren't."

"Don't tell me this is another one of your associates?" Kevin Manley says, startling Harry "Did you exchange the old guy for some muscle?"

"Irv is back at the office. He's holding down the fort," Jack answers.

"That must be some fort you got back there?" Manley smirks, his stomach bulging through an unbuttoned suit coat. "Still, I like Irv just where he is." Manley turns to Charlie. "Please allow me to introduce myself. Kevin Manley, call me Kevin."

"Charlie," Vaccaro replies.

"Just Charlie? No last name? I even got to know Irv's last name. Lavinsky right?"

"That's right," Harry says. "Charlie is less personable."

"Less personable than Irv, didn't think that was possible... How about if we move someplace where we can talk?"

Manley orders a round and has the drinks brought over to a table on the covered back porch, which adjoins the open patio. The rain has stopped, but the awning and trees still drip.

"How's your game Jack?" Manley asks.

"As good as ever," Jack replies. "Who's your boss Kevin?"

"Now, I thought we had an arrangement regarding that," Manley says.

"We did," Harry replies. "That was until we found out you worked for drug dealers, the phone calls started and the Rasta's began pulling guns."

"Huh, well I don't know anything about the calls or the Rasta, but as to the assertion that I represent drug dealers, well..."

"Save it Manley," Jack says. "We know what you are."

"Is that right Connoll? You think so?"

"Listen, you piece of shit," Charlie says, "We want some answers now."

"Now I have to answer to this guy?" Manley laughs. "Don't push me, I'm not gonna take any shit from you Chicago boys. Remember, you work for me."

"No, it appears you, and now we, work for a drug dealer," Harry says.

"You want out Dimmig?"

"No Kevin, just answers," Harry replies.

"All right, you first," Manley says. "Why is Charlie here?"

"He has business with one of Wait's people," Jack answers. "And he provides us with certain other benefits, not the least of which is that he is now my golf instructor."

"Golf instructor, bullshit," Manley smirks. "Still, he's your problem. He better not fuck up your job."

"Listen you fat..." Charlie begins to say, until Harry stops him by placing his hand on his shoulder.

"That's Charlie's story," Harry says. "Charlie is part of the team, might even save your fat ass someday. Now, who we working for?"

"All right, you'll know soon enough anyway. He'll be up at the mansion when the tournament starts. His name is Juan Dalva. Ring any bells?"

"Sounds like some spic coke dealer to me," Charlie replies.

"I bet," Manley says. "Well Mr. Dalva is Columbian, with an engineering degree from M.I.T. and one of the richest men in the world. The source of his wealth you can speculate on, but trust me, he's as legit as any company on the stock market."

"That's comforting," Jack smirks.

"So this rich man wants us to win him more money. Why?" Harry says. "What's another 80 million?"

"It's more," Manley replies.

"More money? More what?" Jack says. "Please Kevin, don't bullshit us."

"You see, it seems that Mr. Waits has invited eight of the world's richest men to these matches. As you know, there's a ten million dollar entry fee thrown into a purse; winner take all. According to his invitations, eighty million is only the tip of what can be had."

"Yeah, so tell us about this invitation, what's below the tip," Jack says.

"Well, it says that the eight invitees can compete, or have surrogates compete, in a match play tournament."

"We know that," Harry says.

"Well, it goes on to say that at the end of the tournament, Mr. Waits will bestow upon the winning team the full extent of his empire, which I've come to learn is in high tens of billions."

"The fucking guy is gonna' give somebody billions of dollars this week?" Charlie says.

"It appears that way. One of the eight will receive everything," Manley replies. "That is why we want you investigating as you play. We want to know as much about this guy as possible to get an edge on this, uh… I guess you would call it, inheritance."

"Who are we competing against?" Harry asks.

"Don't know about the golf," Manley replies. "But I do have a list of the names of the other seven invitees."

"Let me see it?" Jack demands.

"Yeah sure," Manley says. "You'll meet them soon enough. I've already checked them out, very rich, very powerful, but yeah, here it is if you think it will help." Manley removes a folded sheet of yellow legal paper from his inside coat pocket and hands it to Jack. "Just one thing, anything you find out about these guys I want to know. From the minute you pulled into this town, until the minute you leave, you work for me."

"Certainly, Kevin," Harry says. "Now, what's the schedule?"

"The golf starts on Friday. 18 hole matches through Saturday and then 18 for the championship on Sunday."

"Do we get a practice round? Do we get to see the course?" Harry asks.

"No practice, no walk through. Nothing until the matches. Although, you may be able sneak out there on Thursday night."

"Thursday night?" Jack asks.

"Yes, that's the night all the teams are invited to move into their quarters and Mr. Waits…"

"Quarters?" Harry asks.

"Well according to the rules, we all must reside on the mansion grounds for the duration of the tournament. That includes the invitees, their players and anybody associated with the effort. According to my contact in Wait's organization, our accommodations will be very comfortable. We move in Thursday evening and there's a reception, at which, I assume, we'll meet the competition."

"Great, the sooner I move out of this Victorian nuthouse the better," Charlie says.

"So you intend to join us at the mansion?" Manley asks Charlie.

"I sure as hell do. I'm the fucking coach," Charlie replies.

"Well then Jack," Manley says, reaching into his pocket and pulling five hundred dollars from a thick stack of cash. "You better make sure your associate here looks like a golf coach before Thursday night."

"For five hundred I can make him look like a golf ball," Jack replies.

"There's a lot at stake here, so he better not fuck this up," Manley says.

"Don't worry about me," Charlie answers. "I'll be the least of your problems."

"Problems? I want no problems at all," Manley demands.

*   *   *

It is Thursday morning and Lilly stands at her bedroom window staring down to the front lawn. The low eastern sun, fragmented by trees, spreads fingers of daylight across the street below.

Lilly recounts the last few days, the sun had set on Saturday evening, Sunday morning the rain came with low gray skies and Miss Torrance was standing at Lilly's door.

"Lilly dear," Miss Torrance had said, while Lilly pretended not to notice the lady was still wearing the same clothes she wore to the Jockey Club party the night before, "Start preparing for a short trip. This Thursday we'll be traveling. A few days out of this town will be nice. Don't you think? There's a golf match... My friend Martin is playing... He's invited me to accompany him. Four nights... I want you with me. Not a long trip my dear, an hour, maybe an hour and a half drive. It should be very nice... Have you ever been to a golf match?"

Since that Sunday morning, this whole trip had turned sour; the gray skies, Miss Torrance at her door and the looming trip north have made her uneasy.

Making her more anxious is the fact that she has not been visited since Sunday night. No spirits and no dark man. Three clear days since she woke on Monday morning. For the first time since she was a child, she feels truly alone.

Lilly decides everything is connected; the fading of the sun, Kathryn's clothes, the dark man, the sudden lack of visions and the trip north scheduled for this afternoon. She turns to the dresser; everything she has in this world is in two drawers.

She places her possessions in her small vinyl bag. She does not want to leave this room, the turret and the painting. She searches the painting one last time for the dark man, for her Aunt Sylvia, for a clue to what may lay ahead. Lilly finds nothing other than base color, no form, no image, just random brushstrokes, a child's work; the image gone, all meaning lost, lost with her parents, her childhood, her Aunt, and now, the spirits. All she has now in a small black vinyl bag.

*   *   *

There is a bed with a red canopy in Charlie's room at the Adelphi. There are white curtains with pink flowers and the chair Harry sits is blue velvet. Jack swivels in his seat in front of the roll top desk, while Charlie paces the floor.

"I can't wait to get out of this joint," Charlie says.

"Relax," Jack replies. "We'll be leaving in a few hours. Manley says we have to be on the road to the mansion by four. That will give us enough time to get settled in our quarters and cleaned up for the reception."

"Anyway," Harry adds. "We've got to hang around here until we get the call from the office. Then we'll get some lunch,"

"Screw that. We should just call them," Charlie says. "We've been waiting for an hour now."

"We've got to give them some time," Jack replies. "Remember, they're an hour behind back there and Maggie is waiting for your sister to check in."

"Right, an hour behind," Charlie agrees.

"At least the sun is shining," Harry remarks.

"Yeah, I was getting worried that we'd be rained out," Jack says. "How you feeling Harry? You've been very quiet the last couple days, still got those strange feelings?"

"Strange as usual, but now it's different," Harry replies.

"Different how?" Jack asks.

"Different like things have completely stopped, if you know what I mean."

"What things?" Charlie asks.

"You mean like you're finally free?" Jack says.

"No not free, just in some type of waiting room. I walked into this hotel on Sunday and it was a hive. Now, it's as if the hive has been abandoned. A ghost town without ghosts."

"What are you two assholes talking about?" Charlie asks.

"Listen Chaz..." Jack starts, but the ringing phone cuts him off. He hurries to pick up the receiver.

"Yeah Mags. Good, so what have you got?" Jack asks. "No I don't want to hear about the Greek or Irv. What did you find out? No... Jesus. Huh... all right put him on. Irv... I don't want to hear it. Listen to me... Give her a break... Just keep an eye out, that's all we want... No... Listen she's a goddamn Cubs fan. Just lay off, the Sox aren't any better. Irv... Irv... listen, are we paying you? Well then you work for me and I'm telling you to lay off her. I don't have the time for this... She's your boss... Don't start with me... Listen, put Maggie back on... Maggie, give me a break, we're on a case here. You handle Irv. Now what do you have? Yeah, we're leaving in a couple of hours and I'm not sure when I'll talk to you again. Wait... let me get some paper... Okay, go on."

Harry and Charlie watch as Jack fills a white note pad, his head down, often asking Maggie to repeat names. Charlie paces and Harry runs his hand against the grain of the blue velvet.

"That's it Maggie?" Jack asks. "That's what you got? Jesus what is going on here? Right. What about Carla, any more visits from the big guy? They've been around? Good. He did? Who stopped him? Anyway, it's good they're around… All right then, I'll fill in the boys. We should be at the hotel for a couple more hours if you need to reach us; otherwise, I'll call you when we get up to Wait's place. What? Listen Maggie, after this is over we'll take care of the Greek. Now I've got to go… What? If he won't stop bugging you, have Jerry come down and talk to him. Right. I'll be in touch. Yeah, bye."

Jack sits, staring down at the paper. His face is pale.

"So what's up?" Harry asks. "What'd she tell you?"

"Yeah, Connoll, what about Carla?" Charlie asks.

"Huh, Carla… right," Jack answers, as if waking from sleep. "Uh, Irv is driving them all crazy."

"We figured that much," Harry says. "What else did she say?"

"Yeah. Goddamn Irv. Uh Carla, she's fine. Hasn't seen the Rasta man and Charlie's boys, Mark and Jimmy, have been checking on Maggie and Carla every couple hours or so. Jimmy almost choked Irv last night. The old bastard made some crack about Jimmy's shoes."

"Who stopped Jimmy?" Charlie asks.

"That's what I asked Maggie," Jack says.

"What else did Maggie say?" Harry asks. "What did she say about the names on the list?"

"The names," Jack replies. "She said they needed more time, to dig deeper. Carla was still waiting to hear from some of her sources. Maggie wanted to have Jerry make a few calls for her."

"Jerry?" Harry asks. "She's thinks Jerry can help? That's not good."

"No it's not," Jack replies. "Still, they got something on all seven names. More than enough if you ask me."

"So what is it?" Charlie asks.

"Where do I start?" Jack asks.

"How about at the top," Harry answers.

"Right," Jack stands and picks up the pad. "Well let's start here. The first of our invitees is Roland Pierce. Any takers?"

"Just give it to us Connoll," Charlie says.

"Roland Pierce, better known as Jolly Rolly, as in…"

"Jolly Rolly Films," Harry finishes Jack's sentence.

"Movies, magazines, internet, international porn, the world's king of the sex trade," Jack continues. "The guy's as rich, and as big a scumbag, as you can get. Lives on his own island in the South Pacific. There are rumors of slavery and all kinds of whacked shit going on down there."

"Who else?" Charlie asks.

"Well how about Constantine Bandoma?" Jack says.

"The fucking general? The dictator?" Charlie replies.

"You really did go to college," Harry says.

"That bastard has been stealing from his starving people for thirty years," Charlie continues. "Was propped up by every fucking government in the world. He's as dirty as it gets. Killed his own brother and sister a few years back, now he lives in France."

"Right Chaz, well you'll be meeting General Bandoma this evening," Jack says.

"I don't like where this is going," Harry remarks.

"Well considering we work for a Columbian drug dealer, I'd say we got no place to make any judgments here," Jack says. "But relax boys, I've still got five more. How about Alexander Berinczek? Any takers? No. Well he's a former east block physicist turned gun for hire. Nukes and propulsion systems. The Chinese, the Iranians, and who knows who else, have paid this guy hundreds of millions for his skills. If Maggie had more time who knows what else she could dig up on this guy."

"Go on," Harry says.

"Leopold Stellenburg ring a bell?" Jack asks.

Charlie's and Harry's reply is silence.

"Seems that Stellenburg is a banker, Austrian, specializing in investment schemes that have bankrupted whole countries. This activity has made him one of our wealthiest. Oh and here's an interesting one,

Seymour Leiber, an attorney who has made hundreds of millions from insurance companies, suing anything that moves. You've seen his ads. He started in the business by specializing in bilking his elderly clients out of their savings."

"You mean, 'When you need a friend who cares, call Leiber the lawyer?' That guy?" Harry asks.

"You got him. Now here's a strange one," Jack says. "Bertram Hollywell."

"Sounds familiar," Harry says.

"Sure it does," Jack replies. "Try it with a Reverend in front."

"The fucking Reverend Bertram Hollywell," Charlie says. "Jesus Christ, the fucking guy who is on television every day promising salvation; supposedly healing the sick while begging for money. That Reverend Hollywell?"

"Bingo," Jack replies.

"There's one more," Harry says.

"Right," Jack says. "A new one in my book, a German named Martin Waring. He's the head of one world's largest communications conglomerates; newspapers, television, radio, film, publishing, satellites, telemarketing; North America, Europe, Russia, Asia, Australia. His company is everywhere. According to Carla, what we hear, see, read, and know, at some point all originates somewhere in Mr. Waring's greedy little soul."

"Waring?" Harry asks. "That's another familiar name."

"Well you may have heard it back in your glory days. He was a golfer, on the tour for a season until he disappeared and reemerged twenty years later as a media mogul," Jack replies.

"A pro golfer?" Harry says. "Don't recall him."

"So let me see," Charlie says. "We got a porn king named Jolly Rolly, a corrupt dictator Bandoma, Leiber the lying lawyer, Berinczek the scientist, Stellenburg the dirty banker, Hollywell the scumbag preacher, Waring the media pimp and our very own favorite, Dalva the drug dealer; all here to play golf, at the behest of some psycho Jamaican who is promising to give them the works. This is fucking beautiful?"

"Beautiful," Jack echoes.

"We're gonna need bigger guns."

*   *   *

"I'm worried about them," Maggie says to Irv as she hangs up the phone.

"So am I honey," Irv replies. "A snake's den, but it's their job."

"No you're wrong," Maggie says. "This is darker than ever before. They thought they'd be playing golf and maybe doing a little investigating. They're not prepared for this. Jack, he cares about women and maybe golf. Harry, he lives in his own world. They did all right with what they had, this business, made a life, but they're still just kids from the street corner."

"Aren't we all Red?"

"Not like them. They've never escaped the past. They might think this is their second chance. They might try something stupid. Irv, they're in over their heads."

"I only know one thing," Irv replies. "Jack can hit a golf ball like no one I ever saw and Harry's a smart, tough little bastard. They got Charlie Vaccaro and they're all from Chicago. They'll be all right. Besides there's nothing we can do now."

"Nothing? Well for one thing you can go back and sit in your golf shack. That would be a help."

"Now Red, I know you love me."

"You know nothing. I've got to do something. I think it's time I called Carla, tell her to get Mark and Jimmy. I think it's time we paid a visit to that fat lawyer, Frank Danvers, who got them involved in this. Maybe he'll know something that will help."

"Mark and Jimmy? What do you need them for? You got me," Irv says.

"I'm not sure you can scare Danvers with the two teeth you got left. I think we need a little muscle."

"Okay Red. You'll see. These two teeth got some bite yet."

*   *   *

The fat attorney stares across the paper strewn mahogany desk at the frail man's gray weathered face. On either side of the old man, sits a woman, a tall red head, who Frank recognizes and a short, pretty, dark-haired woman, who looks angry.

"So Maggie," Frank Danvers says. "You think this old fruitcake and your pretty little friend can frighten me?"

"Maybe not," Maggie replies. "But I know that our two big friends waiting outside your door should concern you."

"Aha, the old physical threat," Danvers says, sipping bourbon from a square glass. "Having had many years experience in this game, may I make a suggestion? The physical threat only works on the amateurs. You think it's going to work on me; you're kidding yourselves. Someone threatens to do me harm every day."

"Well consider us your threat today," Carla Vaccaro says. "Only we're not kidding. We've got family and friends who you may have sent into some deep trouble. We want to know everything."

"I'm sure you do my dear, but as we all know, in this day, information is a valuable commodity," Danvers says.

"Is it worth your life?" Irv smirks.

"Certainly not old man, but it is worth about ten of yours."

"All right Danvers," Maggie says. "Enough. I know you owe my husband almost ten thousand in gambling debts. I will cover two of that myself if you tell me what you know about Manley, Waits, and how it happened that Jack and Harry got this case. You talk and I'll cover two for you."

"Two thousand. Very good, you're learning. You've got a deal Mrs. Cahoon. I have to say at the outset, you will be disappointed with what I know, but remember a deal's a deal."

"Just start talking," Carla says.

"Of course Carla, of course. Let's see, now there's Kevin Manley, let's just say we have friends who run in the same circles. Through these friends, I hear that Manley has the word out that he is looking for a sub-contractor, a golfer, a special golfer, one who is very good, but also under

120

the radar. This golfer would have to be willing to perform special services and would have to be, you could say, of low ethical standards. Manley was offering a good finders fee and when I heard about it, I immediately thought of your bosses. I thought I was doing them a favor."

"What about Manley," Carla says. "Whom does he work for?"

"Sure Carla anything for you dear... Manley, he works for the lowest scum, the people who trade in addiction, drug dealers mostly, very rich drug dealers."

"And why would a drug dealer need a golfer?" Irv asks.

"Don't know. Don't know anything else about it," Danvers replies.

"What about Waits?" Maggie asks.

"Waits?"

"Christopher Waits," Maggie says. "You know the reggae musician who is now one of the world's richest men."

"Huh," Danvers replies. "Never heard of him. One of the world's richest and I never heard of him. Huh. What is his name?"

"Waits," Maggie says. "He's running the golf tournament that Jack is playing in. The list of invitees includes the drug dealer who Manley works for and seven of the other nastiest scum you can scrape up."

"Interesting," Danvers says. "What do you know about this Waits?"

"Nothing," Maggie says. "We've hit nothing but dead ends, including the business end of an automatic. All we know about Waits is that he was a reggae musician one day and a billionaire the next."

"I can't help you with him, but maybe there is someone who can," Danvers says.

"Well, go on," Maggie says.

"Mrs. Cahoon, darling, remember information has a price," Danvers says.

"All right another thousand off your tab," Maggie says. "Now who is this person?"

"Your offer is very generous, but I want something more valuable," Danvers says.

"What's that?" Maggie says.

"Very simple, I'd like the pleasure of Miss Vaccaro's company," Danvers says.

"What?" Maggie screams.

"Relax dear, for dinner, just dinner," Danvers says laughing. "Anything else, well of that course would be up to beautiful Carla."

Maggie looks over to Carla.

"Is it worth it?" Carla says. "It could be too late anyway, the boys are already on their way up to Wait's place."

"We have to find out everything we can," Maggie answers. "Anything might help. That's all we can do,"

"Oh come on," Danvers says. "How bad can a dinner with me be?"

Carla looks to Maggie and shakes her head. "How bad?" She says to herself. "All right Danvers, you've got a deal. Start talking?"

"Great," Danvers says. "I look forward to our time together, alone, away from all these distractions and this old man…"

"Old man?" Irv says, starting to stand.

"Sit down Irving," Maggie demands. "All right you fat asshole, give us the name."

"The man's name is Chauncy Basch. A true legend. I've known him since we were kids. Then his name was Leonard Basch. Always a flake. In the 60's he fell into this whole reggae scene. You know, ganja, dreadlocks, that terrible music, the whole deal. Funniest thing I ever saw, this little Jewish guy falling into that island culture, or should I say cult. Anyway, Leonard… I mean Chauncey, knew them all. Marley, Cliff all the dope smoking whackos from the islands. He's still deep into it. Runs a small shop up in Wicker Park, sells cd's, books, and all kinds of other… paraphernalia. He would know your man. I'm sure of it."

"What's this shop called," Maggie asks.

"The Jah Shop," Danvers says. "Fucking screwball Leonard was, but he knew'em all, I swear. Now Carla my dear…"

"Give it a break Danvers," Carla cuts Danvers off. "First we check out Basch. If it pans, you'll get paid."

"Good, good," Danvers says. "I'll find us a nice quiet place."

*   *   *

Harry stands outside the cabin gazing down the long drive toward the main road. They were allowed to go no farther then their cabin, eight bedrooms, each with a bath, a large gathering room with a fire already burning, easily better than the homes they had left in Chicago.

As they followed a security car from the front gate, Harry had counted seven other lodges. At the gate, it had appeared to Harry that a ten-foot brick wall with a razor-wire topping surrounded the whole compound. The guards were black men, wearing black combat outfits and armed with automatic rifles. Their matted hair, the mark of the Rastafarian, was held at bay under black berets. Harry remembers his anxiety rising, as Charlie squirmed in the driver's seat upon meeting the guards at the gate.

"You see that?" Charlie said. "The bastard's got an army of them. I told you we'd need bigger guns. Soon as I get to a phone, I'm going to call Mark and Jimmy. We need help." In the lodge they found no telephone, only a warm welcoming fire already blazing.

Now standing outside, Harry is relieved to be here. After all the anticipation, the ghosts and then the lack of ghosts, he is happy to be almost done with it. Three days, some golf and it will be over. Then they could get back to the easy life, their bread and butter, the cheaters.

Manley has not arrived yet from his trip to the Albany airport to meet Dalva's jet. Other than the guards, they have met no one else.

There is no sign of a mansion and more importantly of a golf course. While Jack and Harry explore the lodge, Harry decides to stand on the front porch and take in the woodland scene. It is late afternoon, and dusk is creeping into the blue sky.

The evening reminds Harry of an Oak Grove Monday from his youth. This is an evening Jack and he would have played long into the gloam, until the lights of the clubhouse were all they had left.

A squirrel, on the path in front of the lodge, stops for an instant and eyes Harry. The incident brings to mind his dream and his first meeting with someone from the other side. The old woman, his grandmother had said, "...the key is in the cup. Someday you will know this if you come to this door again. I will be there to help, I have others..."

123

Harry had long ago traced the presence of the ghosts back to that moment and now for the first time it all feels connected to the present; connected to the trees, the mist, to the golf match with Danvers, to Manley, to Waits and something that he is sure lies just ahead.

"This is some spread," Jack says, walking up behind Harry.

"Yeah, I wish our view included the golf course," Harry replies. "How's Charlie doing? He settle down yet?"

"No. Those Rasta guards upset him pretty good and on top of that he hasn't been able to find a phone."

"Yeah, no phone, strange, huh?"

"No stranger than anything in this whole deal," Jack says. "Anyway we'll be playing in the morning."

The two men watch as a long black car stops at the end of their drive, hesitating, before turning up the path toward Harry and Jack, stopping next to the lodge. A driver in full uniform leaps from it, moving quickly around the car to open the rear passenger door. Manley emerges with a nervous smile on his face.

"Hi boys. I see you made it all right," Manley says, turning back to the door to help a delicate dark man exit the car.

The man in a gray suit wears sunglasses. His long black hair, sprinkled with gray, is pulled into a ponytail. From the opposite side of the car, two larger men, wearing suits and sunglasses, unfold, and scan the landscape, taking careful notice of Harry and Jack.

"Connoll and Dimmig, come here," Manley says. "Please meet Mr. Dalva."

"So this is my golfer?" Juan Dalva says to Jack, with no trace of a Columbian accent. "And this must be the caddy."

Harry and Jack extend their hands. "Nice to meet you," They say.

"So tell me," Dalva says. "What detective work have you done since you have arrived?"

Harry and Jack look at each other.

"Well, there's no fucking phone," Charlie says walking up behind them. "How's that for investigating."

"Uh, yes," Manley says. "Mr. Dalva, this is Jack's, uh, golf instructor. I've mentioned him, Mr. Vaccaro."

"Nice to meet ya'," Charlie says.

"Golf instructor?" Dalva asks. "He's a golf instructor like Manny and Carlo here are my financial advisors." The two men in black suits, right hands hidden inside their jackets, smirk behind their sunglasses. "Anyway, Mr. Vaccaro, if you are with my golfer you work for me," Dalva says. "Am I correct?"

"That you are, Señor," Vaccaro replies.

"Good, because if you don't work for me I will have you removed. Understand?"

"Yes, he understands," Harry answers, interrupting any reply that Charlie may have been formulating.

"Good, now lets get settled inside," Manley says. "We'll have a drink and go over the schedule."

*   *   *

The Jah Shop is located in a storefront, on an old stretch of Milwaukee Avenue, surrounded by Mexican five and dimes. The front window is a hodgepodge of album posters and handbills for local reggae concerts.

Maggie and Carla push into the store and are overwhelmed by the smell of fruity incense that is failing to mask the undeniable odor of the more prohibited smoke. Adding to the onslaught is a stereo playing island music with an over amped bass beat.

The two women make their way into this exotic world, through a maze of tightly packed cd bins toward a large glass counter. Under glass they scan the elaborate array of pipes and smoking devices; some resembling modern sculpture in their intricate design. They are so mesmerized by it all, the smells, the music, the posters and the colorful array of paraphernalia, that they don't see the small man walking toward them behind the counter.

"Can I assist you," The man says.

Maggie and Carla jump at his sight, short, slight, he rivals Carla's stature, while Maggie towers over him. His hair is long gray, twisted in

Rastafari fashion, and he wears round wire rim glasses that are tinted dark. His face is hidden somewhere in this mélange. His clothes are baggy, layered, in an attempt to add substance to his small frame.

"I'm sorry if I frightened you. If there's anything you need just ask," He says, turning to walk away.

"Uh, you did surprise us," Maggie says. "And I think you can help us. That is, if you're Chauncey, Chauncey Basch."

"I may be," The man says. "And who might you be?"

"Friends of a friend," Maggie says. "We were sent by Frank Danvers, he said you could help us."

"Frank Danvers?" Chauncey replies. "The fat weasel attorney? You'd be the first that called him friend."

"I see you do know him," Carla says.

"And he's a friend of yours?" Chauncey asks.

"No, but he said you could help us," Carla says.

"Huh, Danvers. I've known him since we were kids; we went to grade school together. He was renowned back then for being a rat squealer. Told the teacher everything... Would run home after school chased by the kid he blew in that day."

"Sounds like not much has changed," Maggie says.

"So, Frank said I could help? I won't ask what it cost you. Still, I'm worried, but you seem all right. What can I do for you?" Before they can reply, Chauncey says, "Excuse me for one moment. I have something on the hot plate in the back. Please, just excuse me for one moment."

As Chauncey runs to the back of the store, Maggie leans in close to Carla and says, "I'm glad we left Irv back at the office. It would have been a nightmare with him in here."

"Yeah," Carla replies. "I can only handle one old whacko at a time these days. Uh-hum... Speak of the devil..."

"Now ladies, what is it you need?" Chauncey says, returning behind the counter. "I am sorry about the interruption, but I usually don't get customers until much later in the day, especially such pretty ones, who are, can we say, friends of a friend."

"I don't know if you have to go that far," Maggie says. "But we appreciate your kindness, Mr. Basch,"

"Please, it's Chauncey ladies and your name's are?"

"I'm Maggie and this is Carla."

"Good, good, now what can I do for you?"

"We're doing some research," Maggie says. "On reggae music… The old days, and we've hit a dead end. Danvers said maybe you could fill in some gaps."

"Fat Frankie, huh. Sure Maggie, what kind of gap you got?"

"His name is Christopher Waits," Maggie replies.

Chauncey's jaw drops and his face turns as green as the t-shirt he wears. Carla thinks that he may be having a stroke and asks, "Chauncey, are you all right?"

"Huh, yes, uh, the name Waits, it just caught me by surprise I hadn't heard it in so long. Christopher Waits, my god, how could you know him? He was in the scene so early and for such a short time… well, I don't know ladies."

"Please Mr. Basch. Chauncey," Maggie says. "We need to hear anything you know about him. It is very important. Our friends, Carla's brother may be in danger."

"Danger?" Chauncey says. "I don't understand."

"We don't know either," Carla says. "But they are with Waits right now and there's already been some threats. We're just looking for some information."

"Certainly ladies. You seem very upset. Please come with me, I have a couch and a couple of chairs in the back. It will be a much more comfortable place to talk. Christopher Waits, yes, I knew him. Your brother and friends are with him, how strange, please follow me."

*   *   *

Lilly, working at preparing tea in the kitchen of the lodge, listens in on a conversation from the adjoining room.

"What is in the envelope they gave you at the gate," Kathryn asks Martin. They sit on the couch in front of the fire.

"Just some instructions for residing on the grounds and the time of the reception tonight," Martin replies.

"What do the instructions say?" Kathryn asks.

"Well first off, only essential personnel are allowed to stay. Specifically prohibited are limo drivers for some reason. Strange. Anyway, the reception is at eight tonight and attendance is mandatory for anyone who will be residing on the compound. That includes invited guests, golfers, caddies, coaches, consultants, maids, and butlers. It's to be in the main house and all tournament information will be provided there. 'All questions answered,' it says."

"Everyone is to attend the reception?" Kathryn asks.

"Yes," Martin says. "I guess that includes your girl and the caddy I brought in with me."

"I don't understand," Kathryn says. "But I must say, everything is first rate, the lodge and the beautiful grounds, very nice. I guess if you're this rich and about to give it all away, you can ask anything you want."

"Lilly," Kathryn calls to the girl listening in the kitchen. "Lilly dear, please come in here."

"Yes Miss Torrance," Lilly says, walking into to the room.

"Lilly. I would like you to attend the party with us tonight. Also attending will be Mr. Waring's caddy, what is his name again?"

"Tommy Deke," Martin says.

"Yes, Mr. Deke," Kathryn continues. "Lilly please find Mr. Deke and tell him that we will be leaving at seven-thirty."

"Yes Miss Torrance," Lilly replies. "It is very kind of you to invite us."

*   *   *

The back room of the Jah Shop is a very small living room. A dark velour couch and two deep cushion chairs surround a low table. There are two floor lamps that emit a low soft gray light.

On the walls are posters; the most prominent is a portrait of black man. The man has a thin beard and high forehead, his right hand, in a clenched fist, is raised. There is a crown on his head and angels hover above him in front of a scorched orange backdrop.

Maggie nudges Carla, who sits next to her on the couch, nodding to the bag of weed next to an ashtray on the table.

"Can I get you ladies anything?" Chauncey asks. "Soda, beer, wine, water?"

"No thanks," Maggie replies.

Chauncey takes a seat in a chair facing the ladies. He grabs the bag from the table and pulls a rolling paper from a pack. "Would you mind?" He asks.

Maggie and Carla, their arms tucked at their sides, nod that they do not.

"Now just allow me to finish this and we can get started," Chauncey says. Chauncey rolls the weed and places it in his mouth, lights a match and takes a long tug. After, he holds the joint in front of him, offering it to Maggie and Carla.

"No, thank you," They say, looking away.

A cloud of green smoke hangs about Chauncey's head and he smiles at their reply, nodding, taking another pull, then placing the rest in the ashtray.

"Ganja," Chauncey says. "Some say they call it that because it is a derivative of Hindu word that means both sweet smelling and noisy. I never believed that. It is my opinion they called it ganja after the river Ganges, the sacred river, the holy flow." He smiles, closing his eyes.

Maggie and Carla watch, stunned, dazed by the music and the aroma, they wait for Chauncey to open his eyes.

"Waits," Chauncey says, his eyes still closed. "Christopher Waits. They used to say he was a prophet"

"A prophet?" Carla says. "Who are they?"

"Yes, they, the other musicians, they thought he was a prophet. Tall, good-looking, but quiet, could sit in a room for hours and never say a word. He just watched. Spent hours in the corner of a room watching where there was nothing to see." Chauncey bolts up and runs to his turntable. "Hold on," He says. "Somewhere, I have a copy of his only disc. A forty-five. It may be the only one that still exists in the world. Where is it?" Chauncey stops the search for a moment. He returns to the ashtray for another puff from the joint and then an instant later he is hunched again over his files. "I'm sure I have it somewhere," He says. "Here, aha, look at this." He is holding an old vinyl disc out in front of him. "Christopher Waits, *Reflection Shoals*, on Beverly Records, Leslie Kong's company, that half-black, half Chinese bastard. Listen…"

Chauncey gently lowers the needle down onto the forty-five. At first there is a scratch and buzz, then the subtle emergence of a repeating baseline. Over the base comes the rhythmic strum of a guitar and, finally, a gentle, reticent voice; it balances tentatively on the slow moving beat, toe-walking on the melody.

Waits sings, "…*the shadows that carry the dead back. They carry them back across ocean, to the homeland, to the garden.*"

Chauncey listens rapt. Carla believes that behind his shaded glasses, tears are gathering at the corners of his eyes.

"I forgot how beautiful this song is," Chauncey says, as the last note dissipates. He lifts the tone arm off the record and carefully removes the disc from the turntable. Once the treasure is safely back in the file, Chauncey turns on the CD player and returns to his chair.

"They thought he was a prophet," Chauncey repeats. "Marley and Toots found him in Kingston. The scene was exploding on the island back then. It started with American rhythm and blues, turned into Ska, then Rocksteady, and by the seventies it was Reggae. Back when they found Waits, it was a little of all that."

"You said you had met him?" Maggie says.

"Yes, the first time was in the mid-sixties. Marley had taken him under his wing and brought him to America. They both got jobs on a Chrysler Assembly line in Delaware. When I heard Marley was there, I jumped the first train out. I had to meet the man, Marley. He was already a legend just from the few Wailer records that had filtered out into the world. He had a number one hit in Jamaica in 1964 with 'Simmer Down,' Do you know it?"

"No," Maggie answers.

"He quit the Wailers for a time in sixty-six. Thought he'd hit it sweet with that assembly line job, but when they laid him off and he couldn't get welfare, he went back to the island. Anyway, I went down to Delaware and there he was with this Christopher Waits. He followed Nesta like a puppy."

"What was he like? Waits?" Maggie says.

"A sweet man. That's how I remember him then. I didn't see him again until the seventies. He was playing guitar with a reggae band opening for the Rolling Stones when they came through Chicago. He remembered me the minute he saw me. I have to say, other than getting thinner, he hadn't changed a bit. God, that was so long ago now. We were all just children."

"So how did this sweet kid, this back-up guitar player, become one of the world's richest men?" Carla asks.

"Ah there lies a mystery," Chauncey says. "I'll tell you what I know, and all I know are rumors passed by the old timers who don't like to talk about things like that."

*　　　*　　　*

Tommy Deke sits on the back porch of the lodge. He is working over Martin Waring's equipment, checking for flaws in the club shafts, cleaning grips and tightening spikes. Having arrived just this morning, Deke feels light headed, as if he's been spirited away in the middle of the night from his bed.

Deke knows this will be his last match. He is almost seventy-five and only took this match when Waring begged him. "There'll be a good pay day for you Tommy," Waring had told him. "One that'll keep you in bourbon for the rest of your days."

Still, to travel halfway around the world, just to carry the bag of a man almost half his age, was not worth it. Deke had seen the world, won two opens with Simon Henderson in the fifties and he does not need this. Still, when Marty begs, it always gets to him.

"Mr. Deke," The girl is calling. "Mr. Deke."

"Yes dear," Tommy Deke replies. "I'm back here." He watches the pretty young woman round the corner of the house. Reminds me of that young lady I was sweet on in Spain, he thinks, summer of sixty-two.

"What can I do for you sweetie?" Deke asks Lilly.

"Good afternoon Mr. Deke. Mr. Waring asked me to inform you that you will be joining him at the reception tonight, seven-thirty."

"Is that right? Well that will be a first," Deke says. "Listen sweetie, you call me Tommy, all right?"

"Yes sir," Lilly replies. "Please, call me Lilly."

"Good. Now Lilly, why do you think Mr. Waring wants an old man like me to attend the reception with him?"

Lilly moves in close to Tommy Deke. "Well Mr. Deke, I mean Tommy, I think you, we, were invited."

"You're going too? Well, I should say, things are looking up for both of us."

"Yes sir… I mean Tommy."

"Let me ask you Lilly, how long you been with Miss Torrance?"

"This is my first trip with her, but I've been in her employ for more than a few years. My aunt, who was with her for over twenty years, raised me. I guess you can say I've been with Miss Torrance most of all of my life."

"Huh," Tommy says, pulling himself up from his chair and walking to railing. He stares out into the forest, into the tangle of branches and listens to a breeze moving through the treetops. "All your life," Tommy says. "Your first trip."

"My parents died when I was a child and since then, in one way or another, I've been connected with Miss Torrance. How about you Tommy? How long have you been with Mr. Waring?"

"On and off for twenty-years," Tommy replies. "He was on the tour for a short time when he was young. I was his caddy. That's when I first met your employer, Miss. Torrance. Only she wasn't Miss Torrance then."

"Well of course, she was probably with her first husband, though it couldn't have been her first, it couldn't have been that long ago?"

"No sweetie, it was longer. This was before any husband. She wasn't married back then. She was barely in her twenties... A very beautiful girl... Hard and clever beyond her age, two tens for a five, if you know what I mean."

"You knew Miss Torrance when she was a girl?"

"She was younger than you I bet," Deke answers. "What was her name? It's been so long, I think it was Cantwell. That's it; they called her K.C. back then. K.C., Kathryn Cantwell, a shoe salesman's daughter from somewhere in Iowa."

*　　　*　　　*

"It was Marley who first told me the kid was a prophet," Chauncey Basch tells Maggie and Carla. "They all believed it though." Chauncey pours tea into three china cups, yellow with gold-trim.

"What did they mean by prophet," Maggie asks. "Was it like he told the future or something?"

"In a way," Chauncey says. "The word was the kid saw things, spirits, ghosts or something."

"And they believed this?" Carla says.

"The island people believed and so do I," Chauncey replies. "The kid would tell them that the spirits follow him. He could describe them, recognizable people, dead parents, old loves, whoever, he could describe them perfectly, and they all believed he was a prophet."

"They told you Waits saw ghosts?" Maggie says.

"Yes... And there was once, it was the time he came through with the Stones. We'd been drinking a lot of wine, and smoking all night, in my apartment on Belden. It was early in the morning and I must have dozed off for a moment. When I woke, he was standing by the window. The sky was turning a violet color. I said Christopher, what are you looking at? He turned to me and smiled and said, 'I see a young boy, he is looking up at me from the sidewalk.'

"I walked over next to him and saw nothing. There's no one there, I said."

"He turned to me and smiled, 'Chaunce,' He said. 'The boy is smiling now. He's smiling because he sees you. I know you can't see him, but he wears a blue sailor's coat and dark rimmed glasses. His hair is brown curls. He is happy now that you have come to the window.'

"That is why I believe him," Chauncey says to Carla.

"You knew this boy he described?" Carla asks.

"Yes, I believe it was my brother Max. He died of pneumonia when we were children. I remember him, the hair, the glasses, the coat."

"Maybe Waits saw a picture you had, maybe he just guessed," Maggie says.

"Maybe, but Waits had done this to the others, and that is why they thought he was a prophet.

"So the ghosts made him a rich man?" Maggie asks.

"I'm not sure," Chauncey replies. "I asked him that night and he told me that they never spoke, they were always silent, they asked nothing and offered nothing."

"So how did it happen?" Carla asks.

"It was the late seventies. Reggae was moving into the mainstream. People were getting very rich, Marley, Toots, the Skatalites were known around the world. In 1977, I traveled to Jamaica for a big concert. It was like a reunion, everyone coming home for one show on the old turf. I asked around about Waits. I'd never forgotten that night on Belden Street. But when it came to Waits, the others were all quiet. They turned away when I mentioned his name. It wasn't like they were embarrassed of him, or angry, I got the feeling they were protecting him, guarding a secret. I heard his name in whispers, hushed conversations, it was Waits who had become the ghost."

"So you don't know how it happened?" Maggie asks.

"I know only this. I cornered a drummer. His name was Corry Bartle. I knew he was a friend of Waits. I told him how Waits had seen my brother that night. How he had told me about his gift. Corry knew that I was one of them, that I was with them before all the record execs and rock stars, that it was my couch they had slept on when they came to Chicago in the early days and it was me that bought them dinner when they were hungry.

"So Corry says, 'Chaunce my friend, our man Christopher has become a king. Richer then any man in the world.' "He told me that it had happened when Waits had gotten a gig with a band booked to play a party on a private yacht. It was supposed to last a week. An Armenian writer owned the boat and he was having this big party. Waits had asked Corry to come along and play, but Corry already had a gig.

"Corry said, 'Something went bad out there. The boat, it sunk, with only two survivors. The Armenian's attorney and Christopher.'

"All the others were dead. And the strangest thing of all was that this Armenian, he left it all, what he had, to Waits. His family contested the will, but everything stood up, the attorney verified it. Waits was a millionaire. That was years ago. What he inherited was nowhere near what I hear he has now. From what I understand, he has increased his wealth a thousand times. That's all I know." Chauncey lights the rest of the joint, taking a long drag and holds in the smoke.

Maggie and Carla sit with their teacups trembling in their hands.

"Everyone died and Waits got it all?" Maggie says almost to herself.

"It's funny how it all matches," Carla says.

"What matches?" Maggie asks.

"How now, an old Waits is having this golf tournament. How he has invited all these rich people to his mansion… It's just…"

Maggie and Carla look to each other. The yellow gold teacup slips from Maggie's hand, splintering on the floor.

*   *   *

Harry stands in front of the red stone mansion. It appears that every light in the great house has been lit, a golden warmth flowing from a hundred windows. His eyes travel along the soaring arches. The irrational roofline brings to mind the medieval castles he had seen in his travels through Europe.

Moments ago, Dalva's group had been left at the front entrance by two cars. Now, armed attendants wearing black gloves and dreadlocks open the mansion doors allowing them entrance.

135

A white man in a blue business suit walks slowly to them, tall, angular face, with a high forehead and receding gray hair. "Welcome Mr. Dalva," The man says, walking directly to Juan Dalva. "I am Alec Bleeris. I have been coordinating your attendance with your Mr. Manley, on behalf of Mr. Waits."

"Mr. Bleeris," Dalva replies with a shallow nod.

"Alec," Kevin Manley says. "Finally, after all this time we meet."

"Yes Kevin," Bleeris replies. "Let me see now, this must Jack Connoll, your designated competitor."

"Good guess," Jack replies.

"Yes of course," Bleeris says. "I've heard a lot about you. I look forward to your play and this must be your partner, Harry, right? Harry Dimmig?"

"That's him," Jack says, "The legend himself."

"Nice to meet you Mr. Bleeris," Harry replies, shaking the tall man's hand.

"Now, these other three, I do not know. Let me guess, these first two here, they must be business associates of Mr. Dalva, right?"

"Yes," Manley says. "This is Mr. Manny Irene and Mr. Carlo Marquez."

"Nice to meet you both. This last gentlemen…" Bleeris scans Charlie Vaccaro for clues. "This one I cannot figure."

"You can call me Charlie. I'm the golf coach."

"The golf coach, huh, I see," Bleeris says. "Well, welcome Charlie, welcome all. Mr. Waits would like you to join the other guests in the ballroom. There are quite a few here already, you make five of the eight groups. So please go, make yourselves at home. The proceedings shall commence shortly."

"Thank you Mr. Bleeris," Manley says.

"Oh, one last thing," Bleeris says before Dalva's group moves on. "Mr. Waits has asked me to inquire regarding you facilities. Is everything acceptable?"

"Yes, everything's quite fine," Dalva replies.

"Good. We wouldn't want to have any bad spirits ruin our fun, would we?" Bleeris says.

All the men except Harry laugh. Mr. Bleeris acknowledges Harry's distraction with a nod only the caddy observes.

"You'll find no bad spirits in this group," Dalva says. "Not for the prize that's on the line."

"Good, good," Bleeris says. "Now, go enjoy yourselves and Mr. Waits will join you shortly."

*   *   *

"They were scheduled to check out of the Adelphi this afternoon," Maggie says, hanging up the payphone at the diner next to the Jah Shop. "They must be at Wait's mansion by now and we have no way to reach them.

"You can't possibly believe that this whole tournament deal is another doomed boat?" Carla asks.

"I don't know what to believe, but in this business, especially in this case, I know there's no room for error. If we make the wrong choice Harry, Jack and Charlie may pay."

"How could no one know about Wait's past?"

"Sounds like the other Rastafari protected Wait's secret. I believe Chauncey may be the only one outside that group who knows. It's been more than twenty-five years."

"So what do we do?" Carla asks. "Can we call the them?"

"No, there is no number listed for Waits."

"What about the police? Maybe I can get my friends in the FBI involved," Carla says.

"We know how that ended last time. Wait's reach is very long. A wrong phone call could get us all killed before we had a chance to do anything."

"So what are you suggesting?"

"I'm suggesting we take a drive."

"We?"

"Yeah, you, me. I'll tell Jerry that I'm leaving…"

"Listen Maggie, I…"

"You don't have to go Carla, but I am."

"No, no, I'll take the tomorrow off."

"Good. It's almost ten," Maggie says. "It will take me a while to explain this to Jerry, get a couple hours of rest, we can hit the road by five a.m."

"Five a.m., you mean we're driving?"

"Of course, you don't think we're going in without guns, do you?"

"Jesus Maggie, what if it's nothing? What if we're wrong and this is just a golf match?"

"Then we've had a nice drive and I'll treat you to an afternoon tea at the spa."

*   *   *

The floor in the reception hall is made of fine wood, inlaid with intricate designs. Harry watches the symbols pass below his feet as he enters the room; swords, spears, cups and pentacles, dark wood into light. From the floor, the room rises to a soaring ceiling, thirty feet up, supported by thick carved beams. A soft tone embraces the room, lit by tiered chandeliers of flickering candles.

Jack pays no attention to the surroundings. He scans the room for his competition, trying to put names to the faces. The dictator, Bandoma, is the first he recognizes. To Bandoma's right stands a party of men and a woman, whose center of attention is the attorney from television, Leiber. There is a group with Slavic features, toward the back of the room, gathered around a diminutive man wearing glasses that Jack assumes is the physicist, Berinczek.

With each of these groups, always near the man of focus, stands a sun-tanned man, who like Jack, is scanning the room. Jack knows these men are his competition and there is no one he recognizes.

It has been years since Jack has felt his nerves tensing for competition. In a matter of hours it will all fall on him. It will be his chance to change history, to prove to Harry that throwing it all away years ago does not matter anymore, to prove to himself that he really could have been the best.

Jack sips his drink and searches the room. That must be the swindler banker Stellenburg, Jack thinks of the new arrival in the pin stripe suit, the neat receding hair, wearing square silver glass frames.

Jack turns to the main door. Mr. Bleeris is leading a group through. Jack watches the tall man following Bleeris. Obviously the invitee, Jack thinks. From this man's walk, the steady controlled movements, the tanned scalp through the thin receding blonde hair, Jack understands that he is also the competitor. This must be the German, Jack recalls, his name is Waring. Playing for himself, for everything.

Jack watches as the Waring group enters, the two women and two men who follow Bleeris. The young girl catches Jack's eye. She is pretty, brown hair, and big brown eyes. The woman is tall and blonde, her hair swept back, she is wearing a simple black dress, a woman of class, Jack thinks, of wealth.

Jack studies her face, the curve of her lips, and the high lines of her face, how her eyes angle down at the corners, catching the soft light of the room.

Jack wonders if he is dreaming, certainly a nightmare, or nerves playing a trick. He feels the years well up inside of him; the past and the present become a wave that rushes in and then out of his chest, leaving only the sands of his deepest fears.

Jack stands frozen as she passes, but she does not look his way. There is a hand on his shoulder and he turns.

"Are you all right?" Harry asks.

"I don't know, I feel dizzy," Jack replies.

"So do I," Harry replies. "After all these years, she has to come back to us now. Jack, you have to let it go, ignore her; pretend you don't know her. Maybe she'll do the same."

"Let it go? How? I have to talk to her."

"Just remember how it ended last time."

"Sure Harry, sure," Jack grabs another glass from a passing waiter and leaves Harry, making his way to the beautiful woman.

"Where's he going?" Charlie asks Harry.

"I'm not sure," Harry replies.

As Jack passes through the gathering he has the sensation that he is floating. A low humming sound is pushing everything from his mind, a static vibration has settled in his fingertips. The decades of change fall from him as he moves to her; the man who overcame the pain, the man who rebuilt his life over a gaping hole, the man who found a road to salvation in his golf swing; all is gone, leaving only the boy who wandered into Ames one summer long ago.

Standing on the edge of the Waring group, Jack overhears Mr. Bleeris saying, "Well that's it Mr. Waring, your group is the last to arrive. Mr. Waits should be with us soon." Bleeris turns to see Jack standing nearby and grabs his arm.

"Mr. Connoll," Bleeris says. "Do you know Mr. Waring? He was once on the tour. He will be competing for himself in Mr. Wait's contest."

"Uh, no…" Jack replies. "It's nice to meet you Mr. Waring. Jack, Jack Connoll."

"Call me Martin," Waring says. "Allow me to introduce Miss Torrance and her assistant Miss Rivera. And this fellow here, is my caddy Tommy Deke."

"Nice to meet you all," Jack replies, staring only into Kathryn's eyes. She shakes his hand with no evident surrender to recognition. Jack knows where to look, the eyes, they are transforming from a velvety blue to swirling indigo.

"So Jack, you're a player," Waring says.

"Yes, I'm competing," Jack replies. "When were you on the tour?"

"So long ago it hardly matters," Martin says, looking over to Kathryn. "A short painful experience. Have you…"

"Can I borrow Mr. Waring for a moment," Mr. Bleeris interrupts, taking Waring by the arm. "I'd like you to meet Mr. Leiber."

"Certainly Mr. Bleeris," Martin replies. "Excuse me Kathryn, Jack."

Kathryn moves quickly, separating Jack from Lilly and Deke. "Jack I... It's been a long time," Kathryn says. "I never expected to see..."

"You never expected to see me again," Jack says.

"Yes, I guess... It was so long ago. We were young. We believed we knew it all."

"You were the only one who believed that K.C. You had a plan to get what you wanted when all I wanted was you."

"I wanted the same," Kathryn says.

"No, you wanted something better."

"Jack... you have to believe me, in all these years, I've never had the feeling that I had a moment ago when I saw you standing there. It was like a dream I've had every night of my life, but could never recall when I woke."

"You are still smooth, still beautiful."

"Jack, I'm sorry. I did love you. I just needed more. Seeing my father fail and my mother suffer. I promised myself it would never happen to me. Leaving you is my one regret."

"You tore apart my life and when the job was complete, you left me, alone. Don't tell me about regrets."

"We were just children. Don't..."

"Don't what," Harry Dimmig says, walking up to Kathryn and Jack. "Jack we need to get back, Waits will be here any moment."

"Harry," Kathryn says. "I..."

Harry waits for Kathryn to continue, but she stops, blinking a tear from the corner of her eye.

"Jack," Kathryn says. "Please, meet me after the reception."

"We have to go," Harry says.

"I'll meet you," Jack answers, turning to follow Harry.

*   *   *

"Maggie, what are you talking about?" Jerry Cahoon says, as they stand in their small kitchen. "You're not driving to Saratoga in the morning. This whole idea is crazy. It's based on the story of some dope smoking lunatic. Harry and Jack can take care of themselves."

"They're in trouble, I know it. There's no other way to reach them," Maggie replies. She stirs the tomato sauce; careful not to let it splash on the Cub's jersey she wears.

"What if this guy Waits is as crazy as you believe, you think he'll just let you walk in there and warn them?"

"We'll find a way."

"We'll? You mean, little Carla, Old Irv and you?"

"Just Carla and me."

"Oh great, that's great, now we're talking."

"What else can I do?"

"Maybe I know somebody in New York I can call," Jerry says.

"No, this is urgent, it's Harry and Jack. I have to go."

"No. No way are you going."

"You can't stop me Jerry."

"Maggie please, this is crazy."

"It's Harry and Jack."

"Maggie please."

"I'm sorry Jerry, but I have to go."

"No," Jerry says. "I'll go. Alone. I'll go up there and get them out. You and Carla will stay here."

"But Jerry, I can't let you, what if…"

"What nothing? I'll go. I'll leave first thing in the morning."

"Take Carla and me with you."

"No. I do this alone."

Maggie places the spoon on a plate next to the stove. She takes Jerry's hand, pulling him to her, kissing him, holding him with all her strength.

"Relax Mags, everything will be all right. I'll play our anniversary in tri-box at the track before I come home. Six-two-one."

*　　*　　*

Juan Dalva watches Jack and Harry. They have left the blonde woman who is with the German, now they cross the room returning to the group. They appear shaken and tense.

"You look as if you've seen a ghost," Dalva says to Jack. "Don't you go soft on me, we've got a big day tomorrow."

"We'll be fine," Jack says.

"Just make sure you are," Dalva says. "I want the prize."

"Relax Juan," Jack says. "You'll get what you want."

"Is that right Connoll?" Dalva moves in close to Jack, their faces almost touching. "You better hope I do."

"Now gentlemen," Manley says, pushing between the two men. "Please, everyone's on edge."

For a moment the three men freeze. Dalva and Jack are face to face, Manley between them. Dalva's bodyguards stand behind their boss ready to move if Jack does.

Harry watches the scene, ready to act, until he realizes it is not the strangest action occurring in the room at the moment. The two large doors are opening and four men are entering the room; the first two are tall, wide, young black men with thick dreadlock hair. They move in the rigid stride of bodyguards. Following, are two older men with gray dreads. The first is fat, wearing black sunglasses. The other is tall, very thin, he wears a black jacket over a black shirt and his eyelids are nearly closed, making his eyes appear as slits. This man seems to move on feel alone.

Bleeris runs across the room to greet the procession. One by one, Manley, Jack, Dalva, Manny and Carlos relax. They turn to the strange parade. Everyone in the room is quieted as the men move silently to a small platform.

"Excuse me," Mr. Bleeris says into a microphone. "Can I please have your attention? I would like to thank you all for your patience. The planning of this event has taken us almost three years and to finally be here on the eve of the great match is very exciting. Later, I will go over the rules and details of the matches. First, I would like to introduce the great man who has brought us all together. Please welcome, Mr. Christopher Waits."

The thin old man, wearing a black jacket, moves slowly towards Bleeris, accompanied by scattered applause. He takes his position on the stage only to stand for moments looking down at his feet. He is gathering his strength.

"'Tank you Mr. Bleeris," Waits says. "Yes, it is finally here. One of you will defeat the seven, and after, my road from ocean to mountain will be complete. I once was a boy with no'ting but the vision. Now you stand before me, blind to your world. A dream it would seem. Three drops of blood in the snow. God has delivered you to me and I have no choice, but to pass on what is mine to the children of Babylon. Still, you have entered into my garden, here you shall strive for the treasure and I will have my due. As I look out, I see those you have brought wit' you. You bring the living and the dead. You have brought the next creator, the next avenger. Among you is the link in time, the world mind of the next age."

Waits trembles, his eyes closing completely. The old fat Rastafari, who had entered the room with Waits, walks up and places his hand on Wait's shoulder to steady him.

Waits shakes his head. "Yes of course. 'Tank you my old friend, 'tank you Looby," Waits says to the fat man.

Jack and Harry look to each other. Jack whispers, "What is this?"

A similar murmur moves around the room.

"I'm sorry," Waits says into the microphone. "I am an old man. Old before my time and I hear so many voices now. You see, I have gathered them all to me. I am holding them wit' the last of my strength. One of you understands," Waits says, his voice beginning to rise, it is now cascading from the speakers at each corner of the ballroom. "For the one who understands, I release them back to you now."

Dalva, Manley and Jack look to each other, a smirk on their faces. They are sure the old man is crazy.

"I release them…" Wait's voice booms.

As the words echo, a flash of pure white light blinds Harry. His legs buckle and he feels the floor giving way. He looks down to the floor and finds a star filled night sky; he drops his glass, and falls to his knees.

Across the room Lilly Rivera has also fallen to the floor. She lies on her back, a crowd gathers around her. As her vision returns, she sees, as does Harry, that the occupants of the room have doubled, tripled. Wait's has returned the ghosts to them.

"Harry. What's wrong?" Jack says.

Harry does not answer.

Tommy Deke kneels next to Lilly. "Be still dear. You must have fainted," He says.

The room's attention has turned away from Waits to the young girl and the caddy both sprawled on the floor. Waits, behind the podium, shakes his head in a gesture of recognition, then motions to Bleeris to take the microphone.

Bleeris waits, watching as Lilly and Harry are helped back to their feet.

"Please, if I can have everyone's attention," Bleeris says. "I would just like to summarize the details of the event. The first match will start promptly at 10 a.m. tomorrow morning. I will consult with Mr. Waits immediately after this reception on the pairings. Your tee times will be delivered to you tonight, with dinner, in your quarters.

"The format is eighteen hole match play, the winner advances, the loser will be escorted from the grounds immediately. The victor will be crowned at a ceremony after the Sunday match. Mr. Waits will turn over his prize, and his estate, to the deserving person on the winning team."

"Now please proceed directly to your lodge and rest. Good night, and good luck."

As Waits moves to leave the room, he stops and whispers to Bleeris, "Who are they wit'?"

"The girl is with Waring and the man is with Dalva. How can this be? How can there be two?" Bleeris asks.

"It is what it is," Waits answers. "If they are to meet, it will not be until the Sunday championship. Do you understand?"

"No, I do not, but I'll arrange it as you say."

*   *   *

Jack and Harry stand outside the mansion. The others in their group have already gone back to the lodge. It is dark now, but in the soft glow of stray light, Jack can see that Harry is shaken and pale.

"What happened in there?" Jack asks. "You went down like you were smacked on the head."

"Jack," Harry says, trying to focus his attention on his old friend. "It was all too much, like a flood. Waits... he was holding them all."

"Holding who?"

"The ghosts, they had left me on Sunday... He had them and..."

"Come on Harry. Not the ghosts, not now. We've got a big match and..."

"I know Jack, but you heard him. He said he was holding them and..."

"I heard the crazy bastard. I also heard him say he was about to give away billions to the winner. That's what I heard."

"Everything all right?" Kathryn asks, joining Harry and Jack.

"Fine," Jack replies.

Harry is silent, too weak to look up. When he does, he sees only spirits wandering in the night.

"That certainly was strange," Kathryn says. "It was bizarre how Harry and my girl, Lilly, fainted at exactly the same moment."

"What?" Harry says.

"When you went down," Jack answers. "So did K.C.'s assistant."

"What did she say?" Harry asks K.C.

"I don't know. I didn't really talk with her," Kathryn says.

"I have to go," Harry says, rushing away to catch the next car back to the lodges.

"Still a very strange man, I see," Kathryn says.

"I wouldn't push it with him," Jack says. "He still hasn't forgotten. Neither have I."

"If you have ever doubted that I loved you, you would have been wrong."

"Love? K.C..." Jack is laughing. "What do you know about that? I can see you have what you desired."

"Jack, I had to do it. I could never have been poor and..."

"And what? That's what you would have been with me."

"No. I mean... I just couldn't take the chance."

"And what you did to me and Harry, you tore us apart, that was for you too?"

"No, I thought I was doing it for you. Jack you have to believe me, I was only trying to help you."

Jack wants to walk away. He wants to prove he is stronger now, that he has changed, but that man never existed. K.C. has never left him, he has carried her for years, he is drained from this effort and he cannot overcome her strength.

"I don't care anymore," Jack says. "When I saw you tonight, I wanted to hate you, I wanted you to hate me. All I got was the knowledge that I can never escape."

"Jack..."

"It's crazy, I spent a lifetime crawling out of the hole. Now, when I have a chance at redemption, here you are again. K.C., I can't afford to make the same mistake twice."

"Neither can I Jack."

Kathryn Torrance and Jack Connoll walk the dirt path back to the lodges. They walk in silence, the forest on their right, the mountains on their left and the dark mansion behind them.

Jack had always known she would reappear to him this way, no longer just a girl, more beautiful, more powerful.

Kathryn is relieved that Jack's easy manner and handsome charm have survived the years. Jack is no longer the boy of promise that rescued her from Ames, but there is wealth and power in his heart and it can be hers if she desires.

In a moment that they have imagined many times over their lives, they stop on the moonlit path and let their bodies come together again, for that moment their hearts again are one.

* * *

Tommy Deke opens the door to the lodge and finds Harry standing there, winded and pale. "Can I help you sir," Deke says.

"Please," Harry says, "I need to speak with the girl. Please."

"You mean Lilly?"

"Yes, the one who fell at the reception."

"Well, she went right up to her room and… I don't think she's up to it," Deke says.

"Please, my name is Harry, Harry Dimmig. Just tell her that I fainted too. And… Tell her I need to talk with her."

"Dimmig? Harry Dimmig, I'll be damned. You don't remember me, Deke, Tommy Deke; I carried for Fitzgerald on the Euro Tour during the eighties. You carried for… What was his name? The tall Englishman."

"Parker, Glyn Parker."

"Right Parker, a good golfer and a very nice fellow. How's he doing?"

"He passed a while back."

"Oh. I'm sorry. Still, you and I survived. Do you remember old Tommy?"

"Sure Tommy. I'm just a little under the weather. I remember you. I remember the night you and Fitz drank four bottles of Champagne on the train from Edinboro to Glasgow and how you both puked your guts on the tenth fairway the next day."

"Damn it Dimmig, I had almost completely forgot about that."

"Who you carrying for?"

148

"Jack Connoll."

"Never heard of him."

"You will. Now Tommy, can I please see the girl?"

"Sure Harry. I'll see if she's up to it." Deke leaves Harry for Lilly's second floor bedroom.

As Harry is standing in the entrance hall, he becomes aware of a man watching him from just inside the living room. At first, Harry thinks he is one of the many apparitions that have returned to him, but when the man approaches, Harry can see that it is the golfer, Waring.

"I couldn't help overhearing," Waring says. "My name's Martin Waring."

"Harry Dimmig."

"So you're carrying for Connoll?"

"Yes, and you're playing your own game?"

"Right Harry. Whom is Connoll playing for?"

"He plays for Dalva."

"I see. Huh. Connoll, the name rings a bell. He ever play a tour?"

"No. He's just played around Chicago."

Tommy Deke descends the stairs saying, "She said she'll see you."

"Thanks Tommy. Please excuse me," Harry says.

"Certainly Harry," Waring says. "We'll see you tomorrow."

Harry starts up the stairs. The landing above appears to be a black void. His legs are heavy and he holds the railing for support. On the second floor, he moves to an open door at the end of the hall where a dim light glows. He approaches it and for the first time in years he feels fear slowing his movement.

Lilly is sitting on the edge of the bed. Her long brown hair falls straight in front of her shoulders, covering both sides of her face. Even in the shadows, Harry can see that she is pretty, her big brown eyes looking up to him, uncertain and wary.

The fear that had gripped Harry has turned to sympathy for the young girl. Without saying a word he sits next to Lilly and takes her hand.

She rests her head on his shoulder. They sit in silence knowing they have found another.

"How long Lilly?" Harry asks.

"Most of my life," Lilly replies. "You?"

"Since I was a boy."

"Have you ever met anyone... anyone else, who could see them?"

"No. If I have, I didn't know," Harry replies. "Can I ask, why did you faint?"

"Because they came back so fast, because there were so many more than ever before. You?"

"Yes, yes, they were everywhere, family, friends, people I recognized from only brief instant in my life. I thought I was going crazy," Harry says. "At least they have given us a break here for a moment. At least we have found each other here alone."

"A break here? Alone? What do you mean?" Lilly says.

"I mean here, me and you, we're alone now."

"You don't see them?" Lilly says pushing away from Harry.

"See them?"

"The lady and man who are sitting on the bench in the hall."

"The bench is empty," Harry says.

"My Aunt Sylvia and the dark man, you don't see them? But..."

"No," Harry says, staring deep into the vacant place and jumping when a form moves into the doorway.

"Well this is interesting," Kathryn says, standing in the hall.

Harry and Lilly leap up from the bed.

"I... I have to get going," Harry says. "I was just checking on Lilly. Must have been the excitement; we both got hit at the same time. I was just checking up..." Harry says.

"I'm sure you were," Kathryn says.

Harry turns to Lilly. "Will you be all right?"

"Yes, thank you," Lilly replies.

"Will I'll see you on the golf course tomorrow?" Harry asks.

"You will see us both," Kathryn replies.

"Great. Great. Well good night," Harry says, glancing at the empty bench, he pushes by Kathryn and disappears down the stairs.

15

On Friday, the sun rises over Lake Michigan. Threads of light hang in the spaces between the towers surrounding the Loop. Jerry Cahoon is driving, his thirty-eight revolver in the glove box. Irv Lavinsky, in the passenger seat next to him, clutches a coffee cup.

Jerry and Irv have not spoken since they drove away from Maggie. There was an argument, and Maggie had cried. "He might help," Maggie had said to Jerry. "He knows golf and I can't let you go alone. He can drive if you need to sleep."

"Mag, I got enough problems then to baby sit this old man," Jerry replied.

"Shh… He'll hear you," Maggie said. "Please… for me, Jerry. Please."

"Absolutely not. This is too much."

"Hey, what's holding this show up?" Irv had shouted, standing next to the car holding a brown paper shopping bag.

"You're not going anywhere," Jerry yelled back.

"What?" Irv replied, cupping his ear.

"He's going Jerry, please," Maggie said, tears falling down her face.

"Shit," Jerry said. "This is just great. Bad enough I'm sent off on some fool's job because of something a stoned Rastafari Jew said, now you want me to partner up with this mutt. Maggie please…"

Jerry stopped arguing when he looked into Maggie's eyes. They were awash in tears and red. They reminded him of the beggar's eyes, pleading for coins on the corner, desperate and ashamed. Jerry had never seen her beg before, and this morning, with her eyes and her ragged Cubs bathrobe, he knew it was just time shut up and leave.

"All right," Jerry said. "I'm leaving. You owe me big for this one."

"I know," Maggie said. "I love you."

"You handle my calls for the next few days. Bill Kelly will help you out, but you got to keep the accounts, because Kelly will get them confused."

"I will," She said, grabbing him, burying her head in his chest. "Please be careful, I..."

"Don't worry Mag, it's nothing. The only one who could get hurt is Irv and that's only if he gives me any trouble." Jerry squeezed her and kissed her forehead. "Don't worry Mags. I love you too. Don't worry."

"You ready?" Jerry said to Irv, as he approached the car.

"You ready?" Irv replied. "I've only been standing here for goddamn near a half an hour waiting for you to kiss goodbye."

"Is that right? Well listen to me, I'm taking you, but I don't need you. Just stay out of my way, you understand."

"Oh, now you're my boss too," Irv said. "I'll tell you..."

"No, don't you tell me anything," Jerry cut him off.

"No damn problem there... Got nothing to say to a two-bit bookie anyways."

"Listen you old..."

"Jerry! Irv!" Maggie shouted.

"Just get in," Jerry said to Irv.

Jerry and Irv drove away. They had stopped for a coffee at Michael's Diner, where each paid for their own Styrofoam cup and they have not spoken since they left Maggie standing on the corner. That silent time has come to an end.

"Stop fiddling with the radio," Jerry finally says, the office towers on his left now giving way to the steel foundries as they turn east.

"What?" Irv says. "I'm just trying to get some music. I can't stand these loudmouths that shout at each other 'bout shit they don't know nothing about."

"Well just leave it."

"You remember when they got Dillinger?" Irv asks.

"What?"

"You remember when they got Dillinger. When they shot him down in the alley off Lincoln Ave."

"No. I wasn't born yet."

"I was a kid. It was Purvis that got him," Irv continues. "You ask most people today, they'll say it was Ness, but it was Purvis."

"So what?"

"The biggest news anywhere. Headlines were as big that day, as the day they landed on the moon or the day when they killed the president."

"Thanks for the history lesson."

"Yeah, whatever. All you young guys are so smart. I remember. I was smart too. I coulda' used a few things people tried to tell me in my life, only I didn't listen either."

"If you say so. Listen Irv, I don't know you, you're probably a good old guy, but you have to understand, I don't want to be on this little adventure. I just want to get it over with. I don't need no help."

"We all need help kid. That's the first thing you realize when you get old. From what I know this is some deep shit we're walking into here. Some freak is offering a billion dollar prize for a golf tournament, from a fortune he inherited as a result of everyone else happening to mysteriously die. This prize is being chased by some of the biggest sharks in the ocean. You think that little piece a metal you got in the glove box is gonna' do any good? You think, because you're a neighborhood bookie from Chicago, they're gonna' stand aside and let you walk right in there?"

"I'm not thinking anything. I just want to get this over with."

"That's right. I've seen that kinda' attitude a thousand times. That's how people get hurt. Just want to get things over with. Don't think."

"Yeah, so you've been involved in a lot of these situations with your career at the golf driving range?"

"I've been around kid. I've seen 'em come and go. Those two boys up there in Saratoga, Jack and Harry, they don't know what they're in for. If we're gonna do anything about it we should be ready for anything."

"And how do we do that?"

"Right here my friend. Right here," Irv says, reaching into the brown paper bag on the floor between his legs and pulling a small gray box from under his folded clothes. "This is how you fight fire." Irv opens the box lid and carefully pulls out two green pinecones.

"Jesus Christ," Jerry says. "Is that what I think it is?"

"You bet. I've got two of them from a friend of mine in the business. He had a whole closet of these things. They'll even out a lot of fights."

"Fucking hand grenades? You're telling me those things really work?"

"I like your wife," Irv says. "She cares about people, cares about Jack and Harry. Even me I think. I promised her I wouldn't let anything to happen to you."

Jerry looks over at the blue-eyed old man. The hairy stubble of an unshaven face surrounds a wrinkled two-tooth smile. "Crazy bastard."

"So what do you think now kid?" Irv asks.

"I think I like the way you think," Jerry replies with a smile.

$$*\qquad*\qquad*$$

Harry feels their eyes on him and the weight of their vigil crushes him. They watch him on the practice range, as Jack takes his warm-up swings. Harry, always the small sickly boy, believes they mock his frailty.

This August Friday morning dawned cool, an early fall breeze in the air. "The cool air is a good sign," Harry says to Jack.

Jack only nods his acknowledgement. With each swing he feels the tension drop away. The strange tournament becomes secondary to the joy of the ball in flight. Even the thoughts of Kathryn recede behind it now.

Harry's leaves Jack and joins Charlie, who is sitting on a bench watching the participants gather. The sight of Vaccaro, large and uneasy, in his yellow polo shirt and khakis, causes Harry to smile.

"You don't look like your average golf coach," Harry says to Charlie.

"That's the nicest thing you've ever said to me," Charlie replies. "So when does this circus start?"

"We're playing in the first match. Teeing off at ten."

"Good, when you guys are out there I'm gonna do a little snooping around the main house. Gonna' find out which of those two Rasta bodyguards pushed around Carla."

"Listen Charlie," Harry says. "Don't start anything until this is over."

"Don't worry about me Dimmig. I know my time. How about you? You recover from your fainting spell. You're still looking a little sick."

"I don't feel great. I got a lot of things on my mind."

"Me too," Charlie says. "Ever since that Waits creep made his speech I've been worried."

"Really?" Harry asks. "Why?"

"Well it's what he said, you know that stuff about, '...having no choice about passing something to the children of Babylon.' That it is, '...his right to have his due.' You know that stuff."

"Yeah what about it?"

"When I was back in college I took a course, you know, one of those course where they compare different religions."

"So?"

"I remember we talked about these Rastafari types. Wait's speech rang a few bells last night."

"What bells?"

"Harry, what do you know about this religion?"

"Nothing. Just the hair the music."

"The thing is, that's a big part of it. My professor said the religion's like culture, the hair, the music, the marijuana, helps it spread. I remember him saying it came out of something called the pan-African movement in the 1920's. A man named Marcus Garvey."

"The Pan-African movement?"

"Yeah, it was Garvey's effort to unite the people of Africa that were sold into slavery. You know them and their descendants. Some kind of worldwide movement that used the fact that some of them poor displaced peoples found passages in the Bible that told them that Ethiopia was the location of the true kingdom of god on earth. They believed it was the garden."

"Charlie, you're a surprising bartender."

"I know a few things," Charlie replies.

"But why would they think this?"

"They would believe this because there are passages in the bible that speak to this connection. Moses married an Ethiopian and one psalm refers directly to, '...the Princes and Princesses of Ethiopia who shall one day come and stretch out their hands to God.' These slaves and their descendants, African Christians, believe that Jesus was a black man and they started predicting the second coming of a black Messiah. In the 1920's, Garvey used this believe to bring together his Pan-African movement."

"So what does this have to do with what Waits said?"

"Allow me to continue."

"Sorry professor." Harry checks his watch and searches for Jack. After a moment of panic, he finds him on the putting green.

"At about the same time Garvey's pushing his movement, a man named Tafari Mekonnen was ascending to the throne of Ethiopia. Tafari was known by the title of Ras, which means Lord or Duke. In 1930, Ras Tafari is coronated King of Ethiopia. At his coronation, Ras Tafari took the name Halie Salassie I. Seems that Salassie, the name, is a synonym for Jah, which itself is a form of the biblical Jehovah, or another term for god. African Christians throughout the world saw his taking the Ethiopia throne as the return of the king to the oldest throne on earth. For them, the King of Ethiopia represented the justice and judgment of god in human affairs. I remember reading that Salassie was coronated with the titles King of Kings, Lord of Lords, the Conquering Lion of Judah. These are terms from the bible that were reserved for the second coming of Christ."

"How do you remember all of this?" Harry asks.

"I thought it was interesting story because my ancestors, the Italians under that fascist bastard, Mussolini, invaded Ethiopia shortly after Sallasie's coronation. This led to a worldwide outcry, which it so happens coincided with the emergence of Calypso music. And it was the music that carried the story of the suffering of the Ethiopians, of the return of Jah to his throne, the second coming, from port-to-port, island-to-island, by sailors, many of whom were direct descendants of escaped slaves. The music told the story of the black man's struggle against the agents of Babylon. Babylon being the white European power structure that they believed was at the root of the slave trade and therefore their dispersion. To shorten the story, in sixty-one Salassie traveled to Jamaica to unite the houses of Solomon and Sheba and the Rastafari emerge there. They are the followers of Salassie and they spread their beliefs through their music and culture more than by word. Some believe the dreadlock hair was adopted from the Mao Mao tribe because of their renown for fighting European colonization. Only other thing I remember is that they follow a strict vegetarian diet and their sworn enemies are known as Babylonians."

"And this is Waits."

"It would appear it is. At least that was Waits, and then Waits became a billionaire. What got me thinking is what he said last night about having no choice but to pass on the gift to a Babylonian, but still reserving the right to exact vengeance. That started me considering this whole circus he's got here."

"And?"

"You saw him Dimmig, Waits, he is obviously crazy, and if he believes he has a god given right, by virtue of his beliefs, if he believes he has the right to reward the good and punish the evil, that sort of shit, then…"

"Then what?"

"Well take a look around here. He's assembled the royalty of the world's evil empires. That includes your employer, Mr. Dalva, the drug dealer." Charlie, a smirk on his large face, stares directly at Harry. "This could turn into a very interesting tea party."

Harry breaks from Charlie's spell when he notices that the spirits have moved in close around them. Harry's grandmother, his father, Glyn Parker, One-Eye, and Buggy are among the many who watch him now. Harry staggers and almost loses his balance. "Waits is up to something very deep here," Harry says, addressing the spirits that surround him, but they do not respond.

"You think?" Charlie answers. "I say we keep on our toes. I'll see what I can find out while everybody is occupied with the white ball today."

"Be careful Charlie."

"You too. Looks like they're getting ready to tee off."

Harry turns and sees the crowd gathering around the first tee. He nods to Charlie and rushes to meet Jack, snatching up the golf bag as he passes the putting green.

"I thought I'd lost you," Jack says to Harry, as his caddy comes up breathing heavy next to him.

"Not yet," Harry replies. "I just had an interesting conversation with Charlie."

"A good guy," Jack replies. "A lot smarter than he lets on. I'm glad he's with us."

"He thinks Waits is up to something way beyond passing on what he owns."

"Like what?"

"It has something to do with religion and revenge."

"Great."

Jack and Harry walk in silence the rest of the way to the first tee. Manley is the first to greet them, wearing a green golf shirt and brown pleated khaki shorts. It is the first time he has been seen without a suit. The knit shirt, a size too small, clings to his belly, folding under the hanging flesh and disappearing into his waist. "How ya feeling Jack?" Manley says, with a nervous smile.

"Good Kevin," Jack replies. "Just looking forward to a little golf."

Standing just behind Manley is Juan Dalva, his white shirt with long sleeves buttoned, looking cool against the emerald golf course.

Alec Bleeris paces on the manicured grass, glancing to Jack and Harry, and then back to an assembling group that includes the physicist, Alexander Berinczek.

Berinczek is a thin balding man, his glasses set on a prominent nose, his forehead bulging, sweeping upward to a square hairless head. He stands with his hands in his pockets, out of place in nature, his head down, contemplating a scene with which he has no experience.

"Excuse me gentlemen," Bleeris says. "May I have your attention?"

The groups that have gathered around the tee box become silent.

"I see the teams for our first match have arrived. Representing Mr. Alexander Berinczek will be Lester Hayword. Representing Mr. Juan Dalva will be Mr. Jack Connoll. Please, can I have the four gentlemen step forward? Berinczek and Hayword, Dalva and Connoll walk to meet Bleeris in the center of the tee. "As you know," Bleeris says to the men. "This is standard eighteen hole match play. If the match is tied after eighteen, you will continue, hole-by-hole, until one gains an advantage."

"Sudden death," Hayword says.

"Exactly," Bleeris replies. "The winner of the match moves on to the next round and the losing team will be assisted off the grounds, immediately. The traditional rules of golf will apply; I will settle any dispute."

Bleeris holds out two closed hands to Jack. Jack points to his right hand, which Bleeris opens to reveal a paper marked with the number two.

"Your tee Mr. Hayword. Good luck gentlemen," Bleeris says, shaking hands with each of the four men.

As Jack and Dalva walk back, Dalva leans in close to Jack and says, "That better be the last thing you lose today."

"Easy Juan," Jack replies, signaling for Harry to move up and join him.

"Good luck guys," Jack says to his opponent.

"Same to you," Hayword replies.

Hayword is young, twenty years younger than Jack, his blond hair, long in the back, hangs over the collar of his black golf shirt, which itself disappears into black peg-legged pants.

"Very stylish," Jack says to Harry.

"Yeah, you can never go wrong with black," Harry remarks.

"Danny," Hayword says to his caddy, "We have a couple of fashion experts here."

"We appreciate good taste," Jack says.

"You could have fooled me," Hayword replies.

"Gentlemen, please tee off," Bleeris says from somewhere at the back of the tee.

"Well, here we go," Hayword says, placing a ball between the black tee markers. After two practice swings, he steps up to his ball and in a quick efficient move sends it rocketing into the green valley below.

The shot is met with thin applause. Berinczek can be heard remarking, "Oh, is good? No?"

"What do you think Harry?" Jack asks.

"I think you do exactly what he did."

"We got a dogleg par four into a valley?" Jack asks.

"Right. It appears you got to hit it two-sixty to have a shot at the green."

"Yeah, no problem." Jack takes his driver from Harry.

Hayword turns to his caddy, Danny, and says, "You ever hear of this guy?"

"Nah," Danny replies. "Looks kinda' like my uncle Mac, the drunk."

Jack nods in the direction of his opponents. Takes two practice swings, lets his body sag, turns back and then forward with a smooth easy motion that sends the ball with a slight hook into the valley. The ball lands dead square in the center fairway, two hundred and eighty yards out, almost on top of where Hayword's ball had come to rest and bounds down the fairway another thirty yards.

Jack turns to Danny the caddy and says, "Mac must be a real handsome man?"

Hayword and Danny march down the fairway with their heads down.

"Nice drive," Harry says.

"Let's get this over with quick," Jack says. "This kid's an asshole."

Fifteen holes later, Jack drops a four-foot putt that ends the match, sending Hayword and Danny off after limp handshakes. Before walking away with his men, Dalva nods and smiles in the direction of Jack. Only Manley walks up to them, patting them on the back, saying, "That's it boys, that's how you do it."

Jack turns to leave.

"Where you going?" Harry asks.

"I want to check out the other matches," Jack replies.

"Sure," Harry says. "I'll head back to the lodge after I walk the rest of the course. We need to talk later."

"Right, later." Jack waves.

"Good, that's good," Manley says to Harry. "He's studying the competition."

"Yeah, I wish," Harry replies.

"What do you mean?"

"Forget it." Harry leaves Manley behind, continuing on down to the next hole, the golf bag on his shoulder and his notebook in his hand.

Harry finds the course beautiful on this August afternoon. It's an old one. Designed in the classic style. You need to be long, straight and fearless. Harry wonders if the designer could have ever imagined how big these old trees would get.

As they had played, Harry had seen the ghosts. They followed in a solemn procession and Harry had to concentrate to stay with the match. Now alone with his ghosts, he is also aware of some other presence. He ignores it and notes the distance to the traps and the slopes on the green.

He makes a note that the sixteenth hole is a long straight par four. The fairway slopes, from a crown in the middle of the fairway, down in both directions to the high rough on each side.

Seventeen is a long par four that travels up from the tee. There is a right turn at the crest in the fairway around a thick stand of tall pines. As he walks the seventeenth, he hears footsteps on the pine needles in the trees to his right.

Harry stands on the tee at eighteen. A magnificent hole, maybe the best he's ever seen. Harry makes a note of the carry required to avoid the sand traps on the right. Down in the fairway, Harry paces the distance to a severe dip, an eighty-yard gap that crosses the fairway, descending, then rising up to a green that appears perched on a sliver of a hill.

"Are they with you now?" The girl asks him.

"Yes. Of course," Harry answers without turning. "And you?"

"Yes, more than I ever remember," Lilly answers, walking up to the caddy.

"The ones I see are not the same ones you see," Harry says, turning to look into her beautiful dark eyes.

"I know that now. Why?"

"I don't know. All these years, to finally meet someone who understands and still not be able explain..."

"When did it start for you?"

"When I was a boy. I was very sick. You?"

"After my parents were murdered. Why do you think we see them?"

"I don't know," Harry says. "But I think he might be able to tell us." Harry looks up from the girl toward the green perched on the hill. Lilly follows his gaze. There, behind the green, the thin black man watches them. It is Waits.

On Wait's left, Lilly sees her Aunt Sylvia and on Wait's right, Harry sees his grandmother. The sight chills the two small people who stand together before the gap in the fairway. Harry puts his arm around Lilly and she reaches for his hand. They stare to the distant green as a man approaches Waits. It is Bleeris; he whispers to the old man and bows his head. Waits takes one more look down the fairway, turns, and disappears over a rise beyond the green.

"Besides Bleeris, who did you see with Waits just now?" Harry asks Lilly.

"My Aunt, and a woman I did not recognize" Lilly answers. "Did you see her?"

"Yes. The woman you saw was my grandmother. And I saw your aunt. It appears Waits can allow us to see each other's ghosts."

Lilly shudders and turns from the Harry.

"Are you all right," Harry asks.

"What does he want?"

"I'm not sure. But I'll find out. He won't hurt you. All those years... I knew there had to be someone who could understand. I won't let him hurt you. I promise you."

Harry and Lilly walk together through a path in the trees, down the dirt lane back to the lodges.

*   *   *

The mansion appears deserted. Charlie stands by a tree and examines the exterior of the building. It reminds him of the mausoleums at Graceland Cemetery, the places where they keep the ashes of the dead encased in marble.

So this is it, Charlie thinks, after all these years, after graduating college to tend bar, I've finally sunk to common burglar, no worse, I've become a private eye.

Charlie bangs on the large wooden doors and waits. After a time, he assures himself that everyone is occupied on the golf course. When he turns the latch the door clicks open with ease. Standing just inside the door he shouts, "Hello. Hey anybody home." His words echo through the dim cavern that is the entrance hall. "Huh," He says to himself. "Maybe I'll just have a quick look around."

Walking from room to room, he holds his right hand on the pistol that he has tucked into his waistband. He moves through the grand rooms of the house, the kitchen, the library, and the ballroom where they had met the night before.

There is nothing unusual to be seen. Still, Charlie has the sense that what he is seeing is more reproduction than real. It appears to be a model based on an old movie. A house designed and furnished to provide the traditional impression of great wealth.

Charlie finds a back stairway, the servant's stairs, and takes the winding narrow route up one floor. On the second floor, he finds showcase bedrooms and no sign that anyone actually lives there. He walks up another flight to the third floor. Again he finds every door open, every bedroom untouched, furnished, but uninhabited.

"What goes on here?" He whispers to himself.

Another set of stairs and he emerges on the fourth floor. There is a long hall with only one door at the far end. It is closed. Charlie approaches quietly, knocks, hears no reply, and turns the knob. The room is raw, a rough wood floor, two windows with dust on the sills and a three wood chairs at an old scratched table. On the table are a gold cup and an old arch-top guitar. He walks to table and places his hand on the guitar. It is real, his touch causes the strings to vibrate and emit a weak tone.

Charlie bends to examine the cup. He estimates its height at ten inches. Would make a good beer mug, he thinks. Etched in the gold are intricate designs, symbols of some foreign language, he assumes.

Charlie reaches for it, the cold metal now in his fingers, he feels the hair on his arms stand, a flash of white light, a searing pain in his head and everything goes black.

*　　　*　　　*

Martin Waring does not notice Kathryn slipping away with Jack, as his and Reverend Hollywell's teams move up the twelfth fairway.

"How's he doing?" Jack asks Kathryn.

"He's winning, of course." Kathryn replies. "You?"

"One down two to go. Do you want to take a walk?"

She moves with him and they follow a path through the trees, to a place where a stream runs in a shallow four-foot break. The sun, now well past noon, traces a mosaic of shadow and light. Jack moves the hair from Kathryn's face and observes a tremble of embarrassment. She is unsure, he thinks. She is no longer the confident girl he had met in Ames.

Kathryn knows that her face has again betrayed her. "I'm sorry for everything," She tells Jack.

"So am I," Jack replies. "If I had been stronger, everything would have been different."

"Jack you were a boy. I…"

"No. I let you leave. You are the only woman I have ever loved."

There is a rustle of leaves behind Kathryn. She turns, using the opportunity to brush the tear from her eye. "We found each other again," Kathryn says. "Can we just start here?"

"I am nothing more today than I was twenty-five years ago. I live on the prayer that is my golf swing. I work a two-bit detective agency to eat."

"You must have had something special to be invited here."

There is the color of dawn in Kathryn's eyes. Jack moves to her, first their faces brushing softly, the memory becoming the present, they kiss, no longer young, their future no longer a treasure to be found.

*   *   *

A car moves through the countryside heading east. A bald bookie drives in silence, while a beaten old man listens to the ancient conversations that constantly move through his head. Together since dawn, Jerry and Irv have withdrawn from each other again, traveling toward the unknown, toward the devil or a six-two-one trifecta box.

Irv glances at the bookie and shakes his head. "You wouldn't believe me if I told you," He says.

"What? Wouldn't believe what?"

"Fifty-five years ago I was a Marine," Irv says.

"You're right, I don't believe you." Jerry says, as he inspects the frail man beside him.

"It's true," Irv says snickering. "I was the only Jew in my company. If you woulda' told me back then that I would be here fifty-five years later, riding the road with some two-bit bookie from Chicago, I woulda' laughed. Back then, it was war. I was just hoping to make the year."

"I still don't believe you. What neighborhood you from?"

"Not Chicago. Baltimore. That's where I grew up."

"Baltimore?"

"Yeah, that's right. I've been all over the east, New York, Philly, Boston. When I was a young I worked them all."

"So how long you been in Chicago?"

"Fifty years. That's how long I been there. Can you imagine that?"

"Fifty years is longer than I've been alive."

"I was headed to California. This guy I knew told me, 'If you ever need a job go to Chicago. They always got work in Chicago.' So I stopped in Chicago and I never left."

"Work? What kind of work?"

"Whaaa,... what do you think? You heard me talk."

"You were a bartender?"

"Yeah, that's right, a bartender," Irv laughs. "What else? I worked almost every joint in the loop. I was a player, always looking for a game, golf, horses, cards. If I worked at night, I was hustling the courses in the morning, the track in the afternoon. If I worked days, I'd find the all night card game. Oh yeah. I knew'em all. I used to get my hair cut by the same guy used to cut Capone's hair. I lived in the same hotel as Jolson, and I served Jimmy Ray when he came into the bar."

"Jimmy Ray?"

"Jimmy Ray... Man he had a voice. I worked the Ambassador West. You know it? Not the Ambassador East, the West was across State, next to Hefner's old spread. I'd take Chicago over New York any day. Aneee-day."

"So how'd you end up at a broken down driving range?"

"Story of my life kid. Story of-my-life. I was good once. When I was young, I could bet my last hundred dollars on a ninety-one shot and watch it roll home. I had it then, I could do that. Take my last hundred, bet it and win. Won nine thousand on a bet like that in 1947. That's true. Back then most didn't make nine thousand a year. But now, I could never make that bet. I used to be good and now, I could never make that bet. That's how you end up in a broken down shack. It's the story of my life; I can't make that bet now. Still I did. I know you'd never take the last hundred you had in the world and bet it. I know that for a fact."

"You're probably right. Then again, I don't ever recall being down to my last hundred."

"You think you're a high roller. You think you know people? You think you're big time? I worked for a guy; think nothing of throwing five thousand on a straight exacta bet. Seen him cash a thirty-five thousand dollar ticket once up at Hawthorne. Last I heard he was headed to Argentina. Never been down to a hundred... huh, big shot two-bit bookie. Well that's the story of my life. But it ain't over yet. I tell you what, I have no fear, if I see a ninety-to-one that can win, I'm gonna' bet my last dollar on it. You'll see."

Jerry turns to the old man. Irv's face is grizzled, his gray hair brushed back, there are gaps in his smile where his teeth once were, but his eyes, the eyes that stare back, are clear, ice blue, sharp; the eyes of a young man, a man who can still size up the odds for every risk.

"Tell me some stories of old Chicago," Jerry says to Irv.

"You want to hear some stories? I'll tell you some stories..."

*   *   *

As he lay in bed, Harry feels the breeze through an open window.

"Shantih, Shantih, Shantih," The voice says. "The peace that passes without understanding. I remember you reading that to me when we were playing that tournament in India. You remember that Harry?"

Harry sits bolt up in his bed and scans the room. There is nothing except the Adirondack knick-knacks and the sparse furnishings. Must have been half asleep, he thinks, the long day, maybe the wind in the trees just outside my windows. Harry lies back and stares up at the ceiling.

"You remember those matches in India?" The English accent travels to him through time, it is familiar to Harry. "I beat the young Oriental, what was his name, Kuzo... That's it Kuzo. Tough little bastard, you remember Harry? You told me to hit the driver from the fairway when we were two down on fifteen."

Harry is afraid to move. Ghosts have visited him before, even Glyn, but he had not heard one speak since he was a boy gripped by fever.

"You remember when we first met?" Glyn Parker asks Harry. "You remember that no good caddy I had, the bumbling fat kid, Taylor? Would you believe he's here with me now? My goddamn caddy for eternity. And you know what? He's still good for nothing. He got himself hit by a bus while eating an ice cream cone when he was 29. The fool just walked in front of a bus. Wasn't paying attention."

"Glyn?" Harry says, still staring at the ceiling. "How?"

"Well you've seen me before Harry. I know you have. I'm over here in the chair."

Harry turns to the chair across the room and there he is, curly hair bursting forth, the rail thin body, sitting cross-legged.

Parker smiles and says, "Harry, all those years we were together, you never told me about the ghosts."

"I didn't think you'd understand. But how, how can I hear you? I…"

"That's a story that I would like to delay for the moment, old friend. For now, let's just leave it. You'll know everything soon enough. Just know I can speak because I've been sent to help you."

"Help me? With what?"

"With the competition you've entered."

"You mean Jack and me."

"No. I mean you. Harry, you have people who are counting on you. You know them. They thought me best suited for this job, you know, because of our former working relationship and all. I guess it's my turn to carry your bags."

"Glyn. What are you talking about?"

"I'm talking about your match against the girl. The match to inherit what Waits has."

"The girl? What Waits has? Do you mean the money? That's the reason for the golf…"

"No. Money, possessions, they are nothing. What Waits has is the key, the connection between our worlds. He is the one mind. He has brought you all here to find the one who will become the next bridge, the next great creator, the next great destroyer. Instead he has found two. The young girl and you. He watches you both and he has allowed you to hear me."

"I don't understand."

"There are infinite worlds my old friend. They are populated with those who have come before, each world different, each world unique to that person and yet they touch everyone, moving in harmony and with unseen influence. One who lives, possesses what it takes to control these worlds, a maestro. You Harry, all these years you have glimpsed the other worlds. And now, Waits has allowed you to hear us and we can bring you so much; knowledge of the past and visions of the future, we will do what you ask. In return, you will allow us to exist, to have power, in a way, to live again. You have to understand that Waits has the key. He knows now it is only you and the girl. The gift will be given to the one who survives the matches. To the one who can guide their team, the one who will use this connection to win."

"You're saying this whole thing is about me and Lilly?"

"In a way. Waits was advised to bring a group together in this manner; that from this group he would find his successor. But I'm afraid he has other reasons too. The power has different affects on those who wield it. In fact, just hours ago we've had some new arrivals."

"What do you mean?"

"You will know soon enough. It's not what you should concern yourself with. First you must win; a major tournament indeed. Just like the old days, we're a team again. You remember Harry. Now you will play and I will advise. You need some rest. Tomorrow you play the banker, Stellenburg, and I will walk with you."

"Rest? How? I have…"

"Please Harry. You are our champion. We need you to win this contest. If you do not, we, your friends, your family, we will all be cast out of memory, forever. Forgotten. Washed away on the sea of time"

"We? Old friends, family? Who do you mean? My grandmother and my dad?"

"Yes, more… Rest now Harry, we will talk again, soon." Glyn smiles and nods before he leaves Harry alone.

Harry stares at the chair for minutes. His weariness overcomes him and he closes his eyes. In his dream, he stands before his old house on Webster. The rats stand in a silent vigil. One turns toward him, the one with the face of a man, a face that now is familiar.

*   *   *

Out over the dense northern forest, a cloud passes under a large yellow moon. It holds for an instant and the forest below darkens, the owl's eyes widen and the rabbit does not sense the hunter descending with claws spread.

As the cloud passes, the moon lights the figure of a girl standing in the window of the lodge. Lilly looks out upon the ancient woods considering the words of the dark man who has just departed.

"I am Javier," The dark man had said. "I have been sent by your Aunt to help you. But, I'm sure you remember. I have been with you since we met once in Palm Beach, at the café on Oleander Avenue... a block from the ocean, five years ago. I was twenty-five and I watched you from my table. I held the door for you as you walked out. You smiled. I wanted to speak with you, but I thought I would wait, wait for the next time when I could sit with you and... There would never be a next time. I died by a friend's hand and now I live only in your heart. I am here to help."

Lilly remembers the café and the only time she had seen Javier alive. She can still recall the pull at her heart, how their eyes locked and everything had stopped.

Javier told Lilly of Wait's contest, of how those that have gone before have chosen Javier to guide her; of how she must compete with Harry Dimmig for the survival of those she has known.

Lilly stands now, looking out to the forest and the moon. Her life seems to have been a dream. The dark man, who had first passed into and out of her life in a café long ago, has spoken to her at last.

16

The morning sun brings Charlie back. It warms his face through a crack in the window shade. Charlie's neck is sore. He tries to stand, but his wrists and ankles are tied to the chair. Across the room, the fat old black man sleeps in a chair next to the table with the gold cup and guitar, his head, gray dreadlocks askew, tilts to the right.

Charlie recalls the last moments before the blackness, I touched the cup and then everything went black. The fat bastard must of come from behind and smashed me over the head.

"Hey," Charlie shouts. "Hey asshole." The fat man shifts his position, opening one eye. "Untie these fucking ropes."

"Let you go now?" The fat man replies with an island intonation. "No, I can't help you there. Not 'til I be told. You just got to be where you shouldn't."

"I was just looking around. It's not like I found anything."

"No you did and Waits wants you here. I was expecting that he would want you to die, but he says you live as long as the others you came wit'. The drug dealer team wins, you live. That is what he said."

"What are you talking about? Who are you?"

"Me? I be Looby Mills."

"Loo… ah shit… My name is Charlie Vaccaro. Just untie me and I won't bother you again."

"I'm sorry my friend. You live as long as the drug dealer wins. Someone will bring you food and I'll stay here wit' you. I'll even play you a few tunes on this old box, to keep you company."

"Looby, I don't know what this is about, but you and your boss don't want trouble from me."

"Now, now Mr. Charlie. No need to be tre'tening ole' Looby. No need at all. Here, I'll play you a song. It is good luck to play a song first 'ting in the morn'."

Looby cradles the cracked arch-top and plucks a few notes before strumming a chord. The sunlight reflects off the gold cup onto the fat man's face. There is nothing Charlie can do now except listen.

Looby sings, *"Now, I pray you, by that virtue which leads you to the stair, think of me in my time of pain and be wit' me in the refining fire."*

*   *   *

Jerry had thought about letting Irv drive last night; for just a weary second he almost gave in. Instead, he pulled into an abandoned gas station and slept.

Now, the dust floating above the dashboard dances in the dawn light and Jerry shifts in his seat, attempting to put it all back in order. It must be Saturday morning, he thinks, when I pulled over last night, I still had about few hours to go… I can't remember the last time I ate something, but I need food now, and then I have to get this show back on the road.

"Hey old timer, wake up," Jerry says to the man sleeping next to him. "We've got to eat and then hit the road."

"Eat? Waste of time," Irv replies; his eyes still closed. "Damn waste of time."

"Yeah well, why don't you start walking and I'll catch up to you after I get breakfast."

"In the war, I didn't eat for a week on some god forsaken island. Blue sky was like a nightmare, sick as a dog, fighting with everything inside me just to live the day. Eat? I'll tell you about eat. It was like God was behind some curtain, laughing, waiting to say it's all some joke."

"Yeah, well this may be a joke, but it isn't war. We can afford to spare the time to eat."

"Whatever you say Captain," Irv says, forcing himself up in his seat. "You're the genius here. I just think we need to get to our boys."

"Our boys are living in the lap of luxury, about to spend the day on the golf course. They don't need us."

173

"Can't be sure bookie. Anyway, feed yourself. Not that you couldn't go without a few meals."

Driving the local roads, off the highway now, they make their way north to Saratoga. In a small town, Gloversville, Jerry parks in front of a coffee shop with "Lucy's" painted in red above the door.

As Irv sips on coffee and waits for his eggs; his eyes scan the room, the hick town diner, he thinks. He's seen thousands like it in his near eighty years. He turns his attention back to his partner, Cahoon, the bookie. Irv does not want to be hard on the boy. Like this greasy spoon, Irv has seen Jerry's kind many times over the years. He's the kid who never left his neighborhood. The kid that gained status through time served; the small fish in the even smaller pond. Irv knows that during his own time there were days when he envied a life such as Jerry's.

"So how long you been married to Maggie?" Irv asks.

"Almost twenty years," Jerry replies.

"Good woman. I give her a hard time, but she sees through it. I know she'd never admit it, but she likes having me around."

"Yeah, if you say so."

"Yeah, huh… for some reason she saw something in you."

"Tell you the truth Irv, I'm not sure what she sees in me either. Never had a job in my life, she can't tell anyone what I do. Sometimes, I stay up half the night just thinking about how that must make her feel." Jerry pushes aside the potatoes that mix with the yellow yoke of the eggs.

"Yeah, plus you lost your hair."

"Right, I'm not handsome either."

"Not like her boss Jack."

"Right, not like Jack."

"How'd you get so lucky to end up with her?"

"That was it, luck. I was a young punk and she was this fiery red headed girl. Pretty. Maggie Grace. That was her name. I took her to a Cub's game on our first date. We sat in the bleachers and I was trying to act like a big shot, telling her who had big money riding on the game. I was working for Johnny Malto back then. Just a runner, but I was acting all pumped up. I remember the day like it was yesterday. The sun was almost directly overhead and Wrigley looked like a painting against the clear blue sky. We had a beer and some peanuts. I was telling her about all the people I knew and she sat there listening, smiling green eyes and red hair. I was struck by how beautiful she was and how I was nothing compared to her. How I was just a loser from the neighborhood, the middle boy of the seven Cahoon brothers', nothing special, just a runner for a bookie. I looked away from her embarrassed and she touched my face. When I turned back to her, I realized that she didn't care about any of that. That for her, it was something more, something that I shouldn't even try to understand. All I knew was, I was lucky to be with her. It's still the only thing I really know."

"She got a sense about her all right."

"Keeps me up at night thinking she deserves more."

"Yeah, she's got a sense about her and now she's got a feeling about Harry and Jack."

"That's why we're on this little drive."

"I'd take it serious," Irv says, nodding his head.

"A wild goose chase, that's what I think."

"I've seen a lot of strange things in my life. This whole deal is right up there," Irv replies. "I was there at the range the day that sweating shyster offered the boys the deal. A real slick one, he was, offering them millions to play in this game. Maggie's got a bad feeling, I'd take it serious."

"I have to admit that this is a strange case, but…"

"A deal like this always has a cost."

"Still they've got Vaccaro and they know how to handle themselves."

"They can't protect themselves if they don't see it coming. Maggie thinks Waits is a madman. That's good enough for me."

"You and your two hand grenades that is."

"Exactly bookie. Exactly."

*   *   *

Today, the grease odor rises in waves from the restaurant to Maggie's second floor window. The Greek has been cooking all night. It is Saturday morning and Maggie is alone. The ancient dust of Chicago's past lays thick on the office and its furniture, reminding her that everyone she loves is gone.

Jerry, Jack and Harry, old Irv, and Carla's brother Charlie are all in the east now. Only a week ago they filled up her life with stupidity, dumb smiles and lame jokes. Now, she has only the smell of the Greek cooking and the dust. Maggie shutters at the thought that this is the way it may be from now on.

The copy of the Tribune that sits in front of her gives her no comfort. The Cubs have dropped another game and another season slips into oblivion. Everything she loves is in jeopardy, as the mad man waits for them all.

Maggie turns to an old photo hanging on the wall behind Jack's desk. It is a picture of Jack, a young man, accepting a trophy from some gray haired tournament official.

Jack Connoll, she thinks, the golden boy of the neighborhood, every schoolgirl's dream, now a failed hero, only a shadow remains, he stumbles from one failed relationship to another, from barmaids, to shop girls, from gangster's girlfriends, to housewives from places like Madison and Indianapolis. They all call the office for a while and Maggie helps his evasion, as Jack pretends not to care.

There were a few that touched him enough to stay around for a time. There was that artist, Gillian Resson. Gillian was with Jack for more than a year. She was beautiful, a free spirit with long blond hair. When she walked into the office, the old space would lighten and it was obvious to everyone that Gillian loved Jack.

"Maggie," Jack told her one morning. "If Gillian calls, tell her I'm tied up on a big case. I'll be out of town, if you know what I mean."

"But Jack, you can't just cut her off like that," Maggie had pleaded.

"I know, I know, just do it for me. Don't get involved."

Gillian's phone calls eventually stopped and Jack began bringing around a tall bank teller with bleached hair. The bank teller had the annoying habit of biting her top lip and tapping her fingernails on any hard surface, if she wasn't the center of everyone's attention.

This was Jack's life. Each time he moved on there was a less of him, less gold, less dash and less to love.

Maggie had seen him fade. She knew he was hiding, never over the old embarrassment of his failed attempt to make it out of the neighborhood. Maggie knew that although he had pulled himself up, built a business, his mind and his heart were still frozen in the moment of his defeat. Maggie would sometimes catch Jack sitting at his desk, the strain of the years hanging around his mouth, the light in his brown eyes dimming to a gray shadow. He was a tortured man compounding the mistakes of his life with unfailing memory.

Maggie listens as the "L" train passes a few blocks away. The sky beyond the grime-covered window is pure blue, cloudless, stark, offering no hope of protection from the hot sun and no protection for those she loves.

As the train jangle fades to the north, Maggie's thoughts turn to Jerry. What have I sent him into, she thinks, with his thin shield of armor wrought in the old neighborhood? Jerry's never dealt with this type before. She wipes the tear from her eye, stands, she wants to run, but there is nowhere to go.

Staring out through the window, Maggie can feel the heat building. Today will be hot, she thinks, all Jerry has are those dark suits, he believes they bring him respect, but the heat... Maggie feels her legs wobble and she falls back into the chair.

"Oh please God," She begs in the empty office. "Don't let them hurt Jerry. Please." Her attention is drawn to the neat desk, in the corner opposite from Jack's. There is a photograph above it on the wall of the tall curly haired Englishman and his caddy.

My only hope is Harry, Maggie thinks, the little man is special. He will bring them home. "Please Harry, bring them home."

*   *   *

North of Saratoga, Saturday has dawned perfect, a clear August morning, but Harry and Jack pace the dim hallway outside of Charlie's bedroom.

"You were the last one who saw him?" Jack asks.

"Yeah," Harry replies. "He was headed up to the mansion to take a look around. That's all I know."

"What should we do?" Jack asks.

"You get to the practice tee. I'll see what I can find out and …" Footsteps approaching in the hall cut short Harry's directions.

"What do you mean, see what you can find out?" Manley says. He is again wearing his resort wear.

Jack and Harry pause to take in Manley's look; pleated shorts down to the knees of his fat white legs, white socks, brown deck shoes and an awful Hawaiian shirt. "Ah… We seem to be missing our golf coach, chief," Jack replies.

"What?" Manley says. "Well, he's probably wandered off to a shady spot with a bottle of bourbon. Don't let this distract you. We win today we're in the finals."

"Screw that Kevin," Harry says. "There's something strange going on around here. We need to find him."

"Strange? What does that mean? What do you know that I don't?" Manley says.

"I mean, you know, this whole thing," Harry replies. "The tournament, that old skeleton, Waits, giving it all away, it's, just strange."

"You better not be holding back on me Dimmig," Manley says.

"I'm not. I'm just worried about Charlie."

"You two think about the match. I'll find your dumb ass friend." Manley says, waddling away. "You guys are more trouble than you're worth. You better not be holding back on me Dimmig…"

Jack waits for Manley to turn the corner before he moves in close to Harry. "You know something you're not telling me. I know you Harry and you are holding back."

Harry hesitates and shakes his head.

"What?" Jack asks. "Let me have it."

"The ghosts, they're back and now they're talking to me," Harry whispers.

"What? Please Harry, not now. Not with everything going on."

"I know, I know, but I spoke with Glyn last night. He said…"

"Glyn Parker? Jesus Christ. Harry you've got to keep it together."

"Listen to me Jack. He said this whole thing, the reason we're here, is because I can see the ghosts. He said the girl, the one with K.C., the girl named Lilly, she's involved. I spoke with her Jack. She told me she could see them too."

"Harry, it's this place. You've got to relax. Maybe we can find some whiskey, maybe a shot will help."

"Trust me Jack, there is something going on here that has nothing to do with golf. It has to do with the dead. I'm worried about Charlie."

"All right Harry, all right. If by some chance, you did talk with Glyn, what did he tell you?"

"He said that the winner of the this tournament will win something more than money. He said that the winner, either Lilly or me…"

"Lilly or you?"

"Yeah, one of us would inherit some connection to world of the dead, some power…"

"What?"

"One will inherit what Waits has, one of us will speak to those who have passed through their lives, we would know the future, be the creator and the destroyer…"

"Damn it Harry, you've finally lost it. I can't have this now. We have to play in a couple of hours."

"Jack, he'll be walking with us today."

"Who?"

"Glyn will be with us."

"Oh that's fucking great." Jack cannot look at Harry. "I don't want to hear anymore of this. I've got to go warm-up. Meet me at the range." Jack moves away quickly, almost running down the hall.

"It's no use," Glyn says standing behind Harry. "Only if you win, will he understand."

"You heard the whole thing?" Harry asks.

"Yes. Now lets go, we have work to do and there's something I would like you to see."

Glyn and Harry leave the lodge and walk down the path toward the golf course road. Before they reach the path, Glyn stops Harry at a drive leading to another lodging house.

"Why are we stopping here?" Harry asks.

"This is what I want to show you."

"This place?" Harry asks. "It's where the guys we played yesterday were staying. Berinczek and his golfer, the kid Hayword and his caddy Danny. They moved out yesterday right after the match. Just like Bleeris ordered."

"They left," Glyn replies. "That's true. But they are still here."

"What?"

Glyn motions to the cabin's window.

Harry walks up the four wood steps onto the porch. The window illuminates the lodge's great room. Inside, Harry sees them all, Berinczek, Hayword, and the caddy. They return his gaze in the silent way Harry knows all to well. They are dead. They are ghosts now.

"But how..." Harry starts to say.

"This is the fate of all the losers in this tournament. It will be the fate of you and your friends if Lilly prevails."

*   *   *

"It's come down to us," Sylvia Rivera says. "Two old women."

"We've seen it coming for a long time. Hell, I've been dead nearly thirty-five years," Vera Casick replies. "I've seen thousands pass into oblivion waiting for that crazy Waits to finally hold this party. So I guess we should consider ourselves lucky."

"Lucky and smart," Sylvia replies. "I just wish Lilly was a few years older, that she had more time with Kathryn to harden her up a bit."

"You're right Sylvia, your girl is too young, just have your boy, what's his name? Javier? Just have Javier pull her back. Harry's much better for the job. Stable and smart. I'll see what I can do for you and yours. I'm sure I can connect you and a few of your people with Harry. We'll take care of the girl when she gets here too."

"Oh Sylvia, please don't insult me. Your boy Harry has always been a fool, weak and sick. Even you would have to admit that. Never even had a girlfriend, on top of that he's old. How long will he hold power, twenty, twenty-five years? The girl will have a nice long run. Back Harry off and we'll make the same deal for you and yours."

"Oh Sylvia, listen to us," Vera says, sipping from her cup. "The fact is the match is on. Your girl is young and my boy is old. The hard choices they face, I'm not sure either of them is up to it."

"Why did you send Glyn Parker, the golfer, instead of the boy's father?"

"Why would I send my daughter's no good husband? Treated that boy like crap all those years. I saw it all before he got here, the racetrack and the other women. No, I chose the English boy. He always treated my Harry good. Harry owes him too. As long as we're on the subject, why did you send the dark haired boy, Javier, rather than one of the girl's parents?"

"Well you've seen him. I know you've been dead for fifty years, but..."

"Thirty-five years, Sylvia."

"Thirty-five, fifty what's the difference, you seen the boy. Lilly melts for him."

"He's just a spirit. We were to send advisors not lovers."

"Ah Vera, you see, you have forgotten. The heart knows what the eyes cannot see. She will want him for eternity."

"The girl, puh, she will not make the hard choice," Vera replies.

"We shall see," Sylvia says. "It's down to you and me now. The Jamaican's time is almost done. One of us we'll be sitting pretty that's for sure. Shame too. Under any other circumstances we would be friends."

"Friends? I got enough friends."

"That so," Sylvia says.

"Thousands now stand with me, more come everyday," Vera says. "All who my boy Harry has touched are now lining up. He's been all over the world you know. What about you?"

"Oh they come, not thousands but a sizeable number. Some of the best and brightest encountered my girl while she was in the employ of Kathryn Torrance. We don't need thousands; once she wins, more will arrive. It's time for a queen, don't you think?"

"A queen, puh... Oblivion waits for you Sylvia. I'll see you gone, your past, your future, your name forever eliminated. When Harry defeats your dear Lilly, it will be the final act for you and yours. You can bet on that."

"A queen Vera. A queen and it will be Harry who falls. You and your army of fools will be the ones cast out forever."

"Lucky and smart," Vera says laughing. "It is down to us now and we shall see."

*   *   *

When Jack swings a nine iron, the balls fly high into the blue morning sky before floating down to the target. The sight of a ball in flight has always been the diversion he required. This morning, he attempts to block the creeping fear. Charlie Vaccaro is missing; Harry is now on speaking terms with his ghosts, and K.C., the beautiful reminder of his wasted life, stands yards away on the practice tee.

The backswing, the pause, the turn back through, the wrists releasing and the ball moves away in the magnificent arc. Jack knows how to swing a golf club. He knows one other fact; he will always be one step behind the world, his life lived obscured from what other's can see clearly.

Harry speaks to ghosts now, Charlie is missing and K.C. has returned, the backswing the pause and the release.

The game is the important thing, Jack thinks. If I had known this back in Phoenix, I would have had a life. The game is all there is. I have to let everything else go. The game is the one thing where I'm a step ahead.

The match today is against the team of the banker, Leopold Stellenburg's man. Jack glances across the practice tee to where Peter Newberry warms up. Newberry is a tall square headed man; his blond hair is trimmed in perfect lines that frame his square face, every edge sharp and neat.

Newberry's swings are also perfect. The compact turn, the flawless symmetry and timing, tell Jack that Newberry learned the game as a child, from a country club pro. Jack imagines the square headed boy's endless summer days, spent hitting shot after shot on some manicured driving range, under the eye of some stocky club pro with the same perfect haircut.

I've seen hundreds of guys like Newberry, Jack thinks. They're robots, don't talk, don't laugh at the jokes, and now I got to walk the course with this zombie. Charlie is missing, Harry's talking to ghosts, K.C. is here and that country club asshole took lessons from a perfect haired pro.

With these thoughts threatening to shake his faith, Jack pulls out his driver and smashes tee shots into the woods, three hundred yards away.

*   *   *

"No entrance. Those are my orders," The funny-haired guard at the gate says to Jerry and Irv. "Leave here immediately. No visitors."

"Listen, we just need to get a message to our friends," Jerry says.

"No messages. That's final."

"Hey asshole," Irv says, stepping up to the man who stands a foot taller than him. "We're not asking you, we're telling you."

"That so old man? Well then, tell it to my friend here," The Rastafari guard lifts his automatic rifle and points it square between Lavinsky's eyes.

"Come on, there's no need for any of this," Jerry says, using his right arm to move Irv away from the muzzle. A black truck moves toward them from inside the gate. Jerry can make out three large figures in the approaching vehicle. "All right Irv. I guess we're gonna have to wait."

"Wait? I'm not afraid of these ghouls. I got a couple things for them in the car that'll even this up. Just..."

"No, it's time we leave. If we can't talk with them, we just can't," Jerry says.

The guards watch as the two men make their way back to the car. Their guns remain aimed until the car disappears over a rise in the road.

"Listen bookie," Irv says, "If you don't have the stomach for this, let me out of this car. I'll go in alone."

"You'll go in alone. Oh that's great. You'll be dead before you get within a hundred yards of that gate."

"Maybe, but I'll take a few, leave you a nice hole."

"Listen. We got to think about this. One thing we found for sure is something isn't right in there. We just got to find another way in. There was a town about ten miles back. Let's head there and see what we can see."

"I say we just blow a hole in the fucking wall."

"No. We have to be smart about this. We'll head to the town."

"Whatever you say, bookie."

"Irv, we have to take this slow, but you might be right about one thing, we may need those hand grenades."

*   *   *

"Mr. Manley, how are you this morning?" Alec Bleeris says, standing in the open doorway of the mansion and looking down on the sweating attorney. "That's quite a shirt you've got there. Hawaiian isn't it?"

"I think," Manley replies. "I bought it from one of those catalogues."

"I see. Well, what can I do for you?"

"We seem to have lost our golf coach. You know, Mr. Vaccaro, the big guy."

"Certainly, Mr. Vaccaro."

"Have you seen him?"

"Your Mr. Connoll is playing very well."

"Yes, what about Vaccaro?"

"Mr. Dalva must be very happy with his progress."

"Of course. Listen Bleeris, I don't have time for this, do you, or don't you, know the whereabouts of Vaccaro."

"I may Mr. Manley. Please come in."

Bleeris, the tall man in his gray pin stripes, silk shirt and auburn tie, looks down on the thick attorney who walks by him into entrance hall. Bleeris turns to a guard just inside the adjoining room.

"Raymond," Bleeris says to the guard. "Please take Mr. Manley to Mr. Vaccaro."

"He's here?" Manley says.

"Follow me Mr. Manley," Raymond says.

Manley follows the towering guard up four flights of stairs. "What the hell? You got him locked up?" Manley says, part joking. Raymond does not answer. Perspiration begins to drip down Manley's back. "Now hold it a minute," Manley says. "What's going on here?"

Raymond does not answer. On the fourth floor, he motions for Manley to move ahead of him. Manley hears a guitar, a man singing and he hesitates. Raymond grabs the attorney's arm, his fingers wrapping completely around Manley's bicep.

"Now hold it right here. Let me go…"

Raymond drags Manley down to the floor's single door, pushing it open. "Got another one for ya' Looby," Raymond says.

"I see 'dat," Looby replies. "Put him in the chair next to the big one."

"Vaccaro?" Manley says, "What's going on here? I don't understand."

"Very simple Kevin," Charlie replies. "We're being held hostage by a bunch of asshole Jamaican's. Even worse, we have to listen to this fat one sing."

"So you're Vaccaro," Raymond says, as he shackles Manley to the chair. "I had the pleasure of meeting your sister."

Charlie's face reddens, a vein appearing above his left eye. "So you're the asshole I've been looking for," Charlie answers.

"I wasn't aware you've been interested in finding me?" Raymond replies.

"What is going on here?" Manley says.

"Yeah, I've been looking for you. I plan on ripping your heart out."

"That so," Raymond says, crashing a fist down on Charlie's face, sending blood spattering on Manley's shirt.

Charlie's head hangs to the side and Manley's mouth hangs open.

"He deserved it," Looby says. "Done nothing all morning, but criticize my singing."

"Yeah, I've heard your singing," Raymond replies. "I did him a favor."

*   *   *

Harry and Jack watch as Martin Waring places his ball on the tee. Waring's opponent, Jolly Rolly's player, has already pushed one left into the trees. The porn king does not seem happy.

"Not gonna be anything close to how pissed he's gonna be if his boy loses the match," Harry whispers to Jack.

"Yeah," Jack replies. "This close to the prize, it would be tough to lose."

Harry considers telling Jack about what Glyn had shown him, the reward of death to the loser. He decides the pressure is already bad enough for Connoll and holds that news for later.

"Smart move," Glyn says standing to Harry's right. "Letting him think this is just for money."

Harry nods his head in response. The crack of Waring's club on his ball echoes across the golf course. The ball starts down the right side toward the out-of-bounds markers. For an instant, it appears certain to be a stroke and distance penalty for Waring, and then the ball catches a thin, leafless, almost invisible, high limb of an old oak and ricochets back into the fairway.

"Fuck," Jolly Rolly screams. "How does that happen?"

"Either the fix is in or it was divine intervention," Jack whispers to Harry.

"What's the difference?" Glyn asks Harry.

"Yeah, good break," Harry says. "Let's just hope we get a few today."

As the first group moves from the tee down to the fairway, Harry watches K.C. glancing to Jack. Next to her, head down, walks the girl, Lilly Rivera. Harry nods to her, but she turns quickly away.

"Gentlemen," Bleeris says to the waiting group. "Allow me to introduce you. Mr. Juan Dalva, please meet your competitor, Mr. Leopold Stellenburg. Golfing for Mr. Stellenburg is Peter Newberry of California. For Mr. Dalva, Jack Connoll of Chicago."

As the golfers go through the ritual handshakes, Harry notices Glyn standing next to Newberry.

"Remember him Harry?" Glyn says to Harry.

Harry shakes his head indicating he does not.

"He was just a kid, we played with him in a practice round at that tournament in Singapore. He's packed a few on since."

Harry searches his memory, but does not recall the golfer.

"I watched him play yesterday, against the dictator Bandoma's guy," Glyn says. "He's good, but the man he played was weak. He was only challenged on two holes; both times he only came up with a half. If Connoll pressures him, he'll crack. Don't let your boy give him a break today."

"We've got the tee Harry," Jack says.

"Don't let him off the hook today Jack," Harry says. "Keep the pressure on him and he'll crack."

"That right? You've seen him play before?"

"Parker and I played him once in Singapore. A good stroke player, but he'll crack under head to head pressure."

"You're good Harry, you're good," Jack says, just before sending a drive three hundred and forty yards down the fairway.

"Nice shot," Glyn says. "That's the old Jack I remember from Phoenix."

Newberry walks tentatively around the tee box. After going through a pre-shot routine, which consists of thirty seconds of nervous twitching, he shouts, "No," as the ball dead hooks left into the trees. He walks off the tee with his head down, his boss, the banker Stellenburg, follows with an expression of disgust.

*   *   *

Chet's Gas Station also sells bait.

"You ever been fishing," Irv says to Jerry, as the bookie fills the gas tank.

"No. But I bet you have," Jerry replies.

"Once I caught a fish with my bare hands," Irv answers. "It was on an island beach in the South Pacific. We were starving."

"Your bare hands?"

"Well, yeah, kind of, a missile had just exploded a little ways up and I think the fish was kind of dazed."

"So you're telling me you reached in and picked it up."

"Still counts. Anyway, it got me to thinking that we should inquire inside about doing a little fishing around here."

"You might have something there, let's do," Jerry replies.

Jerry is wearing the same crumpled black suit he wore when he left Maggie in Chicago. Irv has not removed his wrinkled blue raincoat. Together they stand, mouths agape, surveying the jumbled interior of Chet's Gas Station.

"Reminds me of the back room Bunny Spula maintains behind the newsstand at Lawrence and Broadway."

"Bunny the fence?" Irv says.

"Yeah, you can get anything you want in that back room. The problem is finding it."

"Yeah, good old Bunny. I knew him before he took over for Pittsburgh Mike," Irv says.

"Hey! Anyone home," Jerry shouts.

"Back here, behind the tank," Is the reply. "Just leave the money for the gas on the counter."

"We're interesting in doing some fishing," Irv answers.

"Fishing?" A green and white cap: "Chet's Live Bait," written in red script across the front, appears from behind the black bait tank. "You boys don't look like no fishermen."

"We just drove out. Haven't had a chance to change into our gear yet," Jerry says.

"That so," The broad faced man says. "Well whatta'ya looking to catch then."

"Fish, damn it," Irv answers. "We told you that."

"Right," The man says. "So what can I do for you?"

"Are you Chet?" Irv asks.

"The one and only."

"Well Chet," Irv says. "Me and my bald friend here are looking to get back to our old favorite fishing spot."

"Aren't we all," Chet says. "So what's your problem?"

"Seems they built a fence around it," Jerry says.

"Why would they go and do that?" Chet says.

"Don't know Chet, but we were hoping you knew a way around the fence."

"This fence. It wouldn't be up there with them damn Jamakes, would it?"

"I believe it would Chet," Jerry says.

"Don't recall any fishing holes up there," Chet says.

"Trust us, they got a lot of fish up there," Irv answers.

"In fact, we'll need a whole lot of bait. We'll even pay you in advance," Jerry says. "How's fifty dollars."

"Well if this hole's as good as you say, you'll need more bait than that," Chet replies. "Maybe a hundred dollars worth."

Jerry pulls a roll from his pocket and peels off two fifties, handing them to Chet. "Here. Now about getting around that fence."

"So happens," Chet starts. "A mile past the gate, where them wild haired Jamake watchmen are, is an old service drive. Leads to a maintenance shed. Used to be maids and butlers living down there along with the horse stables. I used to make deliveries there in the old days, when Finch owned it. I was sweet on one of the servant girls. Now it so happens, that I was up that way not long ago, you know, to see what them Jamake's had going on. Found the gate at the end of the service drive unguarded, so I tried the lock and it just happened to come off..."

"Just happened to, huh..." Jerry says.

"Yeah, anyway you follow that old road it might bring you in around back. Might find your fish there."

"Thanks old timer," Irv says.

"What about your bait," Chet says, laughing. "How's about some hooks or line?"

"Don't need them," Jerry says, "My boy Irv catches fish with his bare hands."

*   *   *

Juan Dalva follows his golfer and caddy. He has no concern that the scheming attorney, Manley, has not shown up for today's match. He's too close to the billions. They are within his grasp. As he walks through the fresh summer morning, watching the white balls fly above the treetops, he thinks how his hands that have been dirty for so long, will now be forever clean. His time on the battlefront is almost over.

This boy Connoll's all right, Dalva thinks. The way this match is going it should be over on fourteen. The Austrian banker has met his match. He should have known you could not beat Juan Dalva.

Connoll lashes a low three iron to within fifteen feet of the pin on thirteen. Newberry, three down in the match has gone completely white, a walking ghost. His employer, Stellenburg, can barely watch.

As the match progressed, Dalva has noticed the amount of Rastafari in attendance has also increased. A strange thing, Dalva thinks, still no stranger than this whole affair. The way Connoll is playing it will all be mine. Maybe I'll throw the Chicago boy and his caddy an extra half a mill for making it look so easy."

The putt drops for Connoll on thirteen and he is now four up with five to go.

Along with the increased dreadlocked security contingent, Dalva has also been watching the strange behavior of the caddy who is carrying Connoll's bag. Dalva could swear that he has seen him talking to himself, conversing with the air. Once he heard Dimmig say, "What makes you think the breeze is coming from the left," before shaking his head and informing Connoll of this fact.

Fourteen is a short par four, just three hundred and fifty-two yards. From the tee it drops into a valley. The players both hit five irons down into the fairway. From the middle of the fairway the players look up to a green a hundred and fifty yards away and forty feet above them. They have only the top of the flag to indicate their target.

Dalva watches Harry Dimmig whispering to the air and then turning to Connoll saying, "The pin is right center, twenty on, ten from the back, don't trust the breeze you feel down here, the wind turns in the trees up there and it will knock anything down two clubs. Hit your six."

"The Six?" Connoll replies. "Anything past the pin leaves a slick putt. If I jack it over, I'm dead."

"You won't hit the six over. Take your normal swing, just trust me Jack."

Juan Dalva does not know a lot about golf, but he does know that Jack can hit a six iron well beyond a hundred and fifty yards.

Jack takes the six-iron from Harry. He sights his target and swings. The ball arcs skyward, appearing as an arrow that will surely fly well beyond its target. The ball is now a white spot against blue. It is caught there for all who watch, hanging, a satellite fixed in gravity, before it falls straight down to a green, which is hidden from view of all who stand in the fairway.

Newberry watches this and, after an indecipherable discussion with his caddy, takes a seven iron. His ball barely reaches the sand trap that fronts the green.

Dalva hears Stellenburg murmur, "Shit," under his breath.

When Dalva approaches the green, he passes Newberry's ball, buried in the trap. Jack's ball is four feet from the hole, still in its pitch mark, as if it had dropped down on a line from the sky. I've got to remember to give that caddy, Dimmig, something extra, Dalva thinks. Maybe I'll even ask him who he speaks with.

The gallery that surrounds the green now includes Alec Bleeris and ten armed, black suited, Rasta guards. They all watch as Newberry leaves his sand shot short and three putts. He does not concede the match, looking nervously over his shoulder to a red faced Stellenburg.

Connoll is relaxed when he strokes his putt for birdie. Dalva applauds his player, but the sound of his hand claps are drowned out by the sound of the four rifles being leveled on him and the other competitors.

Dalva's bodyguards reach for their weapons but their chests explode in red. Newberry, his caddy and Stellenburg also fall, jerked to the ground by multiple bullet strikes.

Jack, Dalva and Dimming, gaping at the bodies now lying around the fourteenth green, stand in stunned silence.

"Please gentlemen, no more of that," Bleeris says. "Congratulations on your victory Mr. Dalva. Now the match has reached its final stage. Please follow me." Bleeris walks off, back down into the fairway. Connoll, Dimmig and Dalva follow. The black-coated Rasta form a line behind them.

The procession stops suddenly, when gunshots ring out from somewhere further up on the golf course. Dimmig looks to his right with a desperate questioning expression. Juan Dalva does not see Glyn Parker return Harry's glance with a shrug. He does not hear Glyn say to Harry, "I warned you this is serious business. I'll do what I can. Stay calm, the important thing is we win tomorrow."

17

"Did you hear that?" Jerry says to Irv.

"Hear What?" Irv replies. "I'm too busy trying not to break my leg. We should of pulled the car further up the drive."

"Sounded like gun shots," Jerry continues. "Machine guns or something like'em, not far off."

"Machine guns? Whaaa… It's your imagination. When's the last time you took a walk in the woods?"

"Been a while, but what's that matter? I heard guns."

"Well I heard plenty in my day. If you're right, good thing I brought along my little helpers. I got'em stashed down here, in the deep pockets, down in the bottom hem inside the lining of this raincoat, one on each side. That's for you to know in case something happens to me."

"You sure those things won't go off on their own?"

"If there's one thing I know, it's hand grenades. Pull the pin, release the clip and wait fifteen seconds. Simple enough, even for you."

"I'm hoping I never see you use'em," Jerry says, touching the pistol strapped to his side. "I'm hoping all I heard was a woodpecker."

"Yeah a woodpecker. A goddamn woodpecker."

Irv and Jerry walk down the rutted service drive. They pass the rusted gate with the padlock laying broken in the dirt. Jerry looks over to Irv. The old man is struggling with each step, mouthing words in a conversation with himself, his blue raincoat, now ragged, is dragging on the dirt path from the weight of his hidden cargo.

"This is crazy," Jerry says. "Look at these abandoned sheds. This one must have been the horse barn."

"Yeah, yeah, they kept the horses here," Irv says. "I ever tell you I bet on a ninety to one shot once and…"

"I know Irv. I know," Jerry replies. "Listen, lets take a break. Before we go any farther, let's get our game straight. Know one thing, if there's trouble I'm gonna shoot first. I plan on getting home."

"Home. That's Chicago," Irv says, his eyes unfocused. "Been there over fifty years."

"I know. Irv are you all right? You're not looking good."

"I'm just getting old... Been fifty years in Chicago, but one of these days I'm going back to Baltimore. Gonna see what's changed..."

"Irv, let's sit down here for a while."

"No, no we've got to keep going. We're starting to lose light."

"You're right. Anyway, it looks like the path ends up ahead. There's a clearing through those trees."

They push through low hanging branches and emerge to find a lush green fairway rolling off in both directions.

"I'll be damned," Irv says. "Look at this beautiful golf hole. Oh yeah... yeah, aha, this is an old course. I can tell from this one hole. Designed by a master. There's the green sitting up on that rise."

"So which way do we go?" Jerry says.

"To the green," Irv says. "Always go towards the green, you can follow them all the way home."

"Isn't the same thing true going in the opposite direction?"

"Yeah, but trust me, it's always better to go toward the green."

*　　　*　　　*

Harry scans the windowless room. Dalva and Jack sit across from him under the unblinking eyes of two armed guards. They had all walked in a slow procession behind Bleeris, to this room off the main hall of the mansion.

"No talking. I'll return soon," Bleeris said before walking out.

Harry scans the room, but he does not find Glyn. He is exhausted and feels like lying down. Maybe it's a dream, Harry thinks, maybe I'll wake up, catch the brown line to Belmont, smell the Greek cooking and hear Maggie complaining.

Harry's hopes are interrupted by the sound of footsteps approaching in the hall. Bleeris has returned with Waring, Deke, Kathryn and Lilly. Their faces are masks of terror and helplessness.

"So I take it Jolly Rodger didn't win," Jack says, breaking the silence. "Don't tell me, it ended in sudden death."

"Ah Mr. Connoll," Bleeris replies. "Always making the joke."

"Listen Bleeris, I don't know what insane reason you have for all of this, but whatever it is, let the women, Deke and Harry go. Waring, Dalva and I will play the match, but let the others go."

"The other Mr. Connoll now makes his return," Bleeris says. "The martyred hero. I'm sorry, but you are not in charge here. For that matter you are only an insignificant golfer in this match. The real contest, for the big prize, concerns two others."

"What?" Dalva says. "What are you talking about?"

"Mr. Dalva," Bleeris says. "After everything that you have just witnessed, you still want to continue the challenge?"

"That's right Bleeris. People die all the time. It's the cost of the high stake games I play in. You lose you die. So what? I got Connoll and I demand that we play Waring for Wait's prize."

"Oh your Mr. Connoll will play, but it will be only for your life," Bleeris says, walking across the room to stand in front of Harry. "The match for Wait's prize will be between Mr. Dimmig and Miss Rivera."

"What?" Dalva says. "How can this be?"

"It is Mr. Waits decision to pass on what he holds to one of these two people. They possess the special talent required to carry on."

"What talent is that?" Martin Waring asks.

"They can see the dead," Jack answers.

"Very good Mr. Connoll," Bleeris says.

"What are you talking about?" Dalva says, beginning to stand until a rifle is leveled in his direction.

"Something very old, something that should not concern a vile drug dealer," Bleeris continues. "The only thing you should know now, is that your life, along with Connoll's, Manley's, and Vaccaro's depend on Mr.

Dimmig winning his competition. Miss Rivera likewise, holds the fate of Mr. Waring's group."

Jack looks across the dim room to Lilly. She sits straight in her chair, eyes narrowed. Jack observes in her now what he has always detected in Harry; the cold layer, just under the surface, it always rises in times of stress. It has always allowed Harry to shut himself away from the world. The girl has the same scar tissue. "So these two will play," Jack says. "How?"

"Through you and Mr. Waring."

Bleeris scans the room. "You will be taken to your new quarters, upstairs. You will remain under guard. Please rest, you will have a very big day tomorrow."

"What about Vaccaro and Manley?" Jack says.

"You will see them soon. They'll be joining you on the second floor. Miss Rivera's group will reside on the third floor."

"Why?" Harry says.

"Please Mr. Dimmig. Mr. Waits will address all your concerns soon enough."

"Harry," Jack says. "I'm sorry I never believed you."

Harry turns and nods. There is nothing he can say.

*   *   *

Irv catches a glint of the setting sun in the gunmetal toted by the men tracking them from the tree line. He reaches deep into the hidden raincoat pockets, ready to grab the hand grenades that lay down near the coat's hem.

"I think we got company," Irv whispers.

Jerry stops cold and places his hand on his pistol.

"Stay cool," Jerry says. "Any trouble, we let all hell loose."

"You think?" Irv smirks.

The two men continue their walk toward the green. "The seventeenth," Irv had said, as they passed the last tee.

Irv can make out a mansion in the distance. The last light of day falls on it. The scene reminds him of a diorama of an English castle he once saw, as a child, in a storefront on Front Street in Baltimore.

The footsteps behind them are quickening. Jerry and Irv turn to see the three men approaching, rifles aimed from their hips. The men stop ten yards from Jerry and Irv. Jerry considers getting off at least one round before the M16's start firing.

"You guys are welcome to play through if you'd like," Irv says, breaking the silence and causing Jerry to cringe.

The largest of three betrays a smile. "Who might you be?" He asks.

"Uh…" Jerry begins, "We're looking for Jack Connoll and Harry Dimmig, the golfer and his caddy. We're part of their team."

"Is that so? Part of their team? Waits told us no'ting about no others on Connoll's team."

"Yeah," Irv says. "I'm the assistant caddy and this here's the business manager. You guys must be the musical entertainment."

"Huh. If by the longest chance you might be who you say, we'll let you live for the moment. Let Waits give us the call on this one. He tells us no one on the winning teams should be harmed. So we'll take them to Waits. Make sure you take the weapons."

Two guards follow their boss's orders. They search Jerry and Irv where they stand in the middle of the fairway. Jerry lets them take his pistol, but they do not find the hand grenades down in the hem of the old blue raincoat.

"They are all set Raymond," The guard holding Jerry's pistol says. "Only this little pea shooter between them."

"Good," Raymond replies. "Let's take them to Waits. Tomorrow is the final match and the boss don't want any screw-ups."

Jerry and Irv walk with their captors toward the mansion in the distance. Irv takes one last look at the course, now being cloaked in shadows. As it recedes behind him, Irv thinks, it is the work of a master, the creation of an artist who loved more than just the game.

*   *   *

Chauncey Basch rolls a fat joint and hands it to Maggie. She turns it over in her fingers, glancing at Carla to see her reaction. Carla shrugs.

"Go ahead," Chauncey says. "It'll help you relax."

Maggie sparks the lighter and takes in the strong smoke. It fills up her lungs. She holds it for an instant and then allows it move out of her.

The immediate effect of the taste in her mouth, is the recollection of nights long ago, a hot summer, long before Jerry, she was just one of a gang of teenagers who would meet on Wells Street. They would walk down to the lake with a bottle of wine, where they would pass it, along with a pipe, to each other as they sat on the break wall talking of the future and counting the shooting stars.

"I'm worried about them," Maggie says, handing the joint to Carla. "I haven't heard a word from them in days. Chaunce, when you called, it gave me some hope. Like I wasn't alone."

"I'm worried too," Carla says, taking a wary puff.

"I wish I could help you," Chauncey says. "What about having the police check it out?"

"The last time we tried that, I ended up staring down a gun barrel," Carla says.

"Huh," Chauncey says. "Waits has gotten that powerful. Now, I'm not so sure I should tell the reason I asked you to come here. I thought it would help you, or even ease you fears. Now, I think it may make you feel worse."

"Please Chauncey just tell us," Maggie says. "We need to feel like we're doing something."

"Well, I dug something up after you left on Thursday. I started thinking that there must be something in old newspaper files, a story, about all those people dieing on that boat back in the seventies. So I went down to the public library on State Street. I always enjoy going in that building, it has those giant green ganja buds sprouting out of the roof…"

Maggie settles back into the deep couch as Chauncey speaks. The music now has substance; she can feel it moving around her, her eyes closing, her head resting on a big blue cushion. Across the low table, Chauncey is speaking, now appearing as a tired monk, his blue eyes reflecting the pain he senses in her heart.

"So I went through the microfilm files," Chauncey is saying. "Man you don't know how much shit happened in your life until you've rolled through a few decades of newspapers on film. The senseless wars and murders, the stupid fads and the useless politicians, just recycling the bullshit." Chauncey sits back in his chair and takes a deep drag. He closes his eyes and allows the music to fill the silence between them.

I do feel better now, Maggie thinks. There's something safe about the backroom of the Jah Shop. There's a feeling that we're all connected and everything will work out for the best.

"Anyway I finally found it," Chauncey says, his eyes still closed. "Chicago Trib, March 28, 1976, page five, an Associated Press story, one column. The headline read: 'Miami Police Probe Mysterious Yacht Deaths.' That's what the headline said; I just stared at the thing for five minutes. I was afraid to read on."

"So. What did the article say?" Maggie asks.

"Is she sleeping?" Chauncey inquires.

"No, I'm not sleeping," Carla replies. "Now, what the fuck did the article say?"

"There was a party on private yacht. It left Miami with twenty guests, a crew of eight, a chef and a reggae band. The owner of the yacht, Tersis Vitrizin, hosted the party. You ever hear of him?"

Maggie replies, "No." Carla opens her eyes and shakes her head.

"Tersis Vitrizin was an author from Armenia, an anarchist. His books were an underground sensation during the years of the Eastern Block. His books were said to contain hidden codes and prophesy… They were big in the counter culture of late fifties and sixties. I remember seeing an English translation once. Of course, it was worthless as far as looking for a hidden meaning, but regardless, it was filled with this apocalyptic imagery, very obscure and lurid."

"So what about the yacht?" Maggie says.

"The yacht, well yes, I just thought you would like to know about the background… The yacht… That's the strange thing. You see, although

Vitrizin was an author with a reputation, well, that would still leave him far from being a wealthy man. Certainly not wealthy enough to own a yacht in Miami, with homes in Paris and Madrid. A rich Armenian in those days was lucky to have his own apartment."

"So how?" Maggie asks.

"Don't know, the article only called him an author with business interests around the world."

"So what's the point?" Maggie says.

"The point," Chauncey replies, "Is that... I... I don't know the point. I guess it's that he got rich out of nowhere like Waits."

"Please just tell us what happened on the boat." Maggie says.

"I must say, you ladies are certainly impatient."

"Listen Chauncey, I mean Leonard, start making some fucking sense," Carla demands.

"Please Miss Vaccaro, there's no need to get upset. I just have my own way. Have another toke or some wine."

"Leonard..."

"Right. The yacht. The invited guests were all well known in the European writers community. Certainly not superstars, but influential nonetheless. The AP article indicated some of them had been critics of Vitrizin's work. The article also said that many expressed surprise at being invited on this cruise. Anyway, the boat was out to sea for a three nights when the Fort Lauderdale Coast Guard picked up a single distress call. The boat's location was given at fifty miles southeast. Search planes were sent out and, after three days, they saw the flares from a lifeboat. There were only two survivors; an attorney named Alec Bleeris and a musician named Christopher Waits. Bleeris, Vitrizin's attorney was quoted as saying, 'The boat started taking on water in heavy seas late on the third night.' He said, 'The boat went down so fast that only one life boat was released and that the musician and he were the only two who survived.' The police and coast guard were to continue an investigation, but that's all I could find. That's it. That's the extent of the news report."

"That's it?" Maggie says.

"Well almost," Chauncey replies.

"There is one other article I found. I did a search on Waits. I found many articles of his rise to wealth, his shrewd investments and his philanthropy on behalf of African causes. One of the later articles included a quote from Mr. Wait's long time attorney."

"Let me guess," Maggie says. "The attorney's name is Alec Bleeris."

"You've got it."

"And now thirty years later Mr. Waits is recreating the party thrown by Vitrizin," Maggie says. "Another strange gathering, this time including the world's most disreputable businessmen and our boys."

"Yeah," Chauncey Basch says. "The good thing is, at least this time, it's on dry land."

*　　*　　*

"Mr. Waits is occupied," Bleeris tells Raymond. "You were right not to harm them. They are part of the Dalva team. Take the old man and the gangster to the second floor with the rest of them."

Standing in the grand entrance hall of the mansion, Jerry and Irv watch this exchange. Irv nudges Jerry and whispers, "See that bald white guy, I recognize him from somewhere. When I was a kid, just back from the war I stopped in New York. Got a job bussing tables at the Plaza for a week. I could swear I saw him there. I remember, cause he was with that famous scientist, Einstein, at a table. Never forget the day I saw Einstein and I could swear he was there, but it couldn't be… that was over fifty years ago and the man was the same age as this man is now."

Jerry turns from Irv. He has a sick feeling in his stomach. "Christ Irv, don't go crazy on me now."

"All right, you two follow me," Raymond says.

The men walk up the grand staircase. As he climbs, Jerry eyes the crystal chandelier that hangs over the entrance hall, the refracting light, a million fragments, infinite and beautiful. *I wish I had never left Chicago,* he thinks, caught by the shimmering glass, *I wish I had a decent, real job, and that Maggie didn't have to work. We would never be involved in this bullshit.*

Raymond leads them to the second floor and a hallway with doors to many rooms. As they walk, they can hear voices emanating from the room at the end of the hall.

"I don't believe it," Irv says as he walks into the room. "We break our asses getting here and you guys are lounging like kings in this fancy sitting room."

"Get in there and stay there," Raymond says, turning to leave.

Jack, Harry, and Charlie sit with their mouths open, watching old Irv shuffle into the room.

"Well," Irv says. "Are you gonna talk, maybe introduce us to the ladies?"

"What are you doing here?" Jack says.

"Maggie sent us to rescue you," Irv replies.

"You're doing great job of that," Charlie Vaccaro says.

"About the same as you, from what I can see," Irv answers.

"So what's going on here?" Jerry says. "What's this all about?"

"Not totally sure," Jack says. "Only thing we know is, if I lose a golf match we die. We're the last two teams. We play Mr. Waring here, Kathryn, Tommy and Lilly, tomorrow."

"The tall bald guy…" Jerry starts.

"Bleeris, the attorney," Harry says.

"Yeah," Jerry continues. "He just told us that Irv and I are part of Dalva's team,"

"That's us," Harry says.

"So you're telling me that my life depends on Connoll's golf swing?" Irv asks.

"Better mine than yours," Jack replies.

"That's what you think."

Jerry sits on the couch next to Charlie and Irv pushes in next to Harry.

"Can we talk," Irv whispers to Harry.

"I wouldn't trust anyone in this place," Harry says under his breath.

"What I figured. Are your guns gone?"

Harry nods yes.

"Any clue on how to get out of this?"

Harry nods no.

"If anything happens to me," Irv whispers, moving in close to Harry's ear. "I want you to know, I got two grenades hid down in the bottom of this raincoat."

"What? Where'd ya…"

"Never mind, if you need them, they're there."

Harry smiles. "Irv, did I tell you how good it is to see you?"

"As a matter of fact you didn't."

The sound of approaching footsteps quiets Harry and Irv. Raymond is now standing in the doorway, holding his weapon and surveying the room. "All right," Raymond says. "It is time to get 'dis show on the road. You, Dimmig, and the girl, Rivera, come wit' me, it's time you met Mr. Waits."

Harry stands, but Lilly does not move.

"Let's go. Now," Raymond demands. His voice causes the girl to tremble.

Harry walks over to the Lilly and extends his hand. "Come on. I'll be with you. Let's see what the old man's got to say."

Lilly takes Harry's hand. She does not let go as they walk up the two flights of stairs and down a long hall toward a single open door. From inside the room they can hear a fragile melody from a cracked guitar.

Walking in, they first see the fat man in shorts and T-shirt, sitting in a chair with his hands resting on stomach and smiling.

"Ah Christopher," The fat man says. "Your honored guests have finally arrived."

Harry and Lilly transfer their attention across the room to Waits. He is sitting next to a small table, on which sits a gold cup. An old guitar rests on Wait's crossed legs, his long thin fingers wrapped around the neck. He does not look up at the new arrivals

"Christopher," The fat man says again. "Mr. Dimmig and Miss Rivera are wit' us now."

Christopher Waits strums an A chord. It rings for an instant and he mutes it with the palm of his right hand. Waits pulls his attention from the cup and looks up to Harry and Lilly. His expression transforms from a solemn study to a grandfather's smile.

"I am sorry," Waits says. "I've always been transported by the sound of this guitar. Please come in and take a seat." Waits turns to the armed guard and says, "That will be all Raymond. Thank you, we'll be all right now." Raymond nods, his heavy footsteps become echoes diminishing down the long hall. "These guards, the guns," Waits says, "They are an unfortunate requirement. Right Looby my friend?"

"Certainly Christopher. The guns are always a necessity."

"Now, Mr. Dimmig and Miss Rivera please come to me and have a seat at the table. Forgive me, if I'm too tired now to stand for a handshake."

Lilly and Harry move to the old man who has his right hand extended. Harry shakes the hand and fights the feeling of warmth and tenderness that rises inside of him. Lilly betrays a smile, as Waits releases her hand. They sit with the gold cup between them on the naked tabletop.

"Mr. Bleeris will be joining us shortly," Waits says. "Before he arrives, we should take the opportunity to get better acquainted."

"Mr. Waits, please tell us what this is about?" Harry asks.

"In time Mr. Dimmig," Waits replies. "In time you will have your answers. I must say, sitting here with both of you is quite a surprise."

"What do you mean? You're the one who invited us here," Harry says.

"Yes of course. You misunderstand. I mean, I never expected two of you. That has never happened before. Quite a surprise."

"Two? You mean two people who see the ghosts?" Harry asks.

"Yes, at every passing there has always only been one and now there is two. Harry Dimmig and Lilly Rivera. Miss Rivera, why do you 'tink that is?"

"I don't know," Lilly replies. "I don't know why anything is the way it is."

"You Mr. Dimmig?"

"Please Mr. Waits, why are we here?" Harry replies.

"I tell you what I 'tink Mr. Dimmig," Waits says. "I believe you are two parts of whole; the mind and the soul if you will. Very strange and very unfortunate. You see, I empathize with you both. Spent your lives under the silent gaze. I know. How hard. I do know this. Never before and now in my time I have two. Damaged people, as always, but still two. You see Looby, the soul and the mind. Never before."

Looby nods and smiles, "I see it Christopher. Very strange. Never before you say?"

"Never before," Waits replies. "Only one should exist. Still, it is the end of my time and we will play it so." Waits, lost in a thought, looks down to his guitar, picking absently at the strings.

Harry turns to Lilly and finds that the cup holds her attention. Harry too looks to the small gold object. He focuses closely on the designs that are cut into the gold. They turn before his eyes into geometric shapes, to mathematical formulas, to musical notation, to the faces of those who have passed and then back to unrecognizable shapes. Harry blinks to clear his eyes. He turns to find Lilly staring back at him.

Waits looks up and smiles. "You see, when I was where you sit now there was only me. Now there are two. Bleeris, who is older than us all, has never seen this and neither have any who have come before. It has always been one. I'm sorry for one of you. The world cannot have two. The world must have one heart and one mind that controls."

A voice from the hall says, "Maybe this time my old friend, the world requires either a mind or a heart. Maybe that is what the living need." Alec Bleeris walks into the room. "The split has been evident for some time; the female and the masculine, the secular and the pious, the liberal and the conservative. Everything now is politics. It turned hard to this when that outlier, Vitrizin, led. Maybe the battle ground has delivered us finally a choice."

"You've have always enjoyed the darker side of this business," Waits says. "Always looking for some'ting to ease your boredom, but this, above the veneer, is a game one of these two poor souls must lose."

"Boredom, such a pedestrian concern for one such as yourself," Bleeris replies. "You held promise Christopher; the young musician with your ganja and the beautiful women. No Christopher, you were always too greedy to enjoy the gift, and now, well now, lets just say you're at the end of your road."

"I had no'ting before and, despite all I have accumulated, I still have no'ting. I have given them a voice, I have guided this world, they have used me. Still, in the end, the only 'ting I ever needed was this busted up arch-top."

"It was your choice to live your life like this," Bleeris says. "You chose your path. You wanted to accumulate wealth. Other's have spent their time in much more profound ways."

"Alec, you have been with me since the boat, since I took up this life. You know how I lived as a boy. You know that my last act, that what I do now, will be for the good of this world. And please Alec, if I may say, you've lost a bit of the luster yourself." Waits turns to address Harry and Lilly. "Do not listen to us two old men. Maybe we have both reached the end of our roads. We do not mean to frighten you."

Harry has turned to his left, watching the two men out corner of his eye. Lilly is gripping her chair with both hands. Looby smiles, he has heard this argument a hundred times.

"Have you told them?" Bleeris asks Waits. "Have you told them your decision?"

"No. I have waited for you. I did not want to spoil your fun."

"Well go on then," Bleeris says.

"Before I speak, I believe you should explain," Waits says. "Please take a seat and explain to them their lives."

"Their lives, of course I will explain Christopher, but if you don't mind I will stand." Bleeris paces to the back of the room and rests his right hand on Looby's shoulder. The tall man wears a gray pinstripe suit, a blue shirt with a white collar and auburn necktie. His bald head gleams between neatly trimmed gray hair.

When Bleeris looks down at Harry and Lilly, Harry thinks Bleeris resembles the Earl of Kent, recalling the man he had once met with Glyn at the British Open.

"Your lives," Bleeris starts. "I can tell you of them, although, I had never known of you before two days ago. Your lives began with sickness or grief. They were lacking a belonging. They were filled with loneliness and weakness. You were damaged in some way and you began to see. You saw those who had left you, those who had passed and you know they watch you. Judge you. You see a world that no one else can imagine and it serves to further separate you from the living. You cannot hear their voices and you came to learn you could not speak of what you saw. Is this correct? Tell me Miss Rivera, is this correct?"

"Yes," Lilly replies. "My mother and father were murdered when I was a child and you have described my life."

"Mr. Dimmig, what do you recall?"

"The first years of my life I spent in bed with fevers. I would always be small, haunted," Harry replies.

"Damaged, of course, lonely," Bleeris says. "This is…"

"I did hear a voice once," Harry says cutting off Bleeris.

Wait's eyes widen and Bleeris stops cold.

"Is that so," Bleeris says. "Please tell me."

"I was a child, in fever, maybe a dream, my grandmother was there, others too…" Harry stops to swallow.

"Go on. What did you hear?"

"My grandmother. She said, 'The one who will hold the key, waits and will soon go mad.' She said, 'That I may come to the this door again, that I will need assistance."

"You say others were there?" Bleeris asks.

"Many, but one I remember. He appeared as a rat, but I clearly recall knowing he was a man. The creature was waiting outside my house."

Waits roars with laughter, "Harry that's great. Your grandmother surely did not mean I was the mad one. I will speak with her some day. She sounds quite resourceful. Of course that will only happen if you prevail."

207

"Yes, well," Bleeris says. "I'm glad you find this amusing Christopher, but I have never heard of such a thing. The connection has never been allowed without permission. You say you were a boy? That would have been Vitrizin's time. Crazy Armenian. Or Christopher, are you hiding something from me?"

"No Alec, I hide nothing from you." Waits smiles, looking down at his guitar and Looby laughs.

"You Jamaicans have been nothing but trouble," Bleeris says. "Your time will be over soon enough."

"I'm sorry," Bleeris says addressing Harry and Lilly. "This passing becomes more unusual by the moment. Still Mr. Dimmig, let us leave your strange dream for a moment and get back to the business at hand. What you have in common with each other, you have in common with all those who have taken the position for which you will compete."

"What position is that?" Harry asks.

"Ah, you want a name, but it is known by many names. Many have sat where you may sit. Upon receiving the gift, some have gone to the caves, their power forever lost and the world cold and dark. Others have been known as king, warrior, artist, scientist, musician, philosopher, poet, prophet, or as in the case of our Mr. Waits, tycoon. They are the source of creation. They are the world mind. Their thoughts become the thoughts of all. They paint the world in which they live. They are the dream and the reality."

"They speak with the dead?" Harry asks.

"Yes Mr. Dimmig. The dead work on their behalf and in return the dead receive standing, a role that allows them to maintain influence over the living, to hold a place in our souls. If you succeed in obtaining this power, eternal being will be given to all you have known. They all will be forever bound to the line of the world mind and through them you can touch all who live."

"Eternal existence for myself, my family and friends, those alive and those who have passed?"

"Yes, of course, you shall always be together."

"And if I don't take this job?" Harry asks.

"Miss Rivera will reign and, because of your association to her, you may survive in some memory. As for the others, your 'friends and family' as you say, they will be forgotten, erased, forever lost in time."

"Why? Why us?" Lilly says.

"That is the one bit that always escapes explanation," Bleeris says. "I like to think it is fate, a coincidence of the proper environmental factors, that result in the trauma, combined with an innate gift that allows you to see, but not hear. As for the reason you are here today, Mr. Waits was advised by his predecessors to convene this golf match. He was told he would find his replacement among the group that arrived. For Mr. Waits, he was a musician at a party on a boat when I gave him this speech."

"And you Mr. Bleeris?" Harry asks. "How do you fit?"

"This has always been my role Mr. Dimmig. I was there at the beginning, the only one, the constant character. I was here when they worshiped fire and water, here among the first pyramid civilizations. I was here when those who held this role were known as gods. Buddha, Mohammed. I was here when the one, Jesus, was crucified for the public way he exercised his power. I was here for the passing of those you may know as, Plato, Aristotle, Arthur, Nostradamus, Shakespeare and Newton. History is short, still there were so many who wasted their time. There was Vitrizin and now Waits."

"Vitrizin and Waits?" Harry says.

"Yes, this is a fragment of the line that leads to us here now. Of course you are aware of many of the former's contributions. Still, if you recall during your lifetime a desire for wealth, for accumulation at any cost, if you saw in your world the rise in the mastery of greed, that is an agenda you may attribute to our good host, Mr. Waits. Still, he would tell you that his final act is yet to be realized. And then, there were the outliers, like Vitrizin.

"Outliers?"

"Yes, that's what I call them. We have had those who have turned away from their calling and the world suffered for it. In your history they call those times the dark ages."

"And Vitrizin was an outlier?"

"Yes, he turned from his gift. Miss Rivera was not yet born. However, you Mr. Dimmig, a boy then, may recall his time. He brought destruction and chaos onto his generation. He brought on the age of rebellion, writing those useless cryptic books. He called one: "The Vilnay Bible." He was mad, as was the world, during his years and we are still paying the price today." Bleeris pauses regarding the gold cup. "Still, now that I hear that Mr. Dimmig communicated with the other side during Vitrizin's time, I will need to look again at his reign and his writings. Maybe Mr. Waits will speak to him for me?"

"Alec," Waits says. "I speak with Tersis all the time. I find his books quite enlightening. He looks forward to meeting my replacement."

"Never in the ages have I had such problems," Bleeris says. "And now we have two. The man and the girl. This is not possible. One of you must go."

"What if one of us just walks away?" Harry asks, looking to Lilly.

"This cannot be," Bleeris says. "Walk away, huh, so impudent. The mind of the world, what you desire all will desire. The role has never been shared. Only one can live, Dimmig or Rivera. If either of you walk away, we would find you and kill you just the same. With your death, everyone you have known, everyone you have loved, will be erased, their memory cast into oblivion."

"So how do we decide?" Lilly asks.

"The competition," Waits replies.

"Competition?" Harry asks. "How can I compete against the girl?"

"That is the problem," Waits replies. "In all the transfers Bleeris has presided over, he has never had the problem of having to decide. How does Mr. Dimmig compete with Miss Rivera? You both have talents that could benefit the world. Miss Rivera could be a grand woman; the world could use the romance of her youth and the depth of her heart. It has been so long since we had a female… French, she visits me often. Mr. Dimmig on the other hand, the unassuming, just man, sensitive to the world, maybe under him we would pass into an age of simplistic maturity and tolerance."

"What did we become under you Waits?" Harry asks.

Bleeris laughs. Waits places the guitar on the table and pulls himself up to his feet. "Mr. Dimmig you are the courageous one," Waits says, looming up over Harry. "When I was a boy I had no'ting but the sea and the ghosts. I learned that to live, you had to sell. I was rescued from this world by music, by the Rastafari, by the lord. I chose to use business, capitalism, the accumulation of wealth as my weapon. It is the only way you can wage war on Babylon. My efforts on behalf of my religion have been less apparent, but I have always fought the ones who will have you in chains, the drug dealers, the pornographers, the false prophets and the rest. My wealth I will leave to the people of the garden. They will carry on the fight against those who led us to the wasteland. Before I am done, before the end of Sunday, I will eliminate the kings of evil. The hammer of justice will fall on them. They will be my slaves in the other world. This will be my legacy."

"How do I compete?" Lilly asks.

"My dear beautiful girl," Waits replies. "I see you have interest in our offer. You see Harry. The young one has ambitions. I was to convene this tournament to find the next and I have decided to allow the match to determine the winner."

"You mean Jack and Martin will play for our lives, for your prize?" Harry asks.

"Yes," Bleeris says. "They play for your lives, their own and everyone you have ever known or loved. They play for the future the world."

"Of course," Waits offers. "You may use your abilities to do what you can to assist them," He laughs and picks up the guitar. "And then, when all this is done, my old friend Looby and I can rest. Maybe we'll go to the old lighthouse beach, north of Kingston. We will watch eternity drifting in and out with the waves. Right my friend?"

"Yes Christopher," Looby answers. "It is almost time to go home."

*   *   *

The two women sit at the kitchen table. A soft breeze curls through an open window above a white sink. The curtains ripple and beyond the fluttering silk is a blue sky.

In other times they would have been friends. Both are sturdy strong women who had taken a hard path to provide care for their families. Sylvia Rivera, the housemaid, had raised the daughter of her murdered brother. Vera Casick looked after her four children, her husband rarely in the house. When they were alive they had even resembled each other, strong shoulders, fleshy arms, round faces, and sharp intelligent eyes.

Today they sit in the kitchen. Sylvia's brown eyes look deep into Vera's blue.

When they had lived, they had always preferred this place, a cheap Formica tabletop, near a coffee pot on the stove, to conduct their most important business.

"So this is it," Sylvia says.

"Looks that way Syl," Vera replies. "Everything is on the line now. Those poor kids… My poor Harry, I tried to warn him once, but he could never understand."

"I hear," Sylvia replies. "And how was it that you had that opportunity to speak with him?"

"Well Syl, it's a funny thing who may come knocking at your door when you least expect it."

"Funny thing, so who came knocking?"

"Well, I couldn't give you a name, that wouldn't be very lady like."

"Was it Vitrizin?" Sylvia asks. "That man lurks like a rodent. He's got his hands all over this."

"Now, I don't know what you're thinking. Anyway, I have friends, that's for sure. I've been kicking around here long enough waiting for this day. Can I give you some advice, Syl? Have your girl's boyfriend, Gaffi?"

"Javier."

"Yes, have Javier back the poor girl off this. I'll see what I can do about getting you a pass, you know, bring you in on my side."

"Please Vera, you Chicago types are all the same, always looking to cut a deal. This is about much more than you and me. Everything is on the line, our parents, our brothers and sisters, your other children, centuries of Casiks and Dimmigs, Riveras and Lastras. You can't buy me off any more than I could buy you off."

"Oh Syl, you are so blind."

"I'm not blind. I'm enjoying it, just like you. We matter again, we're in the game and that's what we're fighting for, isn't it Vera? We're fighting to remain in the game."

"Sure Syl, sure. Regardless of how this turns out, it's been nice, you know, this time we had together. Just sitting here on this beautiful afternoon, like the old days, has been worth it. You're a good woman Syl and I'll miss you."

"Ah Vera," Sylvia smiles. "I must admit you Chicago types always made me laugh. I'll miss you too."

*   *   *

The vegetarian dinner is laid out buffet style in the sitting room on the mansion's second floor. "It adheres to the Ital," The guard who serves it says. "In 'dis house, you eat according to our laws."

"Ital? What the hell is that?" Jerry asks.

"It's the diet of the Rastafari," Charlie replies.

"Well I don't mind," Irv says. "I like the veggies. Especially the brussels sprouts. Didn't get to be almost eighty by not eating veggies."

"I guess a long life is good," Jack says. "But if it means looking like you, I think I'd rather have a cheeseburger." Even Irv laughs at Jack's remark.

In the time since they had taken Harry and Lilly away, the others had been shown to their rooms. Prior to dinner, Dalva's group was escorted to rooms on the second floor and Waring's group to the third. They were given no restrictions on their movement between these two floors.

"If this is jail," Irv said. "I'd like a life sentence."

"Life would be the key word here," Charlie replied.

They now all understood what faced them. The match tomorrow would be for life and death. As they eat, the mood is solemn. Some whisper in pairs, Dalva and Manley, Deke and Waring, Charlie and Jerry.

213

Jack and Kathryn have said little to each other. Now, with the daylight fading and the shadows of trees moving fast across the floor, Jack nods to Kathryn. Martin watches her walk quietly across the room, Jack following her through the door to the corridor.

They walk the long hall, up the stairway to the third floor, to Kathryn's room, to a small west-facing window, where across the valley the horizon is orange and violet. The dusk reveals a moon that appears larger than they have ever seen.

"What do we do?" Kathryn asks.

"Not much we can do," Jack replies. "We're locked tight, a gun around every corner. They took all our weapons when they brought us here."

"We have to think of something or we will die tomorrow."

"From what I can tell, only the losers will die."

"And you don't plan on losing."

"No. I'll beat Waring."

"And if you do, I will die."

"Look K.C., we can't do anything now. Tomorrow, on the course, we'll have a chance. We'll think of something. Harry will. We'll get out of this."

"I don't understand," Kathryn says. "Why would they do this to us?"

"I don't know, but I have a feeling we're just secondary players here. Harry says the prize, or whatever it is we're playing for, will either go to Lilly or himself."

"Lilly? I don't understand."

"Neither do I, but I trust Harry. They murdered those people today. The only way it makes sense is to look at the ones who were killed. Not the collaterals, but the principles. They were scum, involved in some immoral act, the world is better for their passing."

"Better? Martin's a businessman. He's not a criminal."

"Maybe not in your eyes, but maybe in the eyes of our host. To a lot of people, the Reverend Hollywell was the most righteous man on the planet. We just happen to have another opinion."

"So you think Waits is attempting to avenge the wrongs of the world?"

"Do you remember what Waits said the first night?"

"No. All I remember was the moment I saw you."

"He said that although he was required to pass something on, it would be his right to exact vengeance on Babylon, or something like that."

"And we're Babylon?"

"It appears that way. Harry and your girl Lilly are somehow in the middle of it, connected."

"And we're the collaterals?"

"Yeah, but we have Harry. I trust him, he'll come through."

"Maybe for you, but I don't hold the same faith. He still blames me for what happened."

"I still blame you for what happened."

"Jack, I thought you…"

"I blame you and I love you. I know better than to fight it. In fact I've given up. I thought I'd be the one to laugh in your face, but it will always be you laughing. Whatever you say or do can never change the fact that I love you. I will make sure you are safe."

"What I did to Harry and you I can never change…"

"The past is inescapable, I know that now, it's always there, no matter how far you think you have run it is bound to appear when you turn the next corner."

"Jack you don't understand…"

"I understand that we're on the firing line here. I understand that our lives are now in the hands of Harry and Lilly. I understand that I will never escape you. I understand that I love you. I understand I will save you."

Jack has surrendered. He is relieved that he has chosen this place, under the gaze of the rising moon and her soft blue eyes.

Kathryn watches the man push his hair back. "I know you do Jack," She says. "And I know you will."

*   *   *

Kathryn Torrance is awake, staring at the blue shadows on the ceiling above her bed.

Earlier, after dinner, Lilly and Harry had returned to the sitting room and sat in a quiet vigil. There could be no conversation within hearing range of the armed guards. Kathryn was stunned at how pale and weak the young maid and the caddy had appeared upon their return. When the order to sleep was given, Lilly had just nodded to Kathryn and then followed the others marching to their beds.

If what Jack said is true, about the real competitors in this tournament, Kathryn knows she must speak with Lilly.

On her feet, barefoot, wearing only a silk robe, Kathryn peers through the partly open door for any sign of a guard. The hall is dark, but for a single light above the stair landing. She observes a shadow moving on the wall and believes it to be a guard stationed on the landing below her floor. She opens her door, careful and slow, moving on soft toe-steps down the hall to Lilly's room; the last room on the left. The girl's door opens with only a slight turn of the knob and a push.

Kathryn blinks when she sees the figure standing by the window, silhouetted in the moonlight, hair and nightgown full with the evening breeze.

"Lilly," Kathryn whispers. "Lilly it's Kathryn."

The woman turns to her and Kathryn staggers. It is the face of her old friend Sylvia, younger than Kathryn remembers and smiling. Kathryn turns to the bed canopied in white silk and sees the girl sleeping. When she turns back to Sylvia there is only the flutter of curtains and the moonlit sylvan landscape. Kathryn stands blinking. I'm finally losing it, she thinks, finally.

Kathryn moves to the bed and kneels beside it. Lilly sleeps, her thick brown hair tangled, her lips barely parted, her long lashes quivering from a dream.

"Lilly," Kathryn says, touching the girl's arm. "Lilly, please wake up."

Lilly brushes her face with her hand and turns away.

"Lilly, it's me, Kathryn, Miss Torrance, I need to speak with you."

The girl opens her eyes, unfocused and confused. "Yes Miss Torrance. I'm sorry, what can I do for you?"

"I need to ask you, what happened, where did they take you?"

Lilly sits up in bed, scanning the room for someone who is not there. "They took us to Waits," Lilly says. "Bleeris was there too."

"What did they say? What's this all about?"

"It's hard to explain Miss…"

"Please Lilly, our lives depend on it."

"Yes our lives… They told us this match is taking place to pass on a power from Waits. It's the power that made him rich."

"Power? What kind of power?"

"He speaks with the dead, Miss Torrance."

"Please girl, the man is psychotic."

"No, I'm afraid he's not. You see, since we were children, Mr. Dimmig and I have seen them, the ghosts. They have always been silent. Just illusions we thought. Now we know that they are more than real."

"More than real?"

"Yes, it appears that through them, Mr. Waits can act upon the world. His thoughts become everyone's thoughts. This is what he offers. He uses the spirits and they exist because of him. This is what he will pass on to Mr. Dimmig or me. We can use this gift as we please. Mr. Waits used it to amass his wealth."

"I don't understand. You're telling me the prize of this whole insanity is the ability to speak with ghosts."

"Yes Miss Torrance. Through them you have access to everything that has passed and everything that will be. You, your family, friends and ancestors will have eternal existence."

"Eternal life?"

"Yes, in a way, eternal life to the winner and oblivion to the loser and those connected to them."

"And this competition is between you and Harry Dimmig?"

"Yes. Bleeris says it is the first time they've ever had two. It will be decided on the golf course tomorrow, by the winner of the match between Mr. Waring and Mr. Connoll."

"And if Mr. Waring wins you will inherit this power?"

"Yes. And if Mr. Waring loses we will be killed. There can only be one."

"I don't believe it."

"I understand Miss Torrance."

"But what if it's true. The power to shape the world, eternal life…"

"The knowledge of the universe."

"Eternal beauty."

"Eternal beauty?"

"Of course," Kathryn replies, "Everything that lives, lives for beauty."

"Everything that lives, lives for love."

"Wealth, beauty and love then. Regardless, we have to win to live."

"Yes."

"And if we win, I will be with you? I will share in your reward?"

"Of course."

"Rest now Lilly. I beat Dimmig once before and I can assure you I will beat him again." Kathryn Torrance touches the girl's arm and stands to walk away.

"I'm afraid," Lilly says.

"Don't worry, I'm with you and, if what you say is true, we are about to rule the world."

Kathryn breathes deep and the pine air fills her lungs. She feels stronger and younger, strolling now back to her bedroom, no longer concerned with alerting the guard.

*   *   *

On the second floor, in Harry's room, Jack sits with his mouth hanging open, staggered by the tale Harry has just told. Harry watches Jack closely, worried about his friend's reaction.

"We can try to rush them in the morning," Jack says. "We got you, me, Charlie, Jerry, Waring, shit, I bet even Tommy Deke and old Irv can handle themselves. I'm not sure if we can trust Manley and Dalva."

"Even if we could, it wouldn't be enough," Harry replies. "One M-16 will do the job, and I've counted twelve guards."

"Right, we jump one, get a gun and blast our way out. That's the plan."

"No," Harry answers. "This goes beyond that. Didn't you hear what I said? This match is for the biggest prize there is, we will live forever."

Jack turns from Harry. "Who wants to live forever? I don't even want to live until next week."

"Of course you don't," Harry says. "But what's the difference, you quit the day she walked out on you in Phoenix."

"With you it always comes down to her. You tell me some fairytale about talking to ghosts, and the future of the world, and it still comes down to that day in Arizona."

"It always has with you."

"Let me get this straight. You want to go along with this madness. You want me to play this match, to win this prize for you."

"For all of us and for the dead. For your dad and Ryan. For our lives and the lives of those we love. You win, we run the show. We live tomorrow and forever."

"And the others, the others are murdered."

"Maybe there's something we can do. Lilly will always be with us, maybe K.C. too."

"Be with us? You mean as ghosts? This is crazy."

"You can beat Waring."

"Harry..."

"This is our time and you can beat Waring."

"We can rush them, get a gun, Irv has those grenades, we..."

"Jack, there is no turning from this. We can make a difference, we will be known, the story of our lives will become the story of the world."

"Just what I need. Just what I need."

"I'll tell the others. We play the match tomorrow for everything."

*   *   *

"Your face does resemble the rat," Waits says to the man sitting at the table on which the gold cup rests. "A very appropriate description."

"I am the rat," Tersis Vitrizin replies, "The creature that searches for the rot that will sustain. And you Mr. Waits, what would you have yourself be."

"I would be the great shark, the king of the ocean, consuming all."

"Yes you would," Vitrizin replies. "Quite a pair the rat and the shark."

"Preordained, or simple coincidence, we have come together on the edge of it all," Waits says, stroking the cup, allowing the intricate carved patterns to move the flesh on his fingertips.

"I like the way you look at it Waits, 'The edge of it all,' yes. I knew you were special when you boarded my boat with your old guitar."

"I have one agenda now and that is to punish those who have harmed my people. What we conspire to do, I do for no other reason."

"Nonsense, you could have found your revenge without our deal. It goes deeper than that, it goes to the abandoned little island boy."

"Abandoned, far from it, I was taken in by Minter, Looby and the Rastafari. They have been my family. It is your motivation that I find more perplexing. A man of education, of great gifts, always seeking chaos, wanting the end."

"The end? Is that how you see it, the end. I see the beginning. The world in two, love versus logic, new world against old, whatever you want to call it, it will result finally in freedom."

"Freedom... I fear that Bleeris is on to us," Waits says.

"Bleeris, the old guard, always protecting the way of the predecessors. He could never understand. If it was up to him, we would continue this charade for another million years."

"A million years seems like a drop in the bucket to me now," Waits remarks.

"Yes, well if it was up to Bleeris, the bucket would overflow. Now it's time we turn the spigot full on. I've worked on this since the earliest days of my reign. I found the sick boy, made the deal with his grandmother, even made the girl, a sad story, but required. It has all come together now. Mr. Dimmig wants it and so will Miss Rivera."

"And what if one is not up to the challenge and falters?"

"What if Mr. Waits... then we will have one. Then we will sit by while the bucket is filled drop by maddening drop. But, you know it Mr. Waits, the compression of time; you can feel it has already begun. The past becoming the present, the present the future, the dead and the living walk now, almost as equals. The world mind is about to be shattered."

"A world split in two, the maid and the caddy."

"Yes Mr. Waits, this will be our remedy."

18

The rodent sits on the black iron of the building's facade. The mansion is bathed in a blue dawn light. Two rooms, one on the second floor and one on the third are lit and two meetings are in progress.

On the second floor Juan Dalva stands red eyed and shaken. He wears a white bathrobe that hangs unevenly on his shoulders. "You must be kidding me," Dalva says to Connoll and Dimmig. "All this for some fable." The others sit in silent agreement. "You're telling me that this whole fucking mess was based on madness?"

"Juan," Jack says. "I understand how you feel, but you have to trust me, this is what it is, it's about Harry and the girl."

"Dimmig and the girl? Dimmig would not have been here without me. How is it possible that..."

"None of us would have been here without everyone who came before," Harry says to Dalva.

Glyn Parker sits on the arm of an old chair next to the drug dealer and nods his agreement. "Tell him." Glyn speaks only to Harry. "Tell him that his cousin Ramon is here, there are many Dalva's and Palacios too, their future also depends on Jack now."

"Mr. Dalva, you have a cousin Ramon who died?" Harry says.

"Yes why?"

"His existence and his family, the Palacios, depend on this match."

"Nonsense," Kevin Manley says. "You're PI's. You've obviously done your homework."

Dalva slumps into his chair, his face is as white as his robe.

"Tell him," Glyn continues, "That Ramon said, 'He never meant to be with Celia that afternoon, still, he forgives you for what you did."

"Mr. Dalva," Harry starts, "Ramon says he never meant to be with Celia, but he forgives you."

"What? How?" Dalva says standing. "This can't be."

"Harry, do me a favor," Irv says. "Find out where my skinflint old man buried all his money."

"Shut up Irv," Jack says.

Charlie stands and stalks to the other side of the room. "This is all bullshit," He says. "Harry thinks he's some kind of psychic, it's bullshit."

"Yeah, but it's the truth," Jack says.

"What else?" Dalva says to Harry. "What else do you know?"

"If Jack wins, all of us will have the world in our hands," Harry replies. "What I think, all will."

"What you think? Living forever? I'm not sure that's such a great prize," Irv says.

"Shut up Irv," Jack says.

"We can take them," Charlie says. "We all might not make it, but some of us could get out."

"I like the plan where we all live forever," Jerry says.

"Right," Harry agrees.

Jack has turned away to the window, looking out to a brightening sky.

"So what should we do?" Charlie asks. "Just stand and wait for them to gun us down."

"What if we refuse to play?" Jerry asks.

"We're dead," Harry replies.

"What if I give them a taste of my two friends, Mr. Hand and Mr. Grenade?" Irv asks.

"A last resort," Harry answers.

"Ask them to consider the implications of Jack winning," Glyn tells Harry.

"Listen, any way you look at this we're dead unless Jack wins. If Jack loses, we fight to the death, but if Jack wins, we, our families, our friends, take the world."

Outside, on a railing, a rodent balances on two hind feet. It leaps to the vines and climbs one floor up, toward the other lighted room, to the other group that sits in stunned disbelief.

223

Javier sits next to the girl, as Kathryn Torrance paces the room and makes her argument. "Jack and Harry will try to win this and we should too," Kathryn says.

"Don't you think we should talk to them, join forces and try to fight?" Martin asks.

"Fight? The only thing we should be fighting for is for you to beat Connoll. Lilly is the key to it all. If we lose, what is there to live for anyway?"

Lilly looks up to Javier and he places his hand on hers.

"I ain't got nothing to live for except the certain future of a lonely death," Tommy Deke says. "The girl knew my poor dead mother's maiden name and the wife that Mr. Waring lost."

"It doesn't look like we have much of a choice," Martin replies. "Whether her story is true or not, I do believe we will die if I don't win. Connoll, he's a tough one."

"Martin," Kathryn says. "I believe Lilly and I can give you an edge. Besides, you beat him once, you can do it again."

"I beat him once? I don't recall," Martin says. "As for you giving me an edge, I don't doubt that. I don't doubt that."

Scanning the faces one last time, the rodent slips off the rail and disappears into the red dawn shadows.

*   *   *

The sun is now full above the trees, offering no comfort to the lives that hang in the balance. The two groups walk toward the first tee followed by gun toting guards. On the tee, Mr. Waits and Mr. Bleeris stand grinning as the competitors approach.

"Congratulations," Bleeris says to them. "You have made it to the finals."

Kathryn Torrance suppresses a smile, but there is no response from anyone else.

"We are almost at the end," Mr. Waits says, his face is now a relaxed expression of relief. "Today we shall have a new guide. Only eighteen holes remain. Please, Mr. Dimmig and Miss Rivera step forward."

Harry and Lilly move to Waits.

"My children," Waits says. "I know your lives have been spent alone, but never alone, always under their eyes, but never able to respond. Always, their memory and sadness has followed you. In other times, you each would be deserving of this honor. Unfortunately, I can pass the reward to only one, 'tis the oddity of your time. The match will decide it and one of you shall receive the reward." Waits turns and signals to Looby. Looby approaches carrying the gold cup. Waits takes the treasure from his old friend and holds it with both of his hands. There is a tear in his eye as he looks back to Looby. "Our time here is almost done. Soon we'll be back on the old Kingston beach, Chasey will be there and we'll smoke a pipe and watch as the world leaves us behind."

"Praise the lord," Looby says. "The time has come. We have earned a rest. Maybe I'll get to learning the old box now."

Waits smiles at his longtime friend before turning back to Harry and Lilly. "'Tis…" Waits starts. "'Tis the symbol of the one. Passed down from hand to hand. It brought the first man understanding, he knew fire, he knew shelter, he knew death, and what he knew, all knew. It has rested on the tables of giants and dwarves, Egyptian Kings and Incan Mystics. It has been lost and then found. It has passed the hands of the great seers, men of deep thoughts, the so-called Gods, through the hands of artists, poets, and scientists. The tyrant, the dictator, the murderer and the thief have also held it. It came to me, a haunted musician and it will come to one of you."

In the sharp August morning light, Jack watches the strange ceremony. He blinks hard twice, trying to rouse himself from this dream. Nothing changes. This strange world only appears stranger.

Kathryn regards the cup with mouth agape. "So that's it, the key to everything," She thinks. "It has come down to this match."

The others stand counting the barrels of the guns that are aimed their way.

"Enough of this ceremony," Bleeris says. "Let's get on with this."

"Right," Waits says. "It seems Mr. Bleeris must have some place to be. Still, one thing before we start, in recognition of this unique situation, I have decided to give our competitors the advantage of a gallery."

"Waits," Bleeris demands.

"I'm still in charge here," Waits responds. With a wink to Looby, there is a crowd surrounding the first tee. The rows of spectators extend down both sides of the first fairway.

Harry and Lilly stagger at the spectacle that only they can see, searching the crowd for familiar faces.

They are all here now, One-Eye, Buggy, Big Tommy, Harry's and Jack's fathers, the Riveras, Howard Ryan, Aunt Sylvia, Vera Casick, the Dalvas, the Dekes, the Lastras, the Lavinskys, the Manleys, the Vaccaros, the Cahoons, the Cantwells and many more; all that those on the tee have loved and all they have known. They are the two sides of this battle, their stakes as high as any of the others, the living ones, who stand unaware on the tee.

"Now we can begin," Waits says. "Mr. Connoll you have the tee."

Harry shakes the hands of Waring and Deke. A ritual of sportsmanship he has performed a thousand times without thought, is now a moment of sadness.

"I guess I'm up," Jack says to Harry.

Harry removes the driver from their bag. "Here," Harry says, handing the club to Jack. "This is our time now. We start again today."

"Start again, maybe for the last time," Jack replies.

"Remember the day we first met?" Harry asks.

"Yeah, in high school, first day. I was a C and you were a D."

"You turned to me, you had a hundred friends, but you still turned to me. Do you remember?" Jack shakes his head. Those around the tee watch, confused at this whispered conversation. "You had no concern for the past, the future or for that woman standing a few feet away. The world came to you and you were happy to meet it."

"I don't understand Harry."

"Let's go back there today. One last time. Back to the days in Webster Park, the days on the fairways of Oak Grove, to the days when nothing mattered, but the game we played."

Jack smiles and puts his hand on Harry's shoulder.

"I'll do my best old friend."

Jack steps to the tee unaware of the large gallery that watches. The weary man swings his club, loosening up, a reflex; slow and shallow. He is releasing the strange world he has found, just another turn in the road of an unplanned life, a life that had almost taken him out of that old Chicago neighborhood. Now, moving behind the ball on the tee, the world melting away, the only vision left is the old one. It is the image of the first green fairway he walked as a boy, the smell of the morning grass in the summer air. Once again, the boy stands behind his ball and is comforted by a breeze he feels on his back. The world will never be better than this moment, alone with the fairway, his life, before him. The boy turns and swings, a natural movement, the only way it could ever be. It is complete, the ball is gone, off on a perfect arc; it is the beginning of the end.

Waring, Kathryn, Waits, and even Harry are stunned by the beauty and simplicity of this swing. A tear surprises Kevin Manley.

Irv grins, "Aha, yes, yes, yes that's the way it's done."

"Nice Jack," Waring says, moving to place his tee in the ground. With a sharp crack, a terse reply, Waring unleashes a low piercing drive. It sails dead true down the fairway, touching down twenty yards behind Jack's ball and rolling thirty yards beyond.

Javier hangs close to Lilly, whispering softly and brushing her hair with his hand.

Glyn walks, as always, in his loping gait, just a half step off of Harry's right. "This Waring's a tough boy," Glyn tells Harry. "Don't let your man get down. He'll feel more than his share of smacks in the nose today."

"My man'll be all right," Harry replies. "I got one seventy to the front," He tells Jack. "Eighty-five to the hole."

"Wind is helping from the left," Glyn remarks.

"Wind helping, a half club, off your left shoulder," Harry tells Jack.

"The seven," Jack says, taking the club, sending his ball skyward, dropping it fifteen feet left of the pin.

Waring's second shot lands inside of Connoll's and they march toward the first hole.

Irv, in his blue raincoat, with his hand in his thin gray hair, is shaking his head when Jerry Cahoon walks up next to him. Cahoon places his hand on Irv's stooped shoulder and they walk together down the fairway.

"You're looking kind of confused," Jerry says to Irv.

"Yeah, I'm at the end of my road you know."

"Looks like a lot of us are."

"The kid, Connoll, he's good, but I don't know if he has what'll take to beat the German. The guy's got the cold hard look Connoll doesn't have."

"Yeah I know. I see it too. Jack's never been the tough one. Not sure if he ever cared for living all that much. You know the drinking, the gambling; he's been trying to kill himself since I met him. And now…"

"And now he's got our lives in his hands."

"Right," Jerry replies. "I wish I could talk with Maggie. She'd know what to do."

The golfers circle the putting surface. Harry walks with Glyn as they line up the putt. "I've got it down hill, very fast," Glyn tells Harry. "Tell your boy very fast."

"I think he can figure that out," Harry says to Glyn, before making his way to Jack, who is replacing his mark with his ball. "Fast Jack," Harry says.

"Yeah I see," Jack replies. "I'm seeing clear Harry, don't worry."

Jack takes a last look from behind the ball, takes his position. After one practice stroke, he surrenders their future to the ball. It begins its role, almost stopping, picking up speed and moving quickly on line toward the hole. Charlie Vaccaro cringes; sure it will roll ten feet past. The ball bangs into the back of the cup and drops.

Harry's expression does not change. He just glances to Glyn who has a broad smile on his pale face.

Deke looks to Waring. "Well you see it. Let's have the same result."

"Right Tommy, right," Waring replies, taking one quick look to check his line, barely touching his ball with the putter, rolling it smooth and definite into the hole.

"All square after one," Bleeris announces.

Kathryn, her fists clenched, blinks, turning to find Lilly. The girl is wandering alone on the edges of the fairway near a patch of white wildflowers. Kathryn cannot see Lilly standing with the ghost of the dark man. The girl is unconcerned with the match at hand. Kathryn knows now that it will be her responsibility to assist here. I'll have one shot at this, Kathryn thinks, I've got to get the girl to help and I will have to wait for the perfect time.

At the second, two flawless tee shots are hit up into the narrow fairway bounded by traps and trees.

Irv walks haltingly, falling behind Jerry who goes ahead on his own. The sun is heating up now, but Irv cannot take off his raincoat, it holds his secret. The end of my road, Irv thinks, what does it matter if I live or die? I just made that damn promise to Maggie, told her I'd bring the bookie back to her. I just don't know how much more I got left, but I've got to keep going.

Irv does the old calculation, almost eighty, he thinks, I'm seventy-nine, eighty on September 9th, I was born in Baltimore, I remember riding my bike with the fat tires through the streets of my hometown. I went to the war, was on my way to California and I ended up in Chicago. I remember the brown haired girl from New Jersey, the bar at the Ambassador and the day these two fellows walked into the driving range. There is so much more, so much that no one will ever know and I will never tell. I've got to keep going, I promised Maggie, but I'm old, at the end of my line and this goddamn sun…

Irv has lost track of the group that is now moving toward the green after their second shots. For him, everything is a yellow haze of muddled memories.

"Come on old man," A Jamaican voice demands. A gun barrel is pushed into the Irv's frail back. "Keep up or the show ends for you right here."

"Huh, ah yeah, yeah…" Irv replies, confused.

"Take that gun away from him or I'll break your fucking neck," Irv hears another man say.

"That right? Well I be hoping you try," The guard, Raymond, replies.

"I owe you," Charlie Vaccaro says to Raymond. "You like to push around old men and women. Put that gun down and lets see what you got."

"In time," Raymond replies. "In time, we will finish this. Right now I work for Waits, not for long though. You and me will finish it then. Now, keep up with the players or I'll finish it right here, Waits or no Waits."

Charlie considers rushing the Rasta who holds the gun to Irv, but thinks, this is not the time. He grabs Irv around the shoulders and helps him toward the green.

"You should'a took him," Irv says.

"Not the time," Charlie replies.

"Yeah. Not the time," Irv says. "Vaccaro."

"Yeah."

"Thanks. If there's anything I can do for you, let me know."

"I will Irv. I will."

As Charlie and Irv reach the second green, Bleeris is saying, "All square after two."

The third hole is a two hundred and ten yard par three that cuts on an angle across a shallow valley up to a green perched between two sand traps.

"A wind is crossing left to right," Harry says. "Try to hold the draw into the breeze, maybe a four iron."

Jack nods, takes the club and walks to the tee. When he bends to tee his ball he experiences a moment of exhaustion and blurred vision. He stands slowly to gain his bearings. He cannot see the crowd that lines the hole. He cannot see his father, Terrance Connoll, a look of concern on his face, wanting to walk to Jack and comfort him.

Harry watches his player with concern. He grabs a towel and takes Jack's club; making a show of wiping it off.

"You all right?" Harry whispers.

"Yeah Harry. Just kind of overwhelmed for a second, I guess. I'm all right now."

"Remember, Monday's at the Oak. There was none of this, no responsibility, just the game. The game you love. Just play the game you love."

"Harry?"

"Yeah Jack."

"Was it all a waste?"

"That's a question only your next shot can answer. You're on a golf course, a beautiful classic course made for legends. You're here because you're one of the best ever. You're here because you've always been here."

"Always been here? Harry, I've been here too long." Jack wipes his hand across his face and the wind moves in the trees. He again steps to his ball and swings.

Harry is stunned to see Jack swing so quick, before allowing the life to fall from his body. The ball sails, not turning into the wind, but moving right, away from the hole, landing in the sand trap short of the green.

Waring steps to the tee, his eyes now hard slits, a gunfighter knowing he has the advantage. Deke says nothing before Waring hits his ball. It starts low and rises suddenly, a hard message of a ball that drops as a dagger on the green.

Moments later they walk to the fourth tee, the first blood spilled, Bleeris announcing, "Waring up one after three."

The two old women sit on a blanket, under a tree beside the eighteenth green. "All this now," Sylvia says. "This golf, you would never find me walking around with them as they chase that little ball."

"You're right Syl," Vera replies. "If this is our last time together, better we spend it here, in this beautiful quiet place. Still, it seems your girl Lilly doesn't care that much either."

"Young love, you remember how that was. Don't you Vera? Besides my best weapon is hard at work. Let the girl enjoy herself, she'll be useful soon enough."

"Your weapon? You mean Kathryn?"

"Of course, worth any of those men in a dog fight. I recall she already trumped your boys, Harry and Jack, once. My money's on her."

"They were only boys then. They'll not fall for her charms again. And remember, I've got friends that you don't."

"You mean Vitrizin?"

"I mean friends."

"Don't be too sure of your friends Vera. Anyway, it's too late now and it is such a beautiful afternoon."

"Yes it is, too late and beautiful," Vera replies. "The last such afternoon one of us will ever see."

Out on the old course, after the players halve the hole, Bleeris announces, "Waring one up after four."

The young lovers have separated themselves and walk together near a creek that runs along the fifth fairway. The air has turned humid. The muddy scent of life and death rises around them. Out here, away from the terrible competition, Lilly believes that she would trade the meager things she has, her life, if she could stay here always with Javier.

"There is love?" Lilly asks him. "There is a power that exists outside of time?"

"Yes. I will love you forever," Javier whispers.

"Then what does it matter if I live or die today?"

"If you perish," The dark man replies. "I will cease to exist."

"But you are part of me now? If I exist so will you."

"Only in your heart. If the caddy wins, you will remain forever with only a memory."

"What if I choose not to exist in Dimmig's world?"

"You will not have this choice."

Javier stops the girl and kisses her gently on the lips. "I have loved you from the moment that I saw you. I know you love me, for it is the thing that has kept me tied to this world. I understand your contempt for this spectacle of power, for this competition on your behalf. These few days have been a lifetime. It is all I will require. Still, for you my love, there can be so much more or so much less. Just consider a future that is ours, a world ruled by your thought, through our love. It can be so if we prevail in this match today."

"I have nothing to do with that," Lilly answers.

"But the others, your parents and Aunt. My family they…"

"I have no way to change what is happening back there. I do not have the same talents as Mr. Connoll or Mr. Waring. The match, our future, is their hands."

"You can assist."

"I don't know how. Besides, Miss Torrance has a plan. She is smarter than all of them."

"Yes Lilly. Yes, she is smarter and you must help her, now."

Lilly looks into Javier's eyes and nods, leaving him to join the match and Kathryn Torrance. "What can I do?" Lilly asks.

"Do you see the ghosts now?" Kathryn answers.

"Yes. They are all here now. Some follow you."

"I bet," Kathryn says. "How about Jack, who follows him?"

"There are many who follow him."

"What do you sense from them?"

"Mostly concern and love. There is one, a young woman, I see pain, hatred in her."

"Good," Kathryn says. "If you do have the power, bring her image to Jack's thoughts."

*   *   *

There is the sun today. There is a breeze that sometimes strengthens to wind. There is the ball in long grass. It is all a clutter now in the brain of Jack Connoll. It is how he has felt after a night of drinking at Rose's, a world of sensation overwhelming him.

233

Jack stands by his ball in the tall grass, left, off the fifth fairway. The sun beats down from directly above. His second shot must be hit 180 yards directly into the wind, to a green that sits surrounded on three sides by a running creek. A daunting shot on any day, but nothing beyond his abilities.

He glimpses the face of the girl Lilly in the crowd. For an instant her face transforms to that of another woman and the sight sends Jack spiraling. He sees contempt in the woman's eyes. He did not recognize her immediately. Her image had come to him just before his tee shot on this hole. He had first thought of her as he bent to set his ball on the tee. She had flashed for a moment in his mind's eye, beautiful, her blond hair in wild curls, giving her the appearance of a gypsy. She wore earrings that were made with colored stones that matched her eyes. It was the earrings that led him to recall. A name at first, Gillian, he thought, yes Gillian.

Jack's mind raged into his past, Resson, he remembered, of course, Gillian Resson, a nervous smile trembled across his lips as he readied for his tee shot. The artist, the girl that... He did not finish this thought. He pushed it away. Jack stepped to the ball, swinging, not caring where the shot landed. After, walking down the fairway to his wayward tee shot, she, Gillian Resson, came to him again.

He remembered a dusty afternoon in his office on Belmont. "Maggie," He had demanded across the room, "If she calls, tell her I'm on a long stakeout, a big case." He recalls the phone ringing a short time later, and how he took a swig from a bottle when he heard Maggie deliver his message. Finally, weeks later, her calls did stop.

And then there was the spring afternoon, a year later, he met Gillian's friend, Kerry Bidner, on Michigan Avenue. Kerry said, "Gillian was never the same after you did that to her. She was so talented. She took the pills. She was so alone. She deserved better Jack."

Jack was left standing on the damp crowded street as Kerry walked away. He wanted to tell Kerry that Gillian was just too sensitive, that it wasn't him, it was the world, the artist's curse, but he never did. He did not believe it himself.

Now Jack stands with the sun above, the breeze that sometimes becomes a wind, the ball in the long grass, the hole 180 yards ahead surrounded by water and the vision of Gillian in the young girl's face.

Gillian did not deserve to die, Jack thinks, and then he swings with the same detachment he imagines Gillian felt when she swallowed the pills.

Jack's ball now lies lost forever at the bottom the murky creek. Leaving the green Bleeris announces, "Waring two up after five."

"The boy looks like he's in trouble," Waits says to Bleeris as they move to the sixth tee. "It looks like Miss Rivera is playing for keeps."

"Never mind that. Do you see him?" Bleeris asks Waits, as the players tee off. "Do you see Vitrizin hiding in the trees?"

"Of course," Waits replies. "You know him as well as I. You know that it is his nature."

"Nature? The man was always up to no good when he was alive and now look, he still acts as if he has some dirty work at hand."

"Vitrizin was a different man and now I guess he is a different ghost."

"Is that right Waits? Always so smug when it comes to Vitrizin. I've warned you about him. Now he tracks the action like some animal moving for the kill. This whole affair; the two seers when there should only be one, the farther it goes, the more I know he's had a hand in it."

"Bleeris, you will never understand him. The man was genius. He was ridiculed for what he wanted…"

"What he wanted. What he wanted was madness. To end it all, to eliminate the line, to destroy all structure and leave it to end in anarchy and chaos."

Vitrizin is a solitary figure moving in the shadows. He is thinking, I will have it all soon, these are minor actors in a play that I write… Hoodlums, musicians and golfers, they have no insight into the dimensions of the precipice on which they stand.

Vitrizin moves from tree to tree. He is apart from the field of competition; the holes pass now, as did the decades of his life and the decades of his death, always separate, between the worlds. He, unlike the others before him and since, had sought this place. It was not tragedy, or abandonment, that brought him here; it was a dark vision that compelled him. The vision of the end, of a divided world, wasted, doomed.

When he was a child, his Aunt Neseem called him a lucky boy. "A genius they said today," His Aunt had said to him once. "Born into this family, in this beautiful city, you are destined to greatness. No farm work, no factory. You are a very lucky boy, Tersis. You will rise above them all."

"Rising above them all is the fool's way," Vitrizin would write much later in his life. "The world is a hovel built upon stilts that stand only inches above the wasteland. The one who knows this truth will watch them all fall."

As the German takes a four-hole lead after nine, Vitrizin watches the match from the trees. The American is haggard, depleted. Vitrizin believes that Connoll desires the oblivion that his defeat will offer. Vitrizin smirks from his blind, "Just as I have always thought," he says to himself, "Behind the bluster, the Americans have always been so weak, so willing to give in."

*   *   *

Tommy Deke looks over his shoulder to see Jack Connoll standing alone, still on the ninth green. "You got him by four, Marty. He looks finished," Deke says to Waring, as they walk to the next tee.

"Surprising, thought he had more than that," Waring replies.

Irv watches Connoll's plight. It's not over yet, he thinks, I've learned that anything's possible… I survived certain death on an island, I saw them stand on the moon and now I'm here at the end of my road with nothing but a couple of hand grenades for protection… Story of my life.

Irv feels the ghosts are close, still, he cannot see his old friend Pittsburgh Mike winking at him, a rolled up racing form in his coat pocket. He cannot see Little Mickey Chana, the toughest boxer Irv ever knew, walking silently beside him with his hands in his pockets, his head down.

"A little upsetting, huh old man?" Dalva says, walking up next to Irv, who is immersed in private conversation.

Irv looks up to the Dalva with a smile. "Story of my life," He says.

"Dead is dead," Dalva answers.

"I may be old, at the end of my road, but I'm not ready to give it up," Irv replies.

"Yes. I know. How about giving me one of your grenades."

"You know about them?" Irv asks.

"I've been talking with Vaccaro and Cahoon. The way Connoll's playing we think it's time to prepare for a fight."

"I don't," Irv says. "Not yet, got nine to play. Don't give up on our boy. But don't worry, when the time comes I'll stand with you."

As the group nears the tenth tee, Harry has stopped to fill his water bottle at a tap. He has tried it all now, has given Jack some rope, has pulled it tight, has tried to divert his thoughts to better times, still, Jack plays for death. Harry turns and looks up to the tenth tee where Jack sits on a bench with his head in his hands.

"Not looking good Harry," Glyn says.

"No."

"Remember that time in Germany, when they told me I was dying?" Glyn asks, stepping in front of Harry and blocking his view of Jack.

"Yeah."

"They told me about those bullshit stages of death, you know, denial, anger, with the final one being acceptance."

"Yeah."

"Well, I'm afraid your boy Jack's life has been nothing but those stages of death. I'm afraid to tell you, but he is in full acceptance stage at the moment."

"I know Glyn. We're lost."

"Lost? No. We're only lost if you accept as well."

"I don't understand."

"Look around, we are the dead, we have weight, we can push you down, or pull you up. Use us."

"But…"

"Remember, we have as much to gain or lose as you. There are those here for revenge. I'm afraid Jack has succumbed to one of his past mistakes, some girl, her image given to him by Lilly on the advice of your old friend K.C. But there is still time. I don't know your boy well, but I believe there are those here who can help. Those who can get him to fight for his life."

Harry looks up to the tall wild haired Englishman. "Glyn, I think I know who can help."

Harry makes his way to the tee and hands Jack his driver. "New nine," Harry says. "Let's turn it around."

Jack does not look into Harry's eyes or say a word in response. He walks to the tee, takes a weak practice swing and pushes his tee shot right, into the trees down in the valley, walking after his ball with his head down.

Harry stops him by grabbing the driver from his hand. "That won't fucking do," Harry says, taking the golf bag off his shoulder. "Here you carry this down there." Harry hands Jack the bag. "I'll meet up with you at the ball."

Harry turns and walks toward the spectators, searching the old faces. He finds One-Eye Dugan and asks him a question. Dugan points off toward the tree line. Harry hurries, half running, toward the trees, moving through the throng of the dead until he reaches a clearing removed from the crowd. There, with topcoats and hats, smoking cigarettes and whispering, stand Howard Ryan and Terrance Connoll.

As the groups move slowly down the tenth fairway, Waring eats a cracker and Deke consults his yardage book.

Kathryn Torrance follows alone. She is surprised when Lilly falls into step next to her. "Lilly dear," Kathryn says to the girl. "It looks like Mr. Waring will have this over in short order"

"And then what?" Lilly asks.

"And then we will shape the world."

"And what shape will that be?"

"It will be in the image of your love and my desire. We will line up everything, the German's empire will be very useful to us."

"Of course Miss Torrance. We shall rule the world."

Jack walks off toward the right rough. He has no hope for his ball. As he passes, Irv offers to carry his bag, but Jack ignores him. Jack welcomes the weight of the clubs. It magnifies the hopeless futility of his effort. It brings him closer to his pain.

Jack reaches the general area of his ball, a secluded stand of trees, and finds Harry already there.

"Jackie," Jack Connoll believes he hears a voice say. "Jackie my boy."

"Dad," Jack replies, dropping the bag to ground. "But…"

"I'm here too Jack," Howard Ryan says.

"Howard?"

"Listen Jack," Ryan says, interrupting. "Your dad and I didn't waste our time on you so you could throw it all away. This is not the behavior of a man."

"I know, it's not your fault," Jack replies. "I'm just at the end of a wasted life. Too many people got hurt because of my stupidity."

"Stupidity, bullshit," Terrance Connoll says. "No Connoll is stupid. You followed your dreams. Nothing wrong with that, if people got hurt, they got hurt because of their own weakness."

"But the girl, Gillian…" Jack starts.

"The girl was looking for a reason," Ryan says. "It just happened to be you. Regret is bullshit. Be a man. Like you learned in the neighborhood."

"It's more than that. I've never made the right choice."

"You were not afraid to choose," Harry says. "That's the point."

"Harry, you can hear the voices in my head?" Jack says.

"I brought them to you. They asked to help," Harry replies.

"You have a chance to be the greatest Connoll," Jack's father tells him. "The one that will allow us to survive for eternity. Don't let the past pull you down. That's what they want, the women, Torrance and Rivera. The German, he's counting on it too."

"But," Jack says.

"Forget but," Ryan says. "You play golf, that's what you do. If this is your last match, than make it your best, don't go down without a fight. We taught you better than that in the neighborhood. Remember you're from Chicago."

Waring and Deke stand out in the fairway, amused at Connoll, so distraught now that he appears to be talking to himself.

"What's he doing over there?" Deke says. "Should I say something?"

"Maybe he's considering chucking the whole thing," Waring replies.

Watching Jack's strange behavior, Irv fingers the hand grenades. Charlie moves in close to Raymond, as the other Rasta guards bring their weapons to waist high.

Jack turns to Harry. Harry takes the four iron out of the bag and hands it to Jack. "Take it low under trees. You know the shot."

"Mr. Connoll, please make your play," Bleeris declares from the fairway. Waits, who stands next to him, is hiding a smile.

"The greatest Connoll of all," Jack's father says.

"Be a man," Howard Ryan says. "For the neighborhood."

A man, Jack thinks, stand up, give the neighborhood its due. Low under the trees, the image of the ball tracing a line to the green appears in his mind. There are no regrets, he thinks, a life is lived, choices are made, the next shot is all that matters.

As Jack takes the club back, Harry senses it, the old feeling, the past recreating itself, the gathering of power, of imagination, of dreams, of history. It is the energy of a man's life, of his neighborhood, his city and nation, as he chooses to act and change the world.

The ball flies low under the branches, then rises on a line, falling to the green's front edge and rolling by the hole, two feet.

In the trees, away from the competition, a man who resembles the rat applauds. For the first time, he is in awe of another.

"Waring three up after ten," Bleeris says, after Jack putts out.

On the eleventh, a two-hundred yard par three with the wind arching in from the right, Jack hits a high four iron that appears to stop above the green, dropping straight down fifteen feet from the hole.

"Waring two up after eleven," Bleeris says.

Tommy Deke takes his player's putter. "You're still good Marty," Deke says to Waring. "He's hit a couple a shots is all. You're hitting the ball good as ever."

"Sure Tommy. Sure. We got a match now," Waring replies, looking hard into his notebook for the source of his creeping concern.

The players halve the twelfth hole, a short par four. As they walk to the next tee, Kathryn moves in close to Jack. She whispers, "It's great to see you playing so well again."

"Thanks," Jack says, distracted by the prospect of the long par five ahead.

"What made such a difference on ten?" She asks.

"Uh, well…" Jack starts.

"You're up," Harry interrupts, thrusting the driver between Jack and Kathryn.

Kathryn steps back and looks to Jack. Still just a boy, she thinks. "Well it's nice to see you playing well again." Her blue eyes sending streams of desire through Jack.

Jack is drawn to her. He wants to move his hand through her hair, to kiss her, to leave this insanity and return with her to the yellow fields of Ames and their youth.

"Jack," Harry says. "Your tee."

Connoll takes the club and walks to the tee. The thirteenth hole runs 580 yards up the side of a hill. From the tee, the green is a watercolor landscape in the distance. It does not appear real. With Kathryn's words still echoing, Jack has a vision of the young K.C., her face, as it was the day they met in Iowa. Jack takes his club back and through, the ball disappears into the sky and then appears again as a white speck bouncing on the far side of a creek that intersects the fairway 310 yards away.

Kathryn feels a chill move through her body. Waring, standing next to Deke, blinks twice. Irv stands alone, smiling and shaking his head. He turns away only when Manley grabs his shoulder and asks, "Did you see that? Did you see that?"

Harry takes the driver from Jack and watches his friend walk up the fairway, alone, head down.

As Jack walks to his ball, he considers the golf course. As beautiful as I've ever seen, he thinks, a masterpiece of god and man, this is perfect for a match, the ancient treetops swaying in the breeze above the field of battle where this ritual should be played out.

Further down the hole, on a hillside, away from the living, Lilly and the dark man sit, hand in hand, seeing only each other's eyes. "Dimmig's man appears to be playing much better," Javier says to Lilly.

"I didn't notice," Lilly replies. She turns back to the fairway in time to watch Jack hit a wood in a high arc toward the green. The ball makes a hissing sound as it passes them.

"If he wins, we will never be together. Our love will be lost forever," Javier says.

"I have spoken with Miss Torrance," Lilly says. "She has instructed me on what I'm to do if Mr. Connoll threatens to win." Lilly stands and pulls Javier to his feet. Together they walk slowly toward the action.

On the thirteenth green Jack taps his ball in for birdie. Bleeris announces, "Waring is one up."

Irv lets the hand grenades fall back down into the hem of his raincoat.

The groups now stand on the fourteenth tee under the gathering clouds of a darkening sky. They stare dead into a steady wind. The players, Waring and Connoll, can no longer look at each other.

Harry is sure that Tommy Deke purposely crossed his path after the last hole, almost stepping on Jack's foot. Harry also notices that Lilly, alone now, has moved closer to the players, walking with Kathryn and whispering. Beyond these two women, Harry sees the guards gathering, now more in formation. The end is nearing, he thinks. The head of the guard, the Rasta they call Raymond, is going from man to man, perhaps giving orders. Harry also notices that, for the last few holes, Charlie Vaccaro had begun to move in unison with Raymond, always ten yards back, always with one eye to the guard. Harry knows that Charlie is now in the middle of his own single-minded pursuit. The match means little to him, the future and the past just secondary to his obligation of revenge. Harry wonders whether the ghosts of the men who follow Charlie are urging him to honor the family and to insure no harm will come to Carla regardless of how this ends.

The competitors halve fourteen, the short par four. Jack scrambles to save par out of a bunker on the par three fifteenth to stay one down. Sixteen, a long par four playing straight into a two-club wind, rewards both players with bogey fives. As they walk from the green, Bleeris, sounding relieved, announces, "Waring one up with two to play."

The words, one up with two to play, are daggers in the pit of Harry's stomach. "All right," Harry says to Jack, handing him the water bottle. "We have to make a move here, we need this hole. We can't go to eighteen one down."

"This is the first time this week I've had to play this hole," Jack says. "It's a long par four, right? Moves right around those trees?"

"Yeah, take a three wood down the center, over the rise in the fairway," Harry replies. "It should take the trees and the rough out of play and give you a long iron in."

"What about taking it over the trees on the right."

"Risky."

"What if I made it?"

"You'd have a pitching wedge, or less."

"What do you think Harry?"

Harry looks down the fairway and then to his opponents. He sees Deke's hand on Waring's three-wood. He knows they are planning to do just what he would do with a one-hole lead and two to play; take a safe club down the fairway. Something still long enough to get home in two, but a club that takes the trees and rough on either side of the fairway out of play.

Harry turns to the three men who follow. Glyn Parker winks at him, Connoll's father nods and Howard Ryan, with both hands holding his fedora says, "Give the kid the fucking driver."

Harry turns, recalls the memory of a shot from a practice round in Arizona long ago. There was an island green and two Spaniards making curse signs with their fingers. Harry hands Jack his driver and Jack smiles in return.

"Thanks Harry. I remember the shot too."

"Just an afternoon at Oak Grove old friend."

Jack walks to the tee and takes aim over the stand of trees on the right side of the fairway. Martin Waring smiles. That'a boy, he thinks, I would of done the same thing.

Jack stands over the ball, the club waggles, the tension dropping away from his body. Everyone, everything, is pulled up into this swing.

Watching Jack, Christopher Waits recalls the complex beauty of the seashells that sustained him as a child. Kathryn Torrance recalls her mother's smiling face. Jerry says a silent prayer for Maggie.

Harry no longer runs through the regrets and lost chances. Instead, he looks to the faces of those that surround him. He is thankful for the life that he has lived.

In the trees on the right, as the ball soars overhead, Vitrizin cries out in an ancient language, making the sound of an animal that is readying for the kill. He follows the ball, now out of sight of those on the tee, as it bounds into the fairway and comes to rest thirty yards from the front of the green.

"Well, do you have a clue?" Jack says, turning to the Harry.

Harry shrugs, "It looks good to me, I guess we'll see when we see."

"Damn good shot Connoll, regardless," Waring says, his first words to Jack in hours.

With Waring's ball safely down the center of the fairway, all, but two, walk on. "It's up to you now," Kathryn says to Lilly, as they hang back. "If Jack wins this hole, you need to do what we talked about."

"Are you sure," Lilly replies. "Are you sure that it is me, and not you, that can stop Mr. Connoll."

"No I'm not. But I know Dimmig well. He will be watching me. He won't be expecting you."

Waring stands 190 yards out knowing that Jack has an easy chip shot to get up and down for birdie.

"Well Tommy," Waring says. "We got him just where we want him. If I stick it close for birdie, I'll put the pressure back on him, we can close them out here."

Deke, knowing what his boss means, hands him a five iron, saying, "The wind is with you, the hole is twenty from the front edge, in a

244

depression. When I saw it this morning, I thought anything hit ten short and right will drain right down to the hole."

"I'm sure it will," Waring says, walking to his ball.

Further up the fairway, Jack and Harry watch as Waring's ball falls to the green in front of them, spinning, catching, bouncing once and then settling to a roll, moving right, toward the hole and stopping seven inches away.

"That was pretty good," Jack says. "Kind of makes this shot a little harder. I guess I have to get this close or it's gonna' get ugly."

Waring, walking by Harry and Jack, on his way to mark his ball, turns and asks, "Not going to give me this one Jack?"

"Normally I would Martin. It's just that machine guns make half a foot seem like a very long way."

Martin winks at him and continues on to the green. Lilly and Kathryn watch, sensing the end is near. The Rasta guards now circle the living. Irv reaches for his grenades and Charlie moves in closer to Raymond.

Harry and Jack walk the 30 yards to the green to inspect the surface. "You saw what his ball did," Harry says. "I say you drop it here and let it roll."

"Yeah I know, I know. What do you say we give it one of our patented piss'em off inspections? Just for old times."

"I guess it couldn't hurt," Harry replies.

They begin to circle the green, stopping at various angles. Jack holds a putter up to plumb-bob. Harry kneels on the line. Jack winks at Irv.

"Well what do you think partner?" Jack says to Harry.

"You make this all day."

They walk together back to the ball in the fairway.

"If we lose, I'm not going down without a fight. I…" Jack whispers.

"This shot first," Harry says.

In the moment of calm preceding the swing, Jack sees a vision of his father that Harry has provided him. With that he turns to his ball, brushes the grass with his club head, moving it back and forward, a sharp stabbing swing, the ball jumps toward the green, it bounces twice, the spin catching on the second; it slows and starts toward the hole.

The ball rolls impossibly slow, every turn a revolution of the earth, every inch equals decades of history. It is the collective experience of world, always divided between where it was, where it is and where it is going. It is the path between life and death, between right and wrong, between love and hate. It is the impossible creation moving to the impossible end.

The ball drops six inches down into the hole.

In the trees, Vitrizin stands staring at the sky. On the green, the European stares across to the American, before picking his ball sharply from the green.

Bleeris, his voice trembling, looks to Waits and says, "All square. This can't be. One hole to play, how will this end? We must have only one."

Waits smiles, echoes Bleeris, "This can't be," and looks for the solitary figure in the trees.

The eighteenth hole lies before Jack and Martin. The sky is now thick with gray clouds. The flag is a speck of blue in the distance, perched on a precipice on the far side of the chasm that splits the fairway.

"Four eighty-seven," Deke says. "Christ, what a fucking hole."

Harry looks to the old caddy and nods in agreement.

"All right," Harry says to Jack. "Keep it left of the bunkers on the right, but right of the trees on the left and hit it very far."

Jack smiles, "Did anyone ever tell you that you're an asshole?"

"The words I wake with every morning," Harry replies.

Jack leans in close to Harry. "What should we do," he whispers, "Our time is running out."

"It certainly is," Harry replies. "Win the hole and we go from there. Charlie, Jerry and Irv are ready to make a move. Dalva and Manley should be some help."

"If we win this, we can't just let K.C. and the others just get shot down."

"True," Harry says. "Although I wouldn't bet my life on how far they would go for us, if they win." He looks out to the hole ahead. "We got a long way to go, 487 yards, before we've got to face that. Just hit it long and straight."

Jack steps to the tee glancing through the crowd and his eyes meet the girl, Lilly. She has tears streaking her face.

The world is so small, Jack thinks, life with all its apparent intricacies is so simple and dumb. He can feel the exhortations, the words of his father and Howard Ryan, losing their hold on him. They have always served their own interests, Jack thinks, the precious Connoll name and the meal ticket known as Ryan Investigations... I have always served them, then and now, it was the neighborhood and the city that has always been at the root of my regret and pain, he understands now, that Harry has been too. Jack pulls his stare from Lilly, but the tears on her face remain the image in his mind.

This is the end, Jack thinks, one hole and maybe I can walk away from them all, from the hero role, from the neighborhood and from my life.

The tee shot floats into the iron sky. It is a missile hurled by Jack at the meaningless world, a perfect drive, just as Harry, just as they all, had wanted.

Waring follows with a brilliant response. Together, Connoll and Waring walk from the eighteenth tee, in silence, side-by-side, down into the final fairway. Bleeris and Waits follow, joined by the others, the spirits, and now, the rodent like man.

"No, that is not possible," Bleeris is saying to Waits, as Vitrizin walks up to them. "Two competing connections, one with the girl, one with Dimmig, that would be disaster. Two ruling ideas, two minds controlling..."

"The heart and the mind," Waits responds.

"Discord," Vitrizin adds.

"Everything would be split..." Bleeris starts

"The battle and the end," Vitrizin finishes.

"The end?" Bleeris says. "The end, this can't be. No, there will be no tie. That would be the beginning of the end. There cannot be two alive."

Up ahead, Waring and Connoll split company, each moving to their golf balls. Kathryn moves to Jack, touching his arm. "Good luck Jack," Kathryn says whispering, her lips brushing his neck. "You played great. I feel young again just watching you."

"I'll do what I can to get you out of this," Jack replies.

"That's all right Jack, I've had a good life. We both have. If it ends here, today with you, I wouldn't mind. It's the girl, Lilly; she's the one who is being cheated here. She's so young. She hasn't lived. To see her die today while Harry, a man who has seen the world… Well that would be the saddest part of this whole story, if the girl dies today." Jack turns back to Lilly. "Do you remember love Jack?" Kathryn asks him. "Do you remember being that young?"

Jack recalls the farm fields that bordered the roads of his youthful travels; the roads that made razor cuts through the heart of this country. His moment was then and he did not know it. His time now lost forever.

As Kathryn speaks with Jack, Lilly watches for Kathryn to give her a quick glance.

Jack, lost in the past, does not see Waring hit his shot; a towering draw that falls to the splinter of a green.

"Jack. Jack," Harry is saying, bringing Jack back to this moment.

Jack is surprised to find himself alone with Harry. Kathryn now stands across the fairway with Lilly, their eyes locked on him.

"Waring's good, pin high about 12 feet. You can drop it in closer. I got a good read off his, you can't feel it here, but the wind is stronger from the left. You need to start it just left and hold it with a draw."

Jack takes the club from Harry without looking at it. The visions of his youth that Lilly has given him have not subsided. They are all he sees in his mind and in his heart. After he hits his shot, Jack never looks to the ball's flight. He turns his back to the green to find Kathryn.

There is a gasp that reverberates around the course, through the living and the dead. A man's voice, Tommy Deke's voice, brings the vibration into words, "I'll be damned," he says.

Harry grabs Jack's shoulder. "Jack," He says. "Five feet, six at the most. At least half of Waring." Harry looks to Jack and follows his gaze across the fairway to Kathryn. "You all right?" He asks.

"Yeah. Good," Jack replies. "Go up ahead and get me a read."

Harry nods, letting go of Jack's shoulder, he takes the club, hands Jack his putter, begins to move away, stops, a hesitation, a feeling of dread that he pushes down before he turns again to the green. He moves quickly down into the chasm, to where the earth starts its rise to the flag. Arriving up at the green, Harry stops and turns to find Jack walking at the lowest point in the valley, his putter almost dragging behind him. He walks slumped shouldered, with Lilly beside him; she is speaking, as they make their way to the green's up slope. Harry watches them separate, his stomach churning in pure terror with a memory that has never left him.

"What'd did she say?" Harry asks Jack. The gray skies have closed over them, impenetrable, the once infinite blue now an iron cell. The green is whipped by wind, the snapping flag the only reply. "What did she say?" Harry repeats.

"Nothing Harry. What do you see here?"

"Jack, we're five feet from winning this. Are up to winning this?"

"Harry."

Harry drops the golf bag in the fringe grass that surrounds the green and gently pulls Jack aside. Waring and Deke are lining up their putt just feet away. The Rasta guards have taken a position, just off the green, back and to the right of hole. They have formed a firing squad.

Harry checks the others; Dalva, Jerry and Manley huddle together off the green. Irv is apart from this group, nearer to the guards. Charlie's eyes are moving nervously between the green and Raymond, who stands in a flanking position, ready to command his men. Lilly has returned to the side of the dark man. Kathryn, both hands clenched, has moved close to the girl and is staring back at Harry, as he turns to speak to Jack.

"Jack, listen to me. You have to tell me what you're thinking. You owe me that."

Jack considers his partner. He recalls the first time he saw the small kid sitting alone near the baseball diamond behind the high school. How is it possible they could be here today? How can life move this fast?

"You're right Harry, I owe you," Jack says, as Waring is going through his routine a few feet away and Deke bends to examine the line. "But please, listen to me this one time," Jack says. "If he makes this and I

249

make, we tie. If he misses and I miss we tie. The match continues, never ending, the conclusion never reached."

Harry looks up to Jack, a child's expression, meant to show he does not understand what is in his friend's heart. To his left, Waring stands over his ball, taking slow measured practice strokes. "Jack, please tell me what's on your mind," Harry says with all his strength.

"We've had a good life, we've had our chances. This whole thing, we don't deserve it. Who are we doing this for?"

"For everyone here, for ourselves."

"Not for ourselves Harry. I know I don't want this and I'm pretty sure you feel the same. We found our place, the office, Maggie, that's all we need. What if we get out on our own terms?"

"You mean walk away. Don't you see those guns? It will be over."

Waring moves the putter back and through the ball. The ball turns, skids and slows to a smooth roll.

"Harry, we have both been given gifts, but we've also had our chance. The girl, Lilly, she's young, this is her time now."

"K.C.," Harry says.

"No, this isn't about K.C., it's about us. When I walked away from you all those years ago, I was motivated by the promise of a fairytale world. I desired everything, but the things that were important to me. Do you recall how that turned out? Do you really want this prize or do you want what we already have?"

Waring's ball begins to curve, breaking left, picking up speed. Harry watches, detached, he knows the conclusion even before he hears the ball drop into the cup. He turns to Jack. "Do you want me to read this putt?" Harry asks.

"Yes. I will listen to you. I want you to tell me where to hit it."

"What about the others?"

"I've told Irv to be ready," Jack says. "They will fight."

Harry looks to the green. For a moment he stands behind the ball, then he walks the line, looking for the imperfections, the grains of sand or rock, and the direction the blades of grass grow. Harry is fighting the anger. This was to be my time, he thinks, what right does Jack have to make this choice? As Harry moves around the green, he recalls the old office on Belmont and Maggie Cahoon, the Greek's cooking and Rose's on Webster Street. With those thoughts the rage passes. Harry again considers what Jack has said. They are still two kids from the neighborhood, Harry thinks, always trying to please, always regretting their lost dream, tortured by what others thought they should be. All those who surround them here, the dead, they are asking for more than they deserve, they've had their chance. Now too, Harry wants nothing more. They will not continue this game for the benefit of others. They will fight for what they have made, to survive, like they've always done, what they have always done.

Jack is standing behind his ball waiting for his friend to give him guidance. Harry could have told Jack where to hit this putt before ever walking the green; from just observing the line Waring's putt had taken. He circles the green one last time, returning to stand with his old friend.

A voice from off the green breaks the silence. Irv says, "Can I say something before you do this? No matter what happens Connoll, you are the best ever from Illinois."

"Thanks Irv," Jack replies.

"I still got one long shot left," Irv continues. "I've been saving it. One you've never seen before. A shot I learned a long time ago; I thought I'd never need to use it again. How do ya' like that? They knew what they we're doing when they let this skinny Jewish punk into the Marines. Good luck boys."

"Good luck Irv," Jack replies, his eyes welling. "Well, what do you think Harry. Where do I hit this putt?"

"You set your aim on that brown blade of grass in line with the right edge of the cup. Do you see it?"

"I see it. Good luck Harry."

"Put a smooth stroke on it and you're buying the drinks after this," Harry replies.

"What happened to fifty-fifty?"

"Fifty-fifty is always a myth."

Jack smiles and moves to his ball. He finds the brown blade that Harry had pointed out, one foot in front of his ball, and draws an imaginary line to it for the hardest putt of his life. The putter head starts the ball on the perfect path to the brown blade, the ball rolls over it, bending it, and then directly over a pebble that lies just inches beyond. The ball hops, wobbles, loses momentum and falls quickly to the left, skimming the right edge of the hole and running by, one foot.

Bleeris smiles. "We have a winner," he says.

The guards look to Raymond, who looks to Waits for the order to fire. Waits stands expressionless with Vitrizin at his side. Kathryn, wearing a broad smile, moves closer to Lilly. Irv, both hands in his raincoat now; holds in each hand the trigger clip of a pinless grenade.

"Give the order," Bleeris says to Waits. Wait's stands silent. The guards raise, lower and raise their guns. "Shoot the losers now," Bleeris demands.

The guns are raised. Jack sprints across the green and takes Kathryn to the ground. An edgy guard, startled by Jack's move, pulls the trigger, a blast of gunfire erupts and Kevin Manley falls to the ground. The sight of Manley's bloody body sends Dalva running, and screaming, down the fairway.

"All fire now," Bleeris yells over the rising confusion.

Irv walks toward the firing squad with his empty hands held toward a gray swirling sky saying, "Don't take this personally, but I promised Maggie I'd take care of the bookie." The detonation, a flash of light, a staggering sound that echoes out across the countryside, sends all ten guards to the earth, dead.

Raymond, stunned by what has happened, stands watching the massacre, until a flash of white light explodes in his brain; his death the result of Charlie Vaccaro's fist to his right temple. Charlie picks up Raymond's rifle and fires a blast into the air yelling, "Come on let's go."

Jack helps Kathryn to her feet, pulling her to him, but she pulls away and Harry grabs Jack's arm moving him to join Charlie. Jerry checks Manley, but finds no sign of life. They fall behind Charlie, who is backing away toward the mansion with the gun aimed from his hip. There is no one left who will stop them.

Jack looks one last time to Kathryn. "We are staying," Kathryn says, before Jack and the others disappear through a path in the trees.

Bleeris turns to Waits and Vitrizin. "This can't be," he says. "We must stop them. They must die."

"They have fought for the right to live," Waits answers. "We cannot stop them now. The world shall have two until the other can be eliminated. The girl has won for now. She shall hold the cup and your allegiance, the allegiance of the ruling line. As for the rest of you," Waits says to the gathering of dead, "You are bound to the alliances that brought you here. Until there is one, we shall have two."

"Two," Bleeris says. "No. Impossible, this cannot be. It will be too much, all will be ruined." In the distance, a car's engine turns over and tires squeal.

Waits takes the gold cup from Looby, patting his old friend on the shoulder. He moves to Lilly, who stands trembling in the arms of Kathryn Torrance, and offers the cup to the young girl. "It is your world now," Waits tells her. "Still, Bleeris is correct, your battle has only begun. Dimmig must be eliminated."

As Lilly takes the cup, the sound of gunfire can be heard from the direction of the main gate, followed by the whining of a car's engine, gunned into the distance. Javier again joins Lilly, standing on her right, opposite of Kathryn.

"What do I do now?" Lilly asks.

Bleeris, resigned now to his dilemma, says, "Well there will be an unfortunate fire in the mansion and…"

19

The Cubs have lost three straight. Maggie Cahoon looks around the empty office, the low angle of the September sun making the dust appear thick on every surface. She touches the photograph of Jerry that sits framed on her desk. The photo was taken two days after he returned from New York. She still shutters at the thought of how close to death they had all come, at how their names would have appeared, along with the others, in the list of those killed in the fire at the old mansion of the reclusive billionaire. Only seven survivors; a media mogul named Waring, a rich woman named Torrance, an elderly caddy called Deke, a girl maid named Rivera, and a lawyer named Bleeris. Maggie had asked Jerry if he had met them. He shook his head that he had, offering no other explanation. All he said was, "Waits was a madman who wanted to murder everyone because of some crazy religious beliefs."

Jack and Harry were the ones who told her the story of Irv Lavinsky. The man she had entrusted with their lives, had indeed saved them, had saved Jerry, at the cost of his own life. Maggie had scanned the newspaper accounts for every mention of Irv. The newspaper called him, "A long time resident of Chicago, originally from Baltimore, a former Marine who had once competed for the state amateur golf championship." Maggie had cut the picture that accompanied the article and had it framed. It now sits on her desk next to the photos of Jerry and Ron Santo.

As she replaces the frame on her desk and waits for her bosses, she smiles, thinking of how the Greek's cooking, although more pungent than ever, does not seem to bother her as much these days.

Looking across the empty office, she studies the painting Jack had placed on the wall just this week. It is one of those novelty paintings, with dogs taking the place of men. In this painting, the dogs are depicted in various human activities. There is a dog smoking a pipe that reminds her of Chauncey Basch. Another is playing roulette and this dog reminds her of Jerry. The dog watching a burlesque show reminds her of Jack and the one who sits at a table with piles of money, disgustingly fat, she thinks, reminds her of Frank Danvers. There is one that sips from a martini glass with a wry toothless smile and, to her, this is Irv. Finally, there is the one who sits and observes the whole scene, not involved, but jotting notes in a tattered book. This is Harry.

Last week, when Jack brought the painting into the office, she wondered whether he had seen the same things, but now she believes he bought it because he believes it is art.

"It classes the place up," Jack said the other day, "Don't you think?"

"Yeah," she replied. "That doesn't take much."

*　　*　　*

This afternoon, the beer at Rose's cuts a particularly delicious path down Harry's dry throat. The match with Danvers this morning went as usual. It ended with the fat attorney screaming obscenities.

Harry scans the bar; T.J. is hauling cases of empties to the back room. He is oblivious to One-Eye and Buggy who are arguing about the greatest Chicago Bear of all time.

One-Eye says, "No one will ever stand above Butkus."

"I'd take Payton any day," Buggy sneers in reply.

Harry knows that Jack should be arriving any moment and he is hoping that Glyn will stop by later for a talk. Glyn has been maintaining a watch on Lilly and the others.

"They'll be coming for you," Glyn had told him last week. "They've set up shop in Berlin. They have all the media and money they need at their call."

"If they want me, they know where to find me," Harry had replied.

"They are waiting for you. They'll need you out of the picture," Glyn had said. "They know you have the protection of your neighborhood, very strong; Vaccaro's people are with you. Have you replied to Dalva's offer of funds?"

"No," Harry had said, touching the folded letter that he had in his back pocket.

"They are confused by your inaction," Glyn had said. "They think it's some kind of ploy. They believe Vitrizin is running the show and if they move too fast, Vitrizin will take advantage. Have you seen him, Vitrizin?" Glyn had asked.

"No," Harry had replied. "He uses my grandmother as a go between."

"You are the leader of a great army and they await your orders," Glyn had told him before he left.

Later, Harry told Jack that he was the leader of a great army.

Jack said, "Do you think you can get them to handle some stakeouts for us? Maybe we can get in some more golf."

"No," Harry replied.

Now, this afternoon, Harry waits at Rose's. He is enjoying the argument between his two old friends at the end of the bar and the cold beer wipes away the thoughts of armies and those who plot against him in Berlin.

Harry turns to see Jack standing at the front door in conversation with Burlie, the mailman, and recalls something his grandmother had told him the other day. She had come to him while he sat alone along the lakeshore, watching the boats pass on the choppy water.

She said, "Harry my boy. You made your choice, it could have been over, you could have been the one, but you turned from it. Still, I know now it was as Vitrizin had wanted."

"I did not turn," Harry replied. "I just took a different road. I am still here."

"Yes," Vera Casick said. "A different road, always. Please, let me give you this advice and please don't ask me to explain. It will be yours to use as you choose."

"Certainly grandmother, what is it?"

"It is simply this. Every person that lives is holy, because they hold the memories of those who have come before. To lead, you must understand this, because of these memories, what each person perceives is different. Man controls, demons sympathize and gods give."

"But..." Harry stopped his question when he realized his grandmother had gone. He has run her words over and over since that day.

"Dimmig," Jack says, bounding into the bar, bringing Harry back to the present. "We made some easy money today. I told Danvers I'd give him 10 strokes in the next match. What do you think?"

"Next match? The next match I..." Harry is interrupted by new voice joining the argument between the spirits at the end of the bar.

"Anyone with any brains knows that Sid Luckman was the greatest Bear ever," Irv Lavinsky says to One-Eye and Buggy. "Right Harry?"

"Well Harry?" Jack asks again. "What about the next match?"

Harry shakes his head and smiles. "Sure," he says. "Anybody with any brains knows that... The next match will very be interesting."

Also by AR Elia:

Telegraph
Opening Round — The Tournament
Trout

Find them at:

www.mulebox.com